Barbara Crossley was born in Saddleworth on the Yorkshire–Lancashire border in 1952. She was educated in Buxton, Derbyshire, and studied English at Lancaster University, followed by Theatre Studies at University College, Cardiff. She joined the *West Lancashire Evening Gazette* in Blackpool in 1976 and has been a journalist ever since, winning a British Press Awards commendation for her coverage of nuclear discharges into the Irish Sea. She is married and still lives in Blackpool.

In *Candyfloss Coast*, Barbara Crossley's first novel, reporter Anna Knight is drawn into an intricate web of local politicking about pollution and nuclear waste, and among her friends – or enemies? – are a charismatic Euro-MP, jettisoned from his hotel window, a beautiful and enigmatic rent-boy, the smooth, poetry-quoting chief executive, and her old friend, Alys, a prominent member of an environmental group. Murky dealings abound in this richly atmospheric and timely thriller.

BARBARA CROSSLEY

CANDYFLOSS COAST

Published by VIRAGO PRESS Limited 1991
20–23 Mandela Street, London NW1 0HQ

A CIP record for this book is available from the British Library

Typeset in Century Expanded by CentraCet, Cambridge

Printed in Great Britain by
Cox & Wyman Ltd, Reading, Berkshire

ONE

Violence simmered through the humid air, threatening to boil over at any moment. It was May Day in Northport, and the Bank Holiday crowds jostled round me on the promenade. Above, a teenaged lad, drunk on beer or bravado, swung by his arms from the rails of a footbridge while his mates cheered. My stomach lurched as one of his hands slipped and he hung, howling in shock and fear. The crowds stopped, convinced he would fall to the concrete below.

His friends panicked, grappling to hold his wrist through the railings. One lad flailed out to grasp his free arm, another hooked his belt, and a collective sigh of relief went up as they hauled him back, tipping him over the rail on to the footbridge. He lay still for a moment, chest heaving, then got up, gave a grin and a bow, and the gang of them raced down the steps, scattering onlookers from their path.

There were more such groups of young tearaways, shouting and swaggering on the beach, spreading consternation. Children yelled in their wake, parents glared, and old people grumbled in their deckchairs.

It was hot, damp and stifling. My thin blouse clung to me as I leaned on the promenade rail, trying to protect my silk skirt from the trailing fingers of sticky children. I was waiting for Greg to come back from the ice-cream stall.

We weren't here to eat ice-cream: we were working – Greg a photographer, I a reporter, for the resort's paper, the Northport *Evening News*. The first sunny Bank Holiday of the year had combined with a home football match to attract a hugh influx of trippers and visiting fans. Hooligan clashes had already erupted, and someone had

1

rung our office to say a fight was planned, here on the seafront, between rival supporters. A scooter-mounted mob from the opposing side was supposed to be on its way after the match, and Northport's fans were gathering on the beach. We were simply waiting for trouble.

Greg battled his way back to me, ice-cream aloft over the heads of the throng. I twitched as I heard the thrumming of engines in the distance.

'Relax, Anon,' said Greg, between licks, 'that's not scooters – too powerful. They're not here yet.'

He'd called me Anon for years – a legacy of my marriage, when I'd joined the Al-Anon support group for the families of alcoholics. The marriage had expired along with my husband, and I had long since ceased to need Al-Anon, but Greg stuck to the old nickname. My name is Anna Knight, I'm thirty-nine – ten years older than Greg – and I looked on him with a sisterly affection. He could be an awkward cuss at times, gruf˜ and introverted, but I was one of the few people he would open out to.

'You've got ice-cream in your beard,' I said.

'Mmmmm – saving it for seconds.'

I rooted in my bag for a bottle of cologne, rubbing its wet coolness on my neck and forehead. I was glad I'd put my hair up that morning, as I felt a blessed waft of air across my shoulders. I checked for stray strands in my hand-mirror.

'Don't worry, you're still perfect,' observed Greg, screwing his mouth up prissily. 'And here we have Ms Anna Knight, ladies and gentlemen, modelling the most sophisticated grooming for a summer's day – no sweaty armpits there, me old cocker.'

He grinned and dodged my playful swipe. We both kept glancing at the traffic, nervous for the sound of scooters. I am tall, and I was standing on a concrete ledge, but I still couldn't quite see far enough over the heads of the crowd. I stood on tiptoe and leaned on Greg's shoulder, my dark hair occasionally brushing his coarse mousy curls. Police prowled up and down, on edge, like us waiting for the first disturbance.

'Ay – ay,' said Greg, tossing the remains of his cone away, 'I think we're in business. Listen.'

Vibrating through the humid air came the sound of engines, getting louder, insistent under the crowd's babble.

'Where are they?' I asked.

'Down by East Pier I'd guess. Coming this way. Come on.'

We forged across the promenade towards the road, Greg's bulky form clearing a path for me. As we reached the kerb I heard raised voices behind us, on the beach, young male voices building up a chant: 'Go 'ome, ya scum. Stick yer scooters up yer bum.'

'Regular little poets, aren't they?' said Greg acidly. 'Northport skins, the flower of our youth.'

I turned to see a horde of young men tearing up from the beach, leaping the steps, mounting the railings, dressed in baggy jeans held up with red braces – the uniform of Northport FC's resident thugs. As they shoved their way towards the road, the scooters were getting louder – and then I saw them: twenty or thirty machines filling one lane, with pennants flying their team's colours.

The pillion passengers were staring at the Northport crew's shaven heads bobbing in the mêlée. They pointed. They tapped the riders on the shoulders and shouted under their helmets. The helmets nodded, and as if as one, they revved their throaty engines as they passed and veered towards our side of the road.

'Here we go,' said Greg. 'Keep your head down, Anon, this could get nasty.'

The youths parked their machines in front of the Middle Pier and dismounted. Immediately I saw police uniforms gathering. But it was too late. The two gangs were already closing in on each other, the scooter mob's helmets still on for protection.

Jostled by the onlookers I had difficulty keeping up with

Greg, and the police were now adding to the mayhem. As the first can was thrown and the first fist flung the uniforms surged forward and the two gangs belted away towards the pier. Frightened passers-by tried to get out of the way, clutching bags and shielding children.

I saw one of the Northport youths turn, a beer can in his hand. He pulled the ring from it with his teeth, and took aim at a helmet just in front of me. It flew through the air, spraying the contents in its wake, and I knew he'd flung it too hard to hit his target. I ducked, and felt the cold beer on my back, then heard a cry behind me. It had hit an ageing man and he'd fallen to the ground. I turned to try and help. He had a boy with him, and despite the confusion it struck me how uncommon-looking they were. The man, balding, probably in his sixties, reminded me of an old colonial fallen on distressed times. His crumpled tropical suit hung from his body as though he had shrunk, his face was haggard, his voice educated. The boy – who looked about thirteen with a pale, unblemished face – had striking pearl-blond hair which curled over the collar of his white sailor-suit. The boy wordlessly wiped the man's dazed face with a large handkerchief. I could see the man was more shocked than hurt, for the can was almost empty by the time it had hit him. The boy and I tried to raise him to his feet, but the pressing people hampered our efforts. Greg had turned round at the commotion.

'Hold this,' he said, shoving his camera at me, and, putting his arms under the man's shoulders, he effortlessly lifted him.

'Thank you, I'll be all right now, thank you,' mumbled the man.

I could have sworn I saw a look of recognition flash between Greg and the boy. Neither said anything, and Greg immediately turned away, but the look stayed with me, as though he'd been startled by the boy's presence.

Greg was already shoving back to the battle, and I saw that the gangs had retreated under the police onslaught,

4

taking the only route open to them – on to the pier itself. They had mounted the barriers, police in pursuit. Greg turned to see where I was and I motioned to him to carry on. Fresh uproar broke out ahead. A bench ran all the way along the pier rail and I stood on it to try to see what was happening. A stall selling toffee apples and candyfloss had been ransacked – the poor young woman behind it red-faced, in tears, as her wares were used as missiles in the fray. Toffee apples flew from their sticks, cracked against skulls or helmets, candyfloss was squashed in faces. One toffee apple, flung up high, smashed against a large bill-board advertising the summer show at the pier theatre. I watched its passage, the red toffee sticking to the young woman's face on the billboard, the pulverised apple streak-ing down her acid-yellow hair on to the heads below. Greg was on the edge of the mêlée, camera whizzing through film, as the police at last began to gain the upper hand. I heard sirens on the promenade – police vans coming to cart off the combatants. The handcuffs were out, voices cursing, the last kicks and punches marking a dying defiance. I left my vantage point and made my way to Greg.

'Much blood?' I asked.

'Naw – lot of spit'n'thunder – a few sore heads. Nothing fatal.'

The fans were becoming sullen now, realising the stupid-ity of cornering themselves. Still, they'd got what they came for, and despite the sticky mess on their cheeks and clothes, some were clearly exhilarated.

Greg bent down to change his film.

'Pity about your daughter,' he said.

'What?'

'The billboard,' he indicated. 'That's her, isn't it?'

It was indeed my daughter's face, now streaked with the remains of toffee apple, staring down at us from the sign, one eye closed in a permanent wink.

'She here for the whole season?'

'Yes,' I answered.

'Didn't she do well?' he said, mimicking the tones of a talent show compere.

I didn't answer . . . she had done well, but like Greg, I couldn't be sincere enough to say it and mean it. Shelley was my only child, she was now nineteen, and beginning to be a big name on the showbusiness scene. This was her first season of top billing at the pier theatre, the Vegas, supported by Tiny Toni, the latest singing super-tot. Shelley was a comedienne. She also sang and danced. She was bright, sharp and beautiful, and I had to admit part of me was proud of her, for she had done it all herself, graduating from dance school to children's panto, talent shows and club cabaret. Now she'd done several TV slots and a commercial, and she was rapidly becoming well known under her stage name, Shelley Chantelle. But it was not as I'd have wished. I wanted her to go to drama school, become a serious actress – she had the talent – but like her father she had a stubborn will, and I had little choice but to let her have her way.

I looked out to sea as I waited for Greg, and saw among the bobbing bathers one balding head, one blond, swimming out together.

'There's that couple,' I said, 'the man hit by the beer can, and the boy. The man must be all right now.'

Greg looked where I pointed.

'How can you tell it's them?' he said, rather roughly. 'We're too far away.'

I acknowledged I could not be sure, and we began walking down the pier back on to the promenade.

'Sweet, isn't he, don't you think?' Greg observed. 'The boy I mean.'

'Yes, I suppose he is – why?'

'You wouldn't think he was working, would you? I mean, he looks quite the little innocent.'

'Working?'

'How old d'you think he is?'

'Thirteen, fourteen – I don't know he's just a young boy.'

'He's nineteen,' Greg said emphatically.

'You know him then?'

'I know *of* him. Go in the same clubs and bars – I haven't much to stay home for, have I?' Greg had lived alone all the time I'd known him. 'He's called Sammy . . . he flits about the club scene. Pretty boy like that, certain types fawn all over him.'

Realisation was beginning to dawn as to what Greg meant by 'working', but still I hesitated.

Greg laughed at my discomfiture.

'I was in Raiders the other week,' he said, meaning one of the resort's many nightclubs. 'Sammy was the belle of the ball. It was his birthday. Geezers kept requesting that record for him – "Nineteen" – because that's how old he was.'

'Geezers?'

'Yes, Anon . . . dear me, do I have to spell it out? He puts out for fellas, love – and not only that, he's on the game, up for rent. How else could he afford his clothes and his clubbing?'

'He's a male prostitute?'

'Bingo! I do believe she's got it!'

'And the old man?'

'Is a punter, Anon. He's paying for Sammy's charms.'

I pondered this silently as we wound our way through the crowds. It must have taken us half an hour as Greg sidetracked to take pictures of the vandalised pier entrance. Eventually we reached the road.

The traffic was heavy and we waited for a gap. Turning to take a last look at the beach, I spotted a commotion at the water's edge. A man in red trunks was running, dodging the deckchairs. A crowd of swimmers had gathered in a cluster, and some were shouting and waving.

I pulled Greg's arm and pointed. 'What's going on?'

'Dunno – don't want to know,' he answered. 'I want to get back to process this film.'

'Come on, Greg – if it's a story they're bound to ask why we weren't there.'

By now the running man had reached the promenade. I heard him hoarsely trying to shout: 'Somebody get an ambulance, get the police! A guy's drowning!'

One man responded to his plea and went haring away. He quickly returned with a young policeman who spoke into his radio before running to the little knot at the sea edge. The deckchair dozers roused themselves to clear his path.

Greg relented with an exasperated sigh. 'Come on then.'

As we approached, I could see the unmistakable outline of a man's body lying on the sand through the strobe effect of the moving legs. I swallowed hard. The body was deathly white.

The policeman and another man were taking turns to pump the man's chest, willing the heart to start again. As we got nearer, I saw a gush of soupy salt water surge from the man's mouth. The kiss of life followed, but it was too late, death had already embraced him. The crowd around him parted a little, and I gasped, recognising the bald head, the drawn face. It was the man who'd been hit by the beer can.

I turned to look for Sammy, but he was not there. I scanned the faces in the crowd – some excited, some repelled – but nowhere could I see the pale-haired boy.

The ambulance crew arrived – to the relief of parents trying to shield children's faces. The flaccid body, its blue veins visible beneath the skin, was loaded on to a stretcher and covered before being borne up the beach. A rabble of tinsel-wigged children followed the party, wagging their head-dresses up and down, their parents nowhere to be seen.

Watching the stretcher's progress I saw the unmistakable yellow hair and tanned limbs of my daughter at the top of the beach steps. As the uniformed men manoeuvred their burden the tinsel-wigged followers spotted her, and nudged each other: 'It's Shelley Chantelle – look, look – Shelley Chantelle, it's her, it is!'

They engulfed her as I watched, touching, stroking her hair, and one even produced a scrap of paper for her autograph. She smiled through it all, that hard, bright, professional smile I'd seen her practise in the mirror. Perhaps she'd wondered what the commotion was on the beach, and had wanted to look; but such whims were becoming beyond her now, she was public property. Before I could call out to her she had retreated, disappearing into the throng.

I looked at Greg in some distress, but he too looked shaken, and after I'd done the necessary interviews, we made our way back to our cars in silence.

TWO

BANK HOLIDAY TRAGEDY
AS TOP DOCTOR DROWNS
by Anna Knight

A top consultant at Royal Northport Hospital drowned yesterday off Middle Beach as thousands of stunned holidaymakers looked on.

The resort was enjoying one of its busiest May Day holidays of recent years when the tragedy struck.

Dr Iain Jefferson, a 59-year-old consultant haematologist, was dragged lifeless from the sea by a horrified swimmer.

Police and lifeguards made desperate attempts to revive him on the beach but their efforts were in vain.

Mr Andy Farrell, aged 23, of Cedar Avenue, Longridge, raised the alarm after spotting Dr Jefferson in difficulties.

'He was quite a long way out – face down, not moving – so I swam out to see if anything was wrong,' said Mr Farrell.

'As soon as I saw what had happened I shouted for help and tried to pull him in, but it was too late.'

Dr Jefferson, of Snowdon Drive, Statham, had worked at the hospital for eight years, winning immense respect for his work, especially in the field of leukaemia.

He leaves a wife, Margot, and two sons. Alistair and Jonathan. The family was too upset to talk, but a family friend said she was surprised Dr Jefferson had been at the beach as he was supposed to have been working all day.

An inquest will be opened on Thursday.

So I told the public less than I knew – I never mentioned his boy companion. Neither did the police. I held my story back specifically to wait for their official statement after the incident, to see what they would say. But they never mentioned the boy at all. Well, it was a delicate time for his family, stricken with shock and grief. To expose the fact that he'd been with a rent-boy – if that's what he was – would have been too cruel. I could see the point of waiting until the inquest, when the family had had more time to adjust and prepare themselves.

But as I sat through the full inquest, later, I began to feel more and more uncomfortable.

DOCTOR'S DROWNING
– SUICIDE VERDICT

Blood specialist Dr Iain Jefferson drowned himself in a fit of depression brought on by overwork, an inquest heard yesterday.

Coroner Mr Travis Mansell gave a verdict of suicide after it was revealed that the 59-year-old consultant left a letter to his wife, making clear his suicidal intentions.

The body of Dr Jefferson, a respected haematology specialist at Royal Northport Hospital, was pulled from the sea on Bank Holiday Monday, when the beach was packed.

A post-mortem revealed the cause of death was drowning, pathologist Dr Miles Simpson told the inquest.

Said Mr Mansell, 'The letter left by Dr Jefferson in the care of his solicitor, and addressed to his wife, makes it clear to me that he had wanted to take his own life.

'I must add, however, from evidence given by his colleagues, that Dr Jefferson had been depressed in recent months due to pressure of work and staff shortages.

'He felt his work was suffering, and he was failing to meet his own high standards. He had reached a breaking point which must have disturbed the balance of his mind at that time.

'Apparently he did a great deal of extra work voluntarily, rather than make a fuss and demand more help. It is sad to record that such work-related stress has robbed us of a very able physician, and his family of a beloved husband and father.'

Thus the inquest had ruled. But what I did not – could not – report was that as I came out of the courtroom I overheard Jefferson's widow, sobbing on the shoulder of another woman in the corridor. Mrs Jefferson, a plump, neat little woman in Scottish tweed, had been weeping in bursts all through the inquest. Now, away from the enforced hush of the courtroom, she was releasing her emotions, talking through her tears. Uneasy about the complete absence of the rent-boy from any of the inquest's proceedings, I lingered to listen.

'It's no good, Sonia,' sobbed the widow, 'I still can't believe it, I don't believe it. He wasn't under any more pressure than usual. He was retiring next year, we were buying a villa in the South of France. He knew all the pressure would be off soon. I can't believe it was because

11

of overwork. Oh God, it's so humiliating. Why won't they listen to me?'

She began to scrabble for something in her bag. She found it, and thrust it in the face-of her long-suffering friend.

'Look at it, look, look,' she demanded. 'Where in there does it say he couldn't cope with work? Just tell me where?'

Her friend, a professional-looking middle-aged woman, tried her best to calm her. 'Margot, I know, I've seen the letter before. I know it doesn't say that. But it's just the whole tone of it. You have to admit, it's so despairing, it couldn't mean anything else. Margot – please . . .'

Mrs Jefferson had shrugged away from her in exasperation, and I realised she was coming towards me, as I hovered by the wall within earshot. 'Look,' she said. 'You look. You're the reporter who was at my husband's inquest, weren't you? You look at his letter. I'm not a neurotic woman like those policemen seem to think. I knew my husband, I knew him. Work wouldn't have killed him. He could cope with that. There's something else behind this . . . and no one will listen to me. They hear me but they don't listen.'

I had no choice but to read the letter as she waited. It was not an easy experience.

'Dearest Margot, my own love . . . If you are reading this you will know the worst has happened, and I will not be on hand to tell you why. Margot please, I want you to know, and truly believe, that you are to blame for none of this – you do not deserve the trial I am putting you through and I do not deserve your forgiveness. I wish with all my heart it could have been otherwise. But the pressure, the evil, evil pressure, has become too great. I no longer know what seems rational. I am unworthy – as a husband, a father, a doctor and as a man – and in this state I am worse than useless – I am positively harmful. Only this way does there seem an escape for me. I have agonised over this act. I can think of nothing else. Now you will know what I have done. Be angry with me, hate me, it is all I deserve, but never, never blame yourself. I have loved both you and the boys more than my life, but I am better out of the way, out of your lives. Now you must try to forget me. Margot I'm sorry . . . Iain.'

I stopped reading, and saw that she was awaiting my response, desperate for me to say something. I struggled for words. 'It – it does seem as though he was terribly depressed, Mrs Jefferson,' I said, feeling the inadequacy of the statement.

'Depressed? I know that!' she said despairingly. 'Oh, stop clutching at me for goodness' sake, Sonia.' She turned on her companion who was trying as discreetly as possible to draw her away. 'But he wasn't a coward,' she returned to me fiercely. 'Something else is behind this, something drove him to it, but it wasn't his job, whatever his colleagues said – he loved it too much. Someone was putting that pressure on him. Someone has my husband's death on their conscience. Someone evil.'

'Margot, please!' Sonia now firmly gripped the widow's arm. 'Stop torturing yourself. You told the police all this, it's all been looked into. There's nothing more you can do, now let's go home.'

Mrs Jefferson looked to me, appealingly, but I didn't know what to do. Abruptly all the energy seemed to drain out of her, and she turned away, burying her face in her handkerchief. Sonia, her arm around her friend, spoke to me in an undertone.

'I'm sorry about this,' she said. 'She's had a hard time accepting what's happened. He might have said she mustn't blame herself but she does – who wouldn't? – and she thinks others are blaming her – for not realising he was at breaking point. So she keeps denying it was overwork. It's an understandable reaction. I'm sorry you've been embarrassed by all this.'

'No need to apologise – really,' I hastened to reassure her. 'It's all right – I understand.'

But in truth I no more understood what had happened to the dead doctor than Mrs Jefferson, now being led away in snuffling bewilderment. However Sonia might explain it away, Mrs Jefferson's conviction that something else was to blame for her husband's death seemed real enough to me.

And what of my own guilt in the affair? Why hadn't I told the police about the rent-boy? Because I was sure someone else would have mentioned it to them, even if the boy himself had not come forward. Hundreds of people must have seen them together. The boy had been in the water with the man – surely he couldn't have just swum away and let him drown . . . could he? Had all those people just assumed the police would find out about the blond-haired boy – and never mentioned him – just as I had? I realised I had to act.

I caught Greg alone near the coffee machine at work.

'Greg – I think we should tell the police about Sammy.'

He knew immediately what I was talking about, for I held my own inquest report, clipped from the paper, under his nose. He cursed as his fingers fumbled with the coffee cup and a spout of scalding water hit his hand.

'You've got to be joking,' he said.

'I'm not, Greg, why should I? I just don't feel that this is the truth,' I indicated the clipping. 'Or at least not all of it anyway. I saw the widow after the inquest – I've never seen anyone so utterly in torment. If we've got information we owe it to her to come forward.'

Turning on me he said, fiercely, 'Why, Anon? What the hell good would it do? You want to salve your conscience, is that it? Tidy up the loose ends? I suppose that'll make everything right again, will it?'

'No, of course not. But yes, you're right, it is on my conscience that we never told the police everything we saw – and I can't understand why it isn't on yours, if you have one.'

'And what did we see?'

'Oh, for God's sake. We saw him with a rent-boy. We saw them together in the water. The boy could have stopped him drowning – and he didn't.'

'We don't know that,' he said roughly. 'We were too far away to tell. And anyway, so what? The man wanted to die – remember? Nothing we can say can bring him back.'

'But Greg, they never even mentioned the boy at the inquest, it's as if no one else knew he was there. Only we know, and it just strikes me that there could be something more sinister behind his death. Can't you see that?'

'No, all I can see is you're setting yourself up for trouble. Don't meddle in this, Anon, I'm saying this for your own good. If you finger Sammy, you'll open an ugly can of worms. I know the scene he's into – it's nasty, it doesn't operate by the moral code you're used to. There's a hell of a lot of people in this town whose poncy careers would be destroyed if a copper got hold of Sammy's list of clients. Not just their careers either. Their marriages, their reputations – their whole lives. He mixes with some big wheels. They'd have no trouble finding out who shopped their little friend. They live on a knife-edge as it is – one twist, and you'll find they're sticking it in you. After all, if they're going to be destroyed what have they got to lose?'

He clenched his hand round the coffee cup, and hot liquid lapped over on to his fingers, but he took no notice.

'Anyway,' he went on. 'Think of that tormented widow – isn't it bad enough her husband killed himself, without knowing that he was seeing rent-boys? Think of that.'

I looked down at the crumpled cutting in my hand, a thin rag of half-truth, shaming me. 'It isn't right, Greg,' I said. 'I still don't feel it's right.'

'Not much is, in this world Anon, certainly not Sammy's little corner of it.' He shrugged irritably, as if despairing of me. 'It's rough trade, Anon. OK, OK, if you want nasty phone calls in the middle of the night, if you want wreaths and hearses rolling up unannounced at your door, if you want all that hassle – go ahead. I can't stop you. It's your choice.'

And he stood staring at me, making it clear I'd be on my own. A secretary came along the corridor, seeking the coffee machine, and our conversation ceased. She had four cups to take back, and by the time I'd finished helping her, Greg had gone.

THREE

I spent the evening alone at my flat, racked by indecision. The flat is a modest, one-bedroomed abode at the top of a modern block. Until a year before, when Shelley left home, we had lived in a tall, handsome Victorian town house – the sole bequest of my husband's frittered life. I'd found it a constant worry, paying for endless repairs, trying to keep on top of the dust which seemed to renew itself daily. So it was a relief when Shelley declared she was going to invest some of her fast-accumulating earnings in a penthouse just down the coast. I sold up, threw out all my clutter, and bought the flat – cheap, light, simple to clean – and I almost felt like a student again revelling in new-found freedom.

I sat on the little balcony that evening, overlooking a large lovely garden which I did not have to tend, and I watched a sparrow pecking crumbs from the plate on which I'd had my cold and hasty supper. I pondered what to do.

Mrs Jefferson's pudgy, damp face kept coming back to me, one minute confused, the next adamant her husband wouldn't have killed himself through overwork. But Greg's warnings had seemed so emphatic, so fierce. Was he being melodramatic?

I couldn't help feeling that cynicism had warped his outlook. He floated around the edges of a shifting society of prostitutes and their prey, visiting dubious clubs and pubs, the haunts of petty criminals. I couldn't see him dabbling himself, but I felt it gave him a vicarious thrill to descend to this seamy underworld. He might well blow up its wickedness, just to bolster his own self-worth. Yet could I ignore his alarm?

What he had said was true – Dr Jefferson could not be brought back from the dead. But the thought of him being buried as a straightforward victim of overwork grated on me like that little bird's claws on my plate. I flung out at it and it burst away in a flurry of ruffled feathers. But in seconds it was back, hopping warily out of reach . . . It wasn't just guilt at not having acted as a responsible citizen: I needed to know whether that boy had let the man die before his eyes – whether he'd played a part in it. Was there a more sinister pressure on Jefferson to tip him over into self-destruction? He was a blood specialist after all, and one with an underlife, meeting a promiscuous homosexual. The AIDS threat was obvious – was he consumed with guilt, threatened with exposure, or blackmail? There were too many ragged questions for his body to be wrapped up with a simple label and left to rest.

I wanted to talk it over with someone whose judgement I trusted, and my thoughts immediately went to Alys, whose companionship had seen me through many years of calm and crisis.

But she wasn't in. I'd been trying to phone her flat in London for the past few weeks, with no reply – and although I was used to such absences with Alys's job, I felt slightly put out that she had not told me where she was going, and that she wasn't there when I needed her. My other friends, here in Northport, were fine for work and parties – we meshed together wonderfully as a social safety net. But the threads were too lightweight for something like this. They'd toss off a blasé remark like, 'Forget about it, Anna – Greg's right you know. Listen, you think too much for your own good. Come on, have a drink and don't be miserable.' And I'd share their drink and laugh at their jokes and they'd go away thinking they'd solved my problems. But I would still be knotted up inside.

It was at times like this I missed my mother's rough wisdom. Brought up on a failing farm, she'd had only a rudimentary education, and as I progressed through school to university, I could tell she regretted being born too early for grants. But she was never bitter. She was instinctively astute – a strong woman who worked hard at whatever job she could get – factory hand, shop assistant, auxiliary nurse – to keep me at school while my sick father slowly succumbed to emphysema. I trusted her insight. I missed it, I missed her. I'd had to stand by as cancer killed her two years before, and the pain was still raw.

I shivered a little as the night air began to chill. Would Shelley ever regard me as I regarded my mother, I wondered? I doubted it. There was already a gap between us, and she was drawing away into her own life, her own future. She, like my mother, was always decisive. My mother's voice came back to me, echoing up childhood stairs, 'Come on, Anna, stop dithering about. The world won't wait while you shilly-shally – it's got better things to do.'

She was right – stop dithering about, Anna, follow your instincts. Get off and talk to the police as you know you should – you can't let the buggers get you down. That's what she'd have said – and let Greg look after his own decisions. I uncurled my legs and began clearing up the supper tray, feeling stronger and somehow relieved by my sudden firmness.

The phone warbled into life and I went to answer it, hoping it was Alys. But it was Shelley's voice that greeted me.

18

'Ma!' she said loudly above a racket of music and voices. 'Can you hear me all right? I'm at the theatre.'

'So I gathered.'

'What? I'm sorry, Mama, this phone's near one of the speakers backstage and I can't turn it down.'

'OK!' I shouted, 'I can hear you. What's the matter?'

'Nothing – nothing's the matter. I've just had some great news though, and I wanted to tell you. The guy from Riverside TV's been in touch – and they want me to do a pilot show with a couple more comediennes they've lined up. If we gel together, we could end up with a series. Isn't that wonderful?'

'Yes, yes, love – it's wonderful.' And I felt as I had when she was a child, beseeching my praise for landing a plum part in the panto. She needed to hear me say it, that's why she was ringing, she needed the reassurance. 'When are you seeing the chap from Riverside?'

'I'm going down next Tuesday just to talk it over. They've been really good about it here at the theatre – they've let me off a couple of shows and they've got Gaye Supreme to stand in, so they're quite happy.'

'You're very lucky, Shelley,' I shouted. 'I'm really pleased for you.'

'Less of the luck, Ma – I've really worked for this. It's ten per cent luck and ninety per cent hard graft – nothing comes easy in this business, you know.'

'I know, I know,' I said placatingly. 'You deserve it – you do work hard, Shelley.' Too hard, I sometimes worried. There was room for little else in her life.

'Well – wish me luck for Tuesday then?'

'Break a leg, darling. I'm sure you'll get the job.'

'Thanks – I'd better go now, Mama. I'm on again in five. Hey – I'll treat you to dinner at Valentino's if the pilot's a success.'

'I'll look forward to that.'

And I would – though I was still coming to terms with my own daughter treating me to outings and clothes in what to me was the luxury bracket. It didn't feel comfortable, being beholden to her, and yet I couldn't, of course, be other than grateful for her generosity. The inflated rewards of the business irked me, making even a dinner at Valentino's leave a sour taste in my mouth.

FOUR

I still shrank from marching straight into a police station to give a statement about Sammy to whatever bored copper happened to be behind the desk. I much preferred the idea of speaking to someone I knew – not formally in an office where I'd suffer the weight of bureaucracy.

I'd struck up a good working relationship with one of the detectives in the last few months. He'd given me background on crime stories and I'd given him publicity for his photofits and reconstructions. I rang him and suggested a meeting one evening. I was rather surprised at his enthusiasm for the idea.

So there I was, sitting waiting for him in the cocktail bar of one of the largest hotels – the Monopole – a tall, modern creation moulded round seminar suites, entertainment rooms and hierarchies of restaurants – a favourite with the conference trade.

After the flurry of the early Bank Holidays, there is always a lull in the resort until high summer when schoolchildren are let loose. This lull is often filled with conferences – essential bed-fillers when hotel cash-flows would otherwise stagnate.

Conferences, however, can be perilous for the unwise.

Delegates, freed from marital chains, tend to get over-excited, fuelled by an unaccustomed surfeit of alcohol and self-importance. Feral creatures prowl around to take advantage of their gullibility – creatures like Sammy and his female counterparts.

I sat on my own in the bar of the Monopole, watching the barmaid being harassed by ranks of local government officers on release for their annual union get-together, and I sipped anxiously at my spritzer, wary that I would be taken for someone waiting to offer 'a good time'.

I had begun to regret the shortness of my velvet skirt, aware it could denote a sexual signal to such a group of rutting males. Agitated, I kept looking at my watch – a fob-watch on a heavy silver chain – my only inheritance from my grandfather, the failed farmer. I wore it as he would have done, hung properly across my brocade waist-coat, and its solid weight gave me some comfort.

Detective Inspector Tom Irving was late, decidedly late. I'd chosen him because I felt I could trust him. He was in his early forties, a Yorkshireman with a rough-hewn char-acter, who suffered little nonsense. I suspected he was a bit of a loner in police terms.

He was sandy-haired and tawny-skinned, good-looking in a tall, fit way, though unselfconscious about it. More than once I had looked with undue interest at the gold wisps on the backs of his hands, and found myself wonder-ing if the hair was gold on his chest and more, wondering what he would look like, naked.

But Tom was married, with a son of nine or ten, and therefore I suppressed such wanton thoughts. Oh, don't think I was being high-minded and moral: this was simply self-protection – I had been that way before. Tonight he was late, but I was not unused to this, either with police officers or with married men. Sometimes, I remembered, married men did not turn up at all – unable to excuse themselves from some sudden family duty or crisis, unable to make contact. Sometimes, I remembered, the woman he had arranged to meet would be left staring at the sticky remains in her glass, wearing her carefully chosen dress, feeling foolish and alone.

I was breaking a cocktail stick into ever-smaller splinters. Men stood in drinking groups round the bar's watering hole. Some hugged pint glasses protectively in the crook of their arm, some threw back large doses of spirits at a fast pace. Several were casting glances in my direction, turning back to their colleagues to utter a gruff word, laugh, and look again. I shot severe, ice-laden stares to counter these parries. It could be effective – I had sufficient experience of bars where lone women were looked on as target practice.

I took a deep draught of my drink and rechecked my watch. It was a stuffy, humid evening and the French windows were open, leading out on to a path through a rose garden. Beyond the garden was the car park, which I had positioned myself to be able to see. I kept looking out for Tom's car, without reward.

A middle-aged, white-haired man caught my attention as he loudly departed from his circle at the bar. Refusing his pals' exhortations to have 'just one more, Harry', he was insisting he wanted an early night.

Though portly, his navy-blue blazer was well enough cut to disguise the paunch, and was smartly offset by a crisp white shirt and spotted cravat. As he left through the garden entrance his unexpected behaviour made me take more notice of him. As soon as he was out of sight of his colleagues he began to loiter round the rose-bushes, making a play of smelling their perfume while looking at his watch and staring round expectantly. His face seemed faintly, annoyingly familiar, but I could not quite place it. I'd noticed he had been drinking whisky or brandy in substantial quantity at the bar – a mistake, I'd inwardly lectured, for with his ruddy, over-blown complexion he must have had high blood pressure or a heart condition.

He left the roses and walked up and down meditatively.

At length, he poked in his inside pocket and pulled out a large cigar. After some difficulty lighting it, its glow seemed to calm him. Like me, he seemed to be waiting for someone.

I began to think Tom was not going to come, and I was tired of mentally holding off the boozing boyos at the bar. I would wait no longer. I began to write a hurried note to leave with the barmaid in case he should arrive, when, casting a last glance through the doorway, I saw him striding through the garden.

I put the note away with some relief. As he entered the bar, he halted, looking about him anxiously until he saw my raised arm.

'Anna – I'm sorry I'm so late – not my fault, honestly – a bunch of idiots chose tonight to create a ruckus down at the Bay Tree. It's not usually my job sweeping up after hooligans, but one of them got himself stabbed and another bashed the landlord and whipped the takings. Upped their status in the crime stakes. What morons.'

'Did you nab them?'

'So drunk they practically sat and begged.' He sat down heavily. 'What a life.'

'You chose it.'

'What?' he puzzled. 'Oh, I see what you mean – no, I meant them actually. Never mind that, they're just rabble. I was just blasted annoyed because they were keeping me away from you.'

The intensity of his eye contact caught me off guard, as did the subsequent brush of his hand on my knee as he said, 'Let me get you another drink.' He had never touched me before, indeed he had never looked at me with such sexual appreciation. Even at, as Greg would call it, my Great Age, I found I still had it in me to blush.

Damn it all, I accused myself, as I watched his broad shoulders easily thrust through the queue at the bar, was it really your conscience over a dead doctor and a rent-boy that brought you here – or was it subconscious craving for the sheer physicality of this man's presence? A frustrated widow – was that what I had come to? Creating excuses for myself to meet a man.

I desperately wanted a cigarette. To hell with the health admonishments, I needed it. With perseverance I had succeeded in cutting my intake from a pack a day to a pack a fortnight, and I'd already had that day's ration at work. None the less I knew I had some in my handbag, the fag-end of a packet that had been there for weeks, steadily drying out. I lit one, and it crackled fiercely. I drew the smoke in deeply, immensely grateful for its soothing support. Glancing up I noticed an answering beacon – the cigar glow of the man in the blazer, still waiting outside. He shuffled from foot to foot impatiently, all pretence of admiring the blooms abandoned.

The ash on my cigarette had mushroomed from the arid tobacco, and I shot an arm out to the ashtray – too late, too quick – my action knocked the half-empty wine glass and it cascaded liquid to the floor.

I was half aware of a white-flashing reflection in the pool of wine as I bent to pick up the unbroken glass. A small, pale hand reached it before I did, and I looked up to find myself staring deep into the blue eyes of Sammy.

'It's Anna, isn't it?' he said in a half-broken boy's voice. 'You're a reporter – a friend of Greg's. He's talked to me about you.'

So Greg didn't just know of the boy, as he'd told me – he actually knew him. Sammy's gaze darted about the room, on his guard.

'Yes, I'm Greg's friend,' I hurriedly replied. 'I work with him. He told me a little about you, too.'

'Listen,' he said urgently. 'I – I want to talk to you. Please – please . . .' But then his eyes flickered away again, intent on dangers I could not see. I could not help but stare at his profiled face, with its fine, translucent skin. He had long, downy blond eyelashes which seemed particularly childlike, and his whole aspect was vulnerable. He looked at me with entreaty. It was a look which seemed to draw out all my maternal protectiveness. He wore a fine lawn shirt which billowed over his slender arms, and his pale hair gleamed, almost luminous. He looked like a beautiful Aryan boy, pure enough to touch a Führer's heart.

I wanted to touch him, I wanted him to go on. 'Please?' I prompted. But he seemed to flinch from some threat. The next second he was gone, leaving an apology trailing on the air . . . 'I'm sorry – someone's waiting – it's no good. I'm sorry Anna.'

I watched him go, speechless.

Then I saw him join the blazered man outside in the rose garden. A fatherly arm went round his shoulder, a tender hand hovered round his head, as though wanting to stroke his hair. The man's face broke into pleasure, and a low greeting brought their heads near. Then they turned, and I lost sight of them as they walked into the gathering night.

Those few moments had left me covered in confusion. How could I know what the boy had wanted? Here I had come, prepared to betray him, and there he was, his eyes haunting me like a defenceless animal. What was he to me? Little more than a name, a so-called rent-boy. Why then had his presence affected me like this, why did I want to shield him? It was his eyes that disconcerted me so – they seemed to look into my very soul. I wanted to apologise for the sordidness of a world that reduced him to living in men's pockets. I wanted to know him.

'Can't I leave you for five minutes without you making a spectacle of yourself?' It was Tom, tutting in mock remonstration over my spilled drink. 'Hold these,' he instructed, putting the glasses in my hand, 'I'll mop up.'

He brought a cloth from the bar. 'I know,' he said, still in a bantering tone, 'it was the devastating effect of my charm – made you go all to pieces.' I was aware of the cloth hovering over my skirt. 'Did any go on your clothes? Irving's Soakaway at your service.'

'No Tom, it didn't,' I said, moving his hand away.

'Pity.' And he turned away to take the cloth back.

When he returned he took a grateful gulp of beer, as though he needed it. I was unsure what to say to him now. The episode with the boy had rattled my resolve. I coughed nervously, trying to cover the empty pause.

'Right then,' he said, fixing me with a smile, 'what's this mysterious item you wanted to talk over – so mysterious you wouldn't even give me a clue on the phone?'

'I – I'm sorry,' I laughed, 'did I sound a bit over-dramatic? It's just something that's been worrying me, only I'd rather not become officially involved if I can help it. I'd rather just tell you as a friend . . . and then I'd be grateful if you forgot where you heard it.' I had started now . . . I could not go back.

'You do intrigue me . . . go on.'

'Well, you remember on Bank Holiday Monday, there was a drowning?'

'Yeah . . . that doctor somebody or other . . . committed suicide.'

'That's it. You're going to tell me I should've said something at the time – and I know I should – but I'm trying to put it right now.'

He didn't say anything, and I saw that he was gazing at me with quite open appreciation. 'I'm sorry,' he said, as if collecting himself. 'The doctor.'

'I was on the promenade, working, when it happened, and I saw the doctor before he went down to the beach. He wasn't alone, Tom, that's what's been worrying me. And at the inquest, there was no mention of anyone with him. But I know there was.'

That vision of Sammy's eyes quite suddenly came back to me in full force, mutely appealing, knocking the next sentence back into my throat. I took a drink and swallowed hard, determined to press on.

'It was a boy called Sammy – I don't know his surname,' I said, not looking at Tom. 'But I'm told he is a rent-boy.'

26

'Aaah . . . I see what you mean. Listen, I'm a bit vague on the details – I didn't deal with the case. But at the inquest didn't they decide it was just pressure at work that made him snap?'

'Yes.'

'So what you're saying is . . . the doc was a closet nancy?'

I winced. 'He could've been, Tom. I'm not saying he was. But if it's true, it does open up the possibility of a different reason for his suicide. There's something else too. I saw the boy in the water with him. I think he could've saved him . . . if he'd wanted to.'

Tom shook his head. 'I'd have to check the file, Anna. It's no use me saying anything now. All this could've been checked out, you see, and eliminated. They wouldn't necessarily mention it at the inquest then. Particularly with a bloke like that – likely to have friends in high places – they close ranks round one of their own.'

I nodded, and sat back, expecting to feel relieved after taking the weight off my mind. But I didn't, I felt uncomfortable, a sense of betrayal like a bad taste in my mouth. Why had the boy had such an effect on me? Why didn't I want to say I'd seen him, only a moment ago?

'You did right to tell me,' Tom was saying. 'I appreciate it . . . and I appreciate it was me you asked for . . . Anna?' His voice had dropped low and intimate. I looked at him questioningly. 'I've wanted a chance like this for a long time,' he said. 'A chance to be on our own – away from work.'

He edged closer towards me, and his arm fell as if casually across the back of my seat. I felt his fingers glide over my collar, and touch the hair at the nape of my neck.

'I like this,' he said, 'the way you wear your hair up. It always looks so smooth and polished, with these tiny little wisps on your neck. I just want to touch them.'

Little sparks, like electricity, were shooting through my skin as I felt his contact.

'You always look so cool, Anna . . . tall and untouchable

27

. . . but you're not, really, are you? Inside you're soft as a baby . . . I've been watching you.'

'How long?'

'Ever since I first saw you, notebook under your arm, come to check the details of a car crash. You were wearing a red suit . . . and I thought, there goes one classy number, Irving, bit out of your league. But I watched you, over the next few months, and I began to think you weren't so untouchable after all. You always opened up towards me. I saw your face when I walked in a room. You always smiled. I wasn't wrong, was I?'

No, he wasn't wrong. Slowly I shook my head, despite myself. He reached out across my lap, and took my hand. I couldn't speak, such surges of feeling were too ridiculous for words. It was confusing and belittling. My fingers stroked the gold hairs on the back of his hand. They clamoured to be let loose on his arms, his chest, his neck – on his whole body. His married body. Oh, but it would be so good to feel a man again. It had been too long.

'I've got a proposition to make to you,' he said.

'Go on,' I replied, my head buzzing with contradictory voices like the noise building up over the busy bar.

'How would you like to come to a show with me tonight? I've got tickets.'

'A show? Where, what?'

'Right here, actually – Shelley and her crew.'

'Shelley?' My face must have shown blank consternation.

'Didn't you know she's on in cabaret with some of the other pier performers? It's a charity job organised by these local government nebbies.'

I felt my insides leaden. 'No, she didn't mention it.'

'Only, I thought, well, you could've been there anyway, couldn't you, doing the proud parent bit? And I know a couple of lads from the station are going, I could've been with them – they wouldn't land me in it – you see what I mean?'

I did see exactly what he meant – alibis to protect his

marriage. It had started already. I didn't want this, I didn't need it.

'You'll come then.' He said it as a statement, not a question.

'No thanks,' I said flatly.

'But . . . I've got tickets.'

'You shouldn't have done.'

'Look, I know you've probably seen it before, but—'

'No Tom, I don't want to go, not even with you.'

He looked as crestfallen as I felt. 'I'm sorry, I'm sorry. I've been a berk, it was stupid of me.'

'Just a bit presumptuous, that's all.' Now I felt pompous. He drew his hand away from mine.

With my height and demeanour, it's all too easy for me to look aloof. I really didn't want to spurn him like this, I didn't want to hurt him. But I found it hard to hide my disappointment. It wasn't him I was rejecting, it was all the trappings that went with him: the marital deception, the subterfuge, the pretence. If he'd suggested, instead, that we go straight home to my bed, I think I'd have accepted, the way my body felt that night. But I didn't want a courtship. And especially not by means of Shelley's show. That needle of unease, which had begun to bother me lately, pierced unbidden into my thoughts: is it me he wants to know? Or merely Shelley Chantelle's mother?

The change in my attitude must have been all too apparent. Tom coughed and looked at his watch, scanning the crowd at the bar which had now started to diminish, filtering off through a side door.

He looked edgily towards it, as if wanting to retreat. 'That's the Diana Suite,' he said, 'where the show is. There's Tony Stone.'

I knew this was one of his mates from the station.

'You go,' I said as kindly as I could. 'Please – it's all right, really. I'm sure you want to see her. You've got tickets after all.'

'You're not going to change your mind, are you?'

29

'Positively not.'

'You're a strange one, Anna. I know, you're an independent woman. But don't be lonely.'

I smiled, 'I'll work on it.'

'I hate leaving a woman on her own like this.'

'Nonsense. It's my choice, after all. Don't worry about it. Go – enjoy the show. I'll finish my drink.'

'Listen . . . I am sorry if I offended you, I didn't mean—'

'Forget it, Tom – really – no offence taken. Now go, or you'll miss the beginning.'

He went, following the last stragglers into the dim Diana Room. I could hear raunchy jazz music beating through the door, almost drowned at times by crescendos of hard, hacking male laughter. It silenced, probably with the dousing of the lights, and a deep drum roll heralded a master of ceremonies.

I heard his muffled voice raising over-enthusiastic mirth at his weak jokes. The audience wanted to be pleased. They were primed and ready for enjoyment. The jokes stopped, and a pause of anticipation followed.

'Gentlemen – and ladies,' the voice came, 'I'm sure you've seen more than enough of me, so let me go right on to a much more pleasing eyeful. Please – put your hands together for the delight you've all been waiting for – the Queen of Comedy, Mistress of Mirth, First Lady of Laughter – all wrapped up in the Piquant Package of – mmmmMISS SHELLEY CHANTELLE!' How that stage name set my teeth on edge.

An enormous surge of applause greeted this announcement, followed by a puzzled murmuring. I knew the routine. While they'd all been staring expectantly at the spotlit stage, Shelley would slip in through a side entrance and slide on to the lap of an unsuspecting male in the audience. Then while the spotlight swept over the crowd, she would be tickling her hapless stooge into helpless laughter.

Then she would whistle, bringing the spotlight to her,

while the man underneath would now be in such a state of abandon that by a practised twist of her body, Shelley could make him fall off his chair to the floor. Using his tie to haul him to his feet, and kissing an imprint of her scarlet lips upon his forehead, she succeeded in branding him as her token man.

Then she led her victim – still by his tie – to the stage, where, embarrassed and blinded by the lights, he became the easy object of her patter.

If he was awkward she would soon get rid of him and turn her attention to the most obvious heckler she could find.

Muffled eruptions of mass laughter from the room indicated that the jibes were hitting home. Many women in her audience adored the exposure of husbandly home truths, hearing her dig deep round the roots of male insecurities – the size of their organ, their pitiful staying power. The women would shriek with recognition, revelling in the mockery they never dared to voice: 'You give it to 'im, darlin' – you tell 'im – that's right.' The men, on the other hand, far from being piqued, seemed to find it stimulating. To see Shelley – pout of Monroe, mane of Bardot, body of a centrefold – cracking the verbal whip about their sex was obviously quite erotic to many. I'd seen them adopting a masculine swagger, as if to say, 'Just let me get you in the sack, darlin' – I'll show you a real man.' The victim on the stage, however, would stumble back to his seat, to his back-slapping cronies, and mask his shell-shock as best he could with alcohol and bravado.

I scarcely knew how I could have produced such an offspring.

She had ransacked the repertoire of old-time stand-up comics, filched their scathing jokes about the Wife, the Mother-in-Law, the Bird, reversed them into male stereotypes, spiked them with bawdry, and she had an Act – sparky and controversial enough to attract the gift she craved – attention.

31

She was both provocative and sly, seductive and venomous, using her own body to excite the masculine lust she mocked. Oh, it was cleverly done, and it was a fertile furrow to plough . . . but it made me dreadfully uneasy. I'd tried to tell her my point of view – that if she disliked the way men denigrated women, why stoop to their tactics in response? She had retaliated. Blows below the belt were the only ones men understood, she said, I'd always disapproved of her going into showbusiness – and why was I trying to undermine her career? It had been hurtful for us both, and I really didn't like to watch her performance any more, even though I tried to give as much maternal support as I could muster.

I was roused from my reverie by a large shadow over the table. I looked up to see Tom standing there, smiling ruefully.

'Just not my scene I'm afraid,' he said. 'I couldn't take any more. I left them to it. Can we start again?'

No, I wanted to say. No, go away. I've told you all I can, all I want to. I don't want to go any further with you. I don't want those fireworks popping off in my body, taking me unawares. I don't want to be mistress to a man so married he wears a blatant gold band on his wedding finger. Go away.

But I didn't say that. 'Of course,' I said. 'Sit down. But I'll have to be going soon.'

'Sure,' he said, resuming his seat.

He seemed to feel the need to excuse his conduct. 'I don't go for club acts of any kind really,' he said. 'I honestly don't know why I bothered. They make me feel like a battery hen – laughing and clucking away along with everyone else as all the old corn gets paraded out. But she's certainly got 'em in the palm of her hand in there.'

'Presumably by the short and curlies.'

'You've got it,' he laughed, 'hit the nail on the head. No wonder you steer clear. Not exactly what a mother wants to hear out of the mouth of her babe and suckling.'

'Oh,' I shrugged and smiled, 'it doesn't shock me, Tom, if that's what you think. It maybe wouldn't be my choice of material . . . but she's an adult now, she has her own decisions to make.'

'It can be pretty vicious though,' he mused quietly into his drink. 'I honestly felt sorry for that bloke she took on stage – she made him look ridiculous.'

'She can be cruel,' I agreed. 'But then, so can men.'

'*Touché.*'

There was a long silence. I gulped the last of my wine. 'I'd better go,' I said.

'Anna, wait, just one more minute,' he implored, grabbing my hand, not tenderly this time. 'I'm sorry. My style's a bit rough and ready. I feel I've offended you and I don't know how. Hey, but it wasn't all on my side, was it? You did give me the come-on, I'm not that blind.'

I saw he was puzzled, hurt. I felt sorry for him.

'No, Tom, it wasn't all on your side. I had second thoughts, that's all. I couldn't go through with it – the deception.'

'You still like me then?'

What does one say to such a bald question? 'Of course I do.'

'No hard feelings?'

'No hard feelings.'

'That's a pity, 'cos I have – or at least,' he grinned, looking down at his anatomy, 'at least John Thomas has.'

I laughed, 'He should be so lucky!'

'One day, he will be, Anna . . . however long he has to wait.'

I picked up my bag.

'Let me at least see you to your car,' he said, rising with me.

We left the cocktail bar and made our way through the hotel foyer. I sensed his arm hovering protectively at my back, wanting to touch. I stared straight ahead, wanting to be out of that place.

Suddenly Tom did touch me – sharply grabbing my arm. He was pulling me back towards the bar, and I realised a commotion had erupted. I saw people, wide-eyed with curiosity, streaming from all sides towards the garden entrance. Hotel staff fought their way through, then turned to press the onlookers away. A white-faced young man dashed towards us, veering off to the reception desk to grab a phone.

'There's been an accident – we need an ambulance!' I heard him shout. 'Someone's fallen – from a window I think.'

Tom elbowed through the spectators, still dragging me by the sleeve. I saw the awning which had been over the doorway now collapsed, and people were treading over it, kneeling and jostling round a figure on the ground.

'Oh God,' a woman moaned. 'I don't believe it, I can't believe it – it's Harry Jansen.'

I realised with sudden clarity why the white-haired, florid man, greeting Sammy in his navy blazer and silk cravat, had seemed familiar. Harry Jansen – a Euro-MP, somewhat outspoken, flamboyant, an unlikely Labour man, given to coruscating condemnations on acid rain, nuclear dumping and other media-magnetising issues.

Someone shouted from the back of the crowd, 'Let this man through, he's a doctor!' The cluster round the victim parted, and I looked down on Harry's broken body, arms and legs crumpled at odd angles like a rag doll.

No blazer this time, no shirt, no cravat – in fact, no clothes at all, except a pair of neat white ankle-socks.

His face, previously flushed with blood pressure, had now drained of colour. The shocked half-open eyes were glazing. His blood spread out over the awning, merging its red stripes across the white.

'He's alive,' someone whispered. 'Look, the pulse of his heart in his chest.' I looked, and saw the faintest thump-thump against the rib-cage. Under the doctor's ministration a gobbet of blood spat from his throat and his breath came rattling erratically. Harassed staff started to shove the crowd away – 'Please, ladies and gentlemen, it's not a floor-show . . . the ambulance is on its way, please just let the doctor get on with it.'

I had lost Tom in the jostling. A porter pressed me back inside. Before going in, I looked up, and saw a gaping window on the fourth storey, from which Harry Jansen must have fallen. A green curtain flapped in the wind.

I suddenly remembered the boy and I searched the faces all round me. He was not there – of Sammy there was no sign.

One recognisable face did emerge among the bobbing heads, however. Shelley – sheathed in a skin-tight, thigh-split sequinned dress. Propping herself on other people's shoulders she was seeking the source of this distraction. I kept my head down as I heard my daughter's penetrating voice above the low rumble of shocked conversation: 'What happened? What happened? Did a man die? Is he there? Is he alive? Let me see!' It faded gradually as her manager adroitly flung her heavy silver-fox fur wrap round her shoulders and propelled her away. I heard her still protesting as they disappeared through the revolving doors.

Sourly, I searched for Tom. I spotted him speaking to an authoritative-looking man, who was probably the hotel manager. I realised he had gone to work, and fishing my notebook from my bag, so did I.

FIVE

MYSTERY OF EURO-MP IN
HOTEL PLUNGE DRAMA
by Anna Knight

Euro-MP Harry Jansen was today fighting for his life after suffering multiple injuries in a horrifying fall at Northport's luxury Monopole Hotel.

The 58-year-old politician, from West Yorkshire, plunged some 50 feet from a fourth-floor bedroom window at 10.10p.m. last night.

Luckily the severity of the fall was broken as his unclothed body landed on a large awning before hitting the ground – otherwise death would almost certainly have been instant.

But despite his miraculous escape, mystery surrounds the circumstances of the fall. Northport police say they are still investigating and refuse to speculate on whether it was an accident, a deliberate leap or the result of an attack.

Mr Jansen, who was staying at the hotel, was in Northport to speak at the Local Government Officers Union conference.

Union press spokesman Terry Nicholls was with colleagues in the hotel's cocktail bar when the incident took place just outside the bar's garden entrance.

'We are all in a state of shock,' he said. 'A party of us had had dinner with Harry earlier in the evening. Afterwards he left, saying he was tired and thought he would have an early night.

'He was his usual jovial self – then this happens – we

just couldn't believe it. We are all just hoping and praying that he will pull through.'

Labour leader Mr Keith Mangan said today, 'I was horrified to hear of this dreadful accident. Not only is Harry one of our party's hardest workers, he is also a great personal friend, and popular both as a politician and as a man. My heart goes out to his wife, Isabel, and to his family. We are all willing him to recover.'

Mrs Jansen rushed from the couple's home in Pemberley, where Mr Jansen represents the West Yorkshire constituency, to be at her husband's bedside.

The hospital has been receiving goodwill messages all day, many from friends and colleagues in the EC. But his condition was still said to be critical today by a hospital spokesman.

The significance of Sammy's link with a second man just before he met catastrophe had hit me sharply. The question bit at my conscience: if I had told Tom that Sammy was there in the hotel, before the disaster, would Tom have sought him, and perhaps forestalled Harry Jansen's dreadful fall?

It had proved impossible to speak to Tom alone since it happened, but I had managed to mention the boy in the midst of a working phone call. The abruptness of his silence indicated the tense lips of controlled anger.

He broke it sharply with: 'For God's sake, Anna. Why the hell didn't you tell me you'd just seen him last night?'

'If I'd known what was going to happen, don't you think I would have done?' I said defensively.

'Yes, but – oh hang it. A row with you's the last thing I want. Water under the bridge. OK, thanks for telling me now anyway. We'll haul him in, quicksticks. D'you know where he lives?'

I said no, but I knew the clubs he went to, and I gave Tom his physical description. Then suddenly, as an after-thought, Greg's connection came into my mind.

'You could try Greg Harding – one of our photographers,'
I said. 'He may know where Sammy lives. But . . . Tom, a
favour to me . . . don't tell him I gave you his name.'

'It's a deal,' he said.

A silence followed, and then I heard a change in the tone
of his voice, as though his hand was shielding his mouth
from prying eyes and ears. 'Anna . . . I did enjoy being
with you last night, in spite of everything. I just wanted to
tell you that . . . there's no need to reply – I know you're
in an open office. I just think you're a beautiful lady. I
always will.'

'Thanks, Tom,' was all I could say, almost in a whisper,
and I put the phone down.

The scurry of work that day left me little time to reflect.
But alone in the car that night, driving along the busy
seafront, the question flashed into my mind, impossible to
ignore. One prominent man dead, another nearly so, and
both in the company of Sammy at the key time. What had
he to do with it? What was going on? All my working life I
had had to be an observer, presenting all sides of a story,
uninvolved. Now I felt drawn into this boy's murky dealings, to a story which had more to it than I could fathom:
more than it was safe to know.

Jagged by answerless questions I drove along the promenade, taking the long route home, thinking I might
perhaps pull up somewhere and take a walk on the beach,
just to wind down and think. My nerves were fragile, not
only from my confusion but also from the simple physical
fact of having seen two such ravaged bodies in a short
space of time. I'd been brittle-tempered all day, particularly after that conversation with Tom. Oh, it would be all
so easy to lay my head on his chest, feel him stroke my
hair, and hear his gentle murmurings that everything
would be all right. But that was all a tempting illusion, and
I hauled myself back from the edge of giving in, knowing
that over the precipice the world and his wife would not go
away.

As these thoughts reeled through my head I kept looking for somewhere to park, but the promenade was choked with traffic, moving only fitfully in stops and starts. Dribs of holidaymakers meandered sluggishly along the seafront, coagulating in clumps around banks of slot machines or bingo callers. Street hawkers and spielers goaded them to part with their money, their banter floating in through my open car window: 'Got just the thing for you, darling – dirt cheap, it's a giveaway – and look how the colour matches your beautiful blue eyes!' Troops of trippers, arms on each other's shoulders, swayed together along the pavement, distracted by the hot-dog barrows, candyfloss stalls and amusement arcades. They had a tendency to stop and stare, spill over on to the road and forget about traffic, till they went too far and saw themselves reflected in a horrified driver's eyes.

Keeping a defensive watch on their erratic wanderings only aggravated my edginess. I found myself stuck behind a horse and landau, clopping along at walking pace, carrying a shrieking party of two men and two women who, beer cans in hand, turned round and pulled faces at me through the windscreen, scratching their armpits, mimicking monkeys, obviously thinking they were a real comic turn. After several minutes of these antics I could stand it no longer. I looked in the other lane to see if I could pull out, saw a gap and decided to risk it, but misjudged the speed of the approaching car. The result was inevitable – a screech of brakes, a great deal of swearing from the offended driver and guilty shouting from me. Luckily we had managed to avoid collision, but I felt drained and at the end of my tether.

I abandoned all thoughts of a walk and instead sought the next available turn-off, heading for home and a stiff drink, a warm bath and an early bed.

SIX

I was at work early the next day, anxious to catch Tom
Irving before he became unreachable – interviewing wit-
nesses or otherwise out of bounds to press calls. I had
heard on the radio news that Harry Jansen had recovered
consciousness, and his condition was said to be improving.
I had to find out whether Tom had succeeded in linking
Sammy to the politician's fall.

I sat at my desk in the almost deserted office, and
automatically switched on my computer. The screen
blinked slowly to life. I reached for the phone and prodded
out the number. The policewoman who answered sounded
doubtful whether he would speak to me. I waited only a
few seconds for her to come back to me with a surprised,
'Yes, DI Irving is available, I'm putting you through.' The
line clicked.

'Tom – it's Anna.'

'I know. I'm glad you've rung. I've been missing you.'

His voice was deep and low, the voice that must have
greeted his wife across the pillow not long ago, fresh from
sleep. I decided to ignore the last remark and be
businesslike.

'Tom, I need to know if you've got any leads on what
happened to Jansen. I need to know if you're going to be
putting out a statement today. It'd be good if you could
make it before the first edition. If we know something's
coming we can leave space for it.'

'Uh-huh,' he said, and paused, as if adjusting to the
briskness of my tone. 'Well, you can tell your newsdesk not
to wait for anything this morning. We still have a few ends

to tie up, but we've got a press conference lined up provisionally for three o'clock this afternoon, OK?'

'Right, fine.'

'Good, now we've got that out of the way, I can get away at twelve for an hour. Will you meet me for lunch?'

'I . . . ummm—'

'It's important, Anna. I want to speak to you before that press conference, to put you in the picture, tell you what's happened.'

He knew I could not refuse that. I said yes, and we arranged to meet in a wine bar. I was about to ring off, but he checked me, as if in exasperation.

'Anna, Anna, it's me you're talking to – not some faceless nerd behind a desk. How are you? Still shaken up after the Jansen business?'

'No – I'm all right, Tom, really. I'm a big girl now.'

'I know, I know, it's all shoulder-pads and self-defence classes nowadays isn't it, among you independent females?'

The bitterness in his tone took me aback. I didn't reply.

'Well just remember, not all women are ball-breakers, Anna, and it's a wicked world out there. Even you might need someone to watch over you.'

I couldn't understand why he was talking like this. I let his words hang in the wires, unanswered.

'Goodbye Tom,' was all I said. 'I'll see you later.'

I walked through the doors of the wine bar at twelve, and he was already at a table, bottle of Mosel before him, waiting.

'Not much time, I'm afraid, I took a chance – I thought you'd like this one,' he said, pouring the wine into my glass and topping up his own. He was right, I did like it, though I was sure it was too perfumed and feminine for his taste.

'I ordered us some sandwiches too – if that's not, what was the word you used? – too presumptuous? One beef, one prawn, you get a choice. I'll eat them if you don't like them. Just wanted to get it out the way.'

41

He amused me, with his impatient practicality, and he saw the glint in my eye, and laughed.

'OK, OK, you think I'm funny,' he said, hands up in admission. 'Well, perhaps I am. God, you're good for me, Anna. I take things too seriously, most of the time.'

'Goes with the territory,' I said. 'It's a serious business you're in.'

'Yes, but you make me . . . oh never mind. Change the record, Irving, this isn't soul-baring time.'

'Right,' I said, looking round the wood-panelled wine bar where business types were beginning to filter in for gossip over the house red. 'So what are we here for? What was it you wanted to tell me?'

He sighed and stared into his glass, swirling the contents.

'The boy, Anna. We found him, brought him in for questioning.'

'Sammy? Is he being charged?'

He took a gulp of his wine and grimaced. 'No, Anna . . . that's what I wanted to tell you. We couldn't make a damn thing stick. We've released him.'

'But I saw him with Jansen. I saw him.'

'I believe you. But you seem to be the only one who did see them together. We couldn't make the boy crack – and believe me, we tried. It was the same with the Jefferson case apparently. He was questioned after the drowning, but he comes over all hurt and denies he was anything more than an innocent bystander. We can't get him to admit he's on the game, nor can we get anyone else to confirm it. Butter wouldn't melt in his bloomin' arsehole – Jesus, he's a slippery little swine.'

His tone disturbed me. Just how hard had they treated the boy?

'So . . . what did he say happened at the hotel?'

'Oh, he did admit he'd been there that night, with a friend, he claimed, certainly not Harry. This so-called friend just happens to have misinformed Sammy as to his home town and seems to have disappeared off the face of the earth. He emphatically denies setting eyes on Harry Jansen – and he says that by the time Jansen fell, he'd left the hotel so he couldn't have had any involvement.'

Tom sighed deeply: 'The trouble is, he's got two people to back him up.'

'Two? Who are they?'

'Your friend the photographer, for one.'

'Greg? You're joking.'

'No I'm not. Greg Harding maintains till he's blue in the face that the boy was having a drink with him in the Townsman pub when Jansen fell. The barman remembers them together, though he wasn't sure about the exact time. Is he likely to lie, this Greg?'

'I – ', I swallowed. 'I wouldn't have thought so, I've never thought of him that way.' Till now.

'Is he a nancy?'

'If he is, he's kept it well hidden. Who's Sammy's other defender?'

'Jansen himself.'

'What?'

'Yes, you heard me right. Harry Jansen.' He tore a bite from a beef sandwich. 'That was the clincher, wouldn't you say?'

'What did – is he well enough to speak?'

'Just about – yup – he's certainly *compos mentis* anyway. We managed to get a statement from him, slowly.'

'And what did he say happened that night?'

'He said he'd been in the bathroom, just had a shower to relax before going to bed. He turned the shower off and heard a noise in the bedroom. He put his socks on and a towel round him and opened the door to investigate. Then, whoops, bang, wallop, face to face with a large intruder – tall, thin, black-haired – rifling through his sock drawer. Harry'd left a wad of money hidden in there, so a struggle ensues and bye-bye Harry, straight out the

43

window, fertilising the rose-bushes with his life-blood. We showed him a picture of Sammy Trickett, and he said there's no way a boy like that was there that night. When I asked if he even knew him, he pleaded a sudden bout of amnesia.'

'So that's it then. The boy's free.'

'As a bird.'

'And is Harry's story plausible?'

'Oh, it's plausible, course it's plausible – he's a politician. That's the version that'll be going out this afternoon at the press conference – together with a description of this tall, dark and, for all I know, handsome intruder. The trouble is, I'm buggered if I believe it.'

'What?'

'Loada cods in my opinion.'

'Tom, what on earth are you playing at?'

'I'm playing the duty game, my dearest. Just like you have a nasty wicked news editor from whom you take your orders, I have a nasty, wicked boss with more pips on his shoulders than I have – and a pea for a brain.'

He drained his flimsy glass with the gulps of one more used to drinking pints of bitter.

'You mean Patton?' I said quietly.

'The same.'

'Should you really be telling me this?'

'I don't know, Anna, I don't know. Probably not. All I know is, Jansen spouts off his plausible story and Patton swallows it, hook, line and sinker. He's strictly an evidence man, wants everything served up on a bloomin' plate. The evidence fits what Harry says – or at least there's nothing to go against it – and try as I might with young Sammy Trickett, the lad won't crack.'

'Then why do you disbelieve Harry?'

'That's the trouble, it's not something I can put my finger on and present to Patton, all done and dusted like he'd want it. It comes down to copper's nose; Jansen doesn't smell right. But I'm afraid that doesn't cut a lot of ice in the present regime.'

'What do you mean though, he doesn't smell right?'

'OK, I'm sitting by Jansen's bed in the hospital, and his eyes are still closed, still unconscious. I'm just staring at him, and all of a sudden, it's as if I can feel him coming to. His eyes are still shut, but his face somehow looks alive again, I can feel the man's there. He stayed like that for oh, half an hour. A nurse put a needle in his arm, and I'm sure he stopped himself flinching. Then, without warning, his eyes opened. I'm convinced he was really conscious for that half-hour, and he didn't want to own up to it. It was as if he was thinking away in there, concocting his story. Then, when they finally let us interview him, out it came, off pat, just as if he'd rehearsed it. It's so seamless there's nothing we can pick up on – the intruder was supposed to be wearing surgical gloves, so there's obviously no prints, the only thing he took was a wad of used banknotes – untraceable. Not even forensic could come up with anything to prove or disprove what he said. It's too neat for my liking.'

'Did no one else see the intruder?'

'Nope – Mr Mystery Man seems to have made himself invisible in the corridor.'

'How's he supposed to have got in?'

'Key. Chambermaids have them – I don't suppose it would be beyond the wit of someone to filch one that way.'

'But again, you don't believe it. What d'you think Harry's covering up?'

'Smells to me that there could be something nasty in old Harry's woodshed, and he doesn't want us barging in and finding it. See, I believe you, Anna, when you say you saw him with that boy. But I mean, frolics with our fairy friends, gay boys, corrupting young innocents – wouldn't do a lot for his political career, now would it?'

'Have you told Patton this?'

'Course I have. All he did was pull a po-face like I'd got

45

dog dirt on my shoes and it was ruining his carpet. He would listen to me if I could come up with any evidence, he said sniffily, making it quite clear that if I wanted to go scraping the gutter, I was on my own. He believes Harry, and that's it, that's all he wants to know. Probably a touch of the magic handshakes and rolled trouser-leg brigade if you ask me.'

I took a triangle of prawn sandwich and nibbled at it out of politeness more than hunger, for my appetite now was for facts rather than food. The prawns were smothered in an acrid pink sauce and I returned it to the plate after one bite.

'What do you think could really have happened, Tom?'

He shrugged, pushing away the remains of the beef. 'I dunno, Anna . . . I just dunno. It could be a whole putrid can of worms with these people. Perhaps Harry wanted the lad to do something he didn't like. You know, some of them are into bondage and such. Perhaps the kid was trying it on – blackmail I mean – and they had a fight.'

'But Sammy's so small – could he have physically pushed a big man like Harry from a window?'

'Size doesn't have a lot to do with it if you catch someone off balance – and Harry had had quite a lot to drink that night. The trouble is,' and here he sighed, 'you can't help feeling sympathy in a way. I mean, what chance does a kid have, snarled up in all that, so young? Makes me want to puke.'

'What are you going to do now then?'

'I'm going to go through with this charade this afternoon, that's what. I'm going to sit alongside Chief Inspector Patton and be his little boy blue, and tell all you hacks Harry's story.'

'And then?'

'And then I shall go through the motions of looking for our dark-haired intruder while I'm really trying to follow up the rent-boy. That way both me and pea-brain Patton are happy.'

'Thanks for telling me all this, Tom.'

He suddenly looked at me sharply. 'Here, you're not going to use any of this for some scoop story are you? I mean this is strictly between us, isn't it?'

'Don't worry, Tom. I just meant thank you for putting me in the picture. I would have wondered what on earth had gone on when you came out with this story this afternoon. I know, it's all off the record.' And I patted his arm in reassurance. He caught my hand and held it there. 'Anna, we can trust each other, can't we? I mean, I feel you're intelligent enough to . . .'

'Know when to keep my mouth shut?'

'To be discreet,' he corrected with a touch of self-irony. 'To be honest, there's no one else I could talk to like this. My wife seems to think I should arse-lick my way to promotion, and I can't mouth off at work – the bloody walls have ears. Now I find someone I can let off steam to, and bugger me if you're not a bloomin' reporter and I'm supposed to watch everything I say.'

'You can trust me, Tom. I won't land you in it.'

He increased his pressure on my hand. 'And you can trust me, too.' Which was more than his wife could, I thought coldly.

He still had hold of my hand, and he was staring at it, ruminatively, as if something was on his mind. I began to wonder if he was summoning up the effort to try again, to tempt me into his arms as well as his confidence. But when he looked up it was not with desire, but with worry.

'Anna, there's something else I have to tell you – another reason I had to see you today.'

The expression on his face was so serious, I began to fear something dreadful had happened.

'It's your daughter – no, no, don't panic,' he said as he saw the alarm on my face. 'She's all right, nothing's happened to her. It's what's happened to other people that's the problem.'

'For pity's sake, what do you mean, Tom?'

'Manchester police have picked up a guy who's been going round attacking women for the last six months. When I say attacking, I mean, it's more than that – raping them, pissing on them, beating them up and damn near killing them.'

'Yes – I read about the attacks.'

'Right. It goes without saying the guy's a nutter. Unstable background, in his twenties, never had a successful relationship with a woman, big on body-building, unemployed for the past year.'

Tom bit his lip and I waited for him to go on. 'OK – the guy's admitting he did it, and we've got enough semen and blood to convict him anyway. But this is where the trouble starts for you – for your daughter, I mean.'

'What on earth has he got to do with Shelley?'

'He's going to stand up in court and claim it was your daughter who tipped him over into committing these attacks. He's going to use it in mitigation to try to get a shorter sentence, or be judged insane.'

I was horrified. 'But why?'

'It seems he was one of the guys she picked out of the audience to take part in her act one night just over six months ago. Look, he's an inadequate character, a loner, deeply insecure as far as women are concerned. He might not have shown it that night, but he couldn't take the humiliation she doles out. He cracked. He went away and went on the rampage for six months, and he would've gone on doing it till we caught him, taking his revenge on women, you see, in his eyes, showing them who's master. He's going to claim that if she'd never picked him out that night, he'd never have done it. Being shown up like that in front of so many people sent him round the bend.'

I stared at him, transfixed. 'But is it true?'

'Whether it is or not, that's the line his lawyer's going to take in court. And your daughter's name's going to be dragged into it, smeared with the whole mess . . . I felt I had to tell you, Anna, to warn you. I didn't want you to hear about it from someone else.'

'Does she know yet?'

'Probably – someone from Manchester division was going to see her today.'

'Dear God, what a nightmare.'

'I know.'

'I have to go,' I said abruptly, getting up to leave. 'I have to speak to her.'

But I felt his hand gripping my arm, holding me back.

'Anna, Anna, if there's anything I can do . . . if you want someone to talk to. I'm sorry it came out so brutal. I'd hoped I could soften it a little – but I'm not good at that.'

'No, I'm glad you told me, Tom. Now I understand why you were going on about women being ball-breakers this morning. Not many of us are, believe it or not, and my daughter's not as hard as she makes out.'

'Not if she takes after her mother, she's not,' he said, getting up to walk out with me.

'Take care, Anna,' he said as he left me. He sounded as if he really meant it, and I wanted him to. I still found him sexually attractive.

SEVEN

I spoke to Shelley briefly on the phone, and arranged to see her that evening. She sounded too stunned to talk much, still taking in what the policeman had told her. So when the day's work ended I hurried to the car park, anxious to see her before she left for the theatre.

'Anna! Anna!' I heard my name shouted with ferocity as I reached my car. I did not look up. I knew who it was and I wanted to get away. I'd been trying to avoid him and had succeeded, until now. It was Greg.

'Anna!' I heard him coming closer as I fumbled with my car keys. I couldn't possibly pretend I hadn't heard him any longer. I started to turn towards him, and felt my shoulder forcibly wrenched as he swung me round to look him in the face. He was sweating, and breathing heavily, his skin clammy under the fuzzy beard.

'What's the game?' he said, his eyes filled with accusation. 'What are you trying to do to me?'

'Greg – calm down, please,' I responded, putting my hand on his arm, hoping to achieve some matronly gravitas. 'Relax a minute, I'm not going to run away.'

'No? Then why've you been running away from me all day, huh? Don't treat me like a kid, Anna. We're past that stage. Listen, I told you the other day to keep your nose out as far as Sammy Trickett's concerned, didn't I – didn't I?'

'Yes, you did, but I—'

'Stop, stop there – because if you're going to tell me you didn't give his name to the police, I'm not going to believe you.'

I parried sharply: 'And if you're going to tell me you don't know him, you only know of him – wasn't that the phrase? – then I'm not going to believe you either.'

He paused, looking me hard in the eye, and I felt his grip relax on my shoulder. 'All right, all right,' he said. 'Believe what you like. But I wasn't using the kid . . . I was trying to help him.'

He looked down at his shoes, seeming to struggle for the right words.

'Jesus, Anna . . . I know I'm not exactly an Adonis. I may not get as much action in the sack as I'd like . . . but I don't have to stoop to paying for it. I'm not that pathetic.'

He was now staring at me with defiance. 'All right Greg,

all right,' I said, trying to be conciliatory. 'I never thought you were.'

'No? Then why the hell did you give the police my name? Why the hell did you drag me into the same shit as Sammy? Why – when I'd spelled out to you what a cess-pool you'd stir up? It was you, wasn't it? Come on, I want the truth.'

'Yes,' I said, looking at him steadily.

'Well, if you thought I'd shop him, you've got another think coming. They must've tried every wheeze in the book, and some out of it, to make me tell them he's on the game. I've told you, I'm not that daft even if you are. And anyway, I just don't see why you're so determined he bumped off Jefferson and tried to do the same to Jansen. That is what you think, isn't it? You've seen him – does he look strong enough to do that, even if he wanted to?'

'No, Greg. I don't know what happened – that's the point. I just wanted to make sure the police had all the evidence to find out. It's a question of getting to the truth, and he could have been involved, that's all. If he's been eliminated then you should be pleased. But I am sorry I had to drag you into it, Greg. I'm sorry if they put the screws on you.'

'Yeah, well . . . I have to say thanks a bunch. You know what the police are like if they think they've got a nancyboy to play with? Brings out all their macho muscle that does. They hate poufs, don't you know that? Poufs make 'em squirm. Give 'em a chance and they'll kick seven shades of shit out of a queer – just to show who's boss.'

'What did they do to Sammy?'

'They gave him a hell of a rough time – bastards. Oh they stopped short of the physicals, but mentally he's a mess. They made him feel like a worm, despicable, something you'd wipe off the bottom of your shoe.'

'Did they do that to you?'

'They started, they tried. But I gave back as good as I got. I could handle them . . . not like Sammy.'

'Where is he now?'

'I've got him at my place . . . he was shaking, he wouldn't eat . . . so I've got him bedded down on my couch so I can keep an eye on him.'

I felt helpless: 'What can I say, Greg? I'm sorry . . . I didn't know they'd treat you that way. Is there anything I can do?'

I half expected him to retaliate with, 'Haven't you done enough?' But he didn't. He pursed his lips as if considering the matter before looking round, checking no one was in earshot. Then he stared at me levelly before leaning back against my car.

'Yes,' he said, 'as it happens, there is something you can do – not for me, but for Sammy. I was going to ask you anyway, but now I reckon you haven't much choice – you owe him something. Look, I want to explain to you what I'm doing with him.'

'Well how on earth did you meet him in the first place?'

'He fell at my feet – no, I'm not trying to be funny – I mean it, literally. I'd seen him around town, noticed how attractive he was, never spoke to him though. One night . . . well early one morning actually, I was going home after the clubs closed. I saw him coming down the street towards me, on his own. He was sort of swaying.'

'Drunk?'

'No, not that – possibly the only vice he doesn't have. Just as he got to me, his eyes rolled backwards and he keeled over, head in the gutter. I bent down and his eyes flickered open. I said I'd phone for an ambulance, he looked in a bad way. I saw panic in his face, and I realised then he must be on drugs. He begged me not to call anyone, he managed to get to his feet, and he kept saying he was all right. I could see he wasn't. I asked where he lived, if there was anyone I could ring, but he said no, he lived on his own, there was no one.

'I didn't want to leave him like that, but he said he'd run away if I called an ambulance, so I took him back to my place. He was all right in the morning.'

52

'And was it drugs?'

'Yeah, yeah. That's why he went on the meat-rack in the first place, to pay for his habit. Listen, I told you it was a nasty business, didn't I? So it is, Anon, believe me . . . but he has been having treatment to come off them. He wants to be clean.'

'Is that how you're helping him?'

'Not directly. Look, I'll admit, I didn't take him on just because I felt sorry for him, not at first. Anon . . .' He gave me a serious look. 'Promise you won't spread this around, please.'

I nodded my assent.

'I'm trying to get out of the newspaper game, Anon. I'm sick of hack-work. I'm trying to set myself up as a real photographer – an art photographer – but I'm still working on it. I've made myself a dark-room and a little studio at home, and I'm building up a portfolio. Only I don't want anybody at work to know about it yet – in case I fall flat on my arse – understand?'

'Of course; I think it's a great idea, Greg.'

He ground his shoe in the gravel: 'Well, we'll see . . . anyway immediately I saw Sammy, I'll tell you, all I wanted him for was as a model. You should see his body, Anon. He may be thin but he's strong, he's not scrawny – he pays attention to how he looks. In his game, he has to. That body, that face . . . I've made some ace pictures with him, Anon, believe me . . . studies of the human form, in light, in shadow. He's a natural in front of a camera.'

'I'd like to see them. I suppose you're paying him for all this?'

'Of course. Why else would he do it? Anyway, what I'm leading up to is, while working with me, he started getting really interested in photography – asking questions all the time, about the cameras, lighting and stuff. In the end, he pestered me so much, I lent him a camera and he started taking his own pictures, developing them too – I showed him how. He was good on the straight side, but he soon went off on tangents of his own – started fooling around with the developer, distorting the images deliberately, doing double exposures, till in the end he was producing these incredible fantasy pictures – photomontages really – and I think they're worth money. See, if he could get an income out of that, he wouldn't be tempted to go on the game any more. I'm trying to encourage him, but what he needs is someone to actually buy one of his pictures, to give him the belief in himself.'

'So you want me to do that?'

'Yes, but I think you could go one better. I think you could give him a leg up into a wider market . . . your daughter knows a lot of people, the type who might buy pictures like that, see what I mean? If she took him up, bought one or two herself, perhaps his name might get passed around in the right circles.'

I considered. It was true that the stereotyped décor of Shelley's apartment needed a dash of character. I'd tried to persuade her to buy some paintings, without success. She hadn't the time to go and look.

'I'll see what I can do,' I said. 'It might help if he could take the pictures to her.'

At long last his face lost that tense look, and he grinned. 'All he needs is a start, just something to build on – something to get him away from those dick-heads round the clubs. Then he can look after himself. He's not from a bad background, you know. His parents ran a pretty decent restaurant in Yorkshire somewhere. Only it failed and they split up when he was ten. Both started new families, new businesses. Sammy was shunted between them, but he always felt in the way. He started arguing, pilfering, and he legged it as soon as he was sixteen. Neither parent fell over themselves to bring him back. He got in with a bad crowd, and it was downhill from there.'

'Greg?'

'Huh?'

'Why didn't you tell me all this before?'

'Can't you guess why?' Anger flashed back in his face, followed by a look of vulnerability. 'I feel too much for him, Anon – it's more than just wanting him for my photographs now . . .'

'Oh Greg . . .' I put an arm on his shoulder, feeling his anguish, knowing he'd probably never admitted this to anyone else before.

'I didn't want to tell anybody about him, I didn't want the blokes at work to find out – you know what they're like.' I did. Greg's fellow photographers would taunt him unmercifully, never missing the opportunity for a 'poufter' joke if he was around. And if he retaliated, they'd turn on him, saying he couldn't take a bit of fun. I'd seen them treat a young photographic assistant in this way, making his worklife a misery.

'It'll be all right,' Greg went on, 'when I've got myself set up in my own freelance business – I couldn't care less what anybody thinks then. But while I've still got to work here – well – I just want to keep my head down. You can understand that, can't you, Anna?'

Of course I could. And I could also understand his look of distress when speaking of Sammy. It was as if Greg had found himself being drawn into this emotional involvement against his better judgement. After all, who, in their rational mind, would become infatuated with a rent-boy, someone who sold his favours to anyone with cash? This was obviously why Greg was so keen to get him out of that business, to help him sell his pictures.

The boy was so unnervingly beautiful: one's defences were shaken at the sight of him, even when forewarned and wary. I too had felt that stirring of protectiveness towards him which still unsettled me. Something in me wanted to see him again, to feel the magnetism that had ensnared Greg, and to test my own reaction to his presence.

'I'll talk to Shelley about the pictures,' I said. 'I'm just off to see her now – I'm late. Listen, she might be a bit preoccupied at the moment – a problem's come up – it might not be the right time. I can't promise anything yet.'

'OK,' he squeezed my hand. 'Thanks Anon. I know you'll try. All he needs is just one break, I'm sure of it.'

I smiled, and as I drove away I was glad to be back on better terms with Greg. As for the boy . . . I still wasn't sure I was doing the right thing.

EIGHT

As soon as I rang the doorbell at Shelley's apartment, she answered. Wild-haired, she let me in with no more than a brief greeting.

I followed her into the living room where she paced nervily, sitting for a few seconds only to jump up and stare out of the window or swivel to confront herself in the mirror opposite.

'I don't know what to do, Mama,' her voice came tense and thin. 'I don't even remember the man and he's going to say I made him a criminal – a rapist.'

'That's foolish,' I said, sitting on one of the black suede couches, trying to be as calm as I could. 'It's obvious he'd have done it anyway. With someone as unstable as that, anything could have triggered him off. It's just unfortunate – you were unfortunate – to choose him that night. But you can't blame yourself for what he did afterwards.'

'But I do – he does – and everyone else will when they read it in the papers.'

'Nonsense – it's just a courtroom ploy, to try to get a

shorter sentence, and I'm sure the court will see through it. Now calm down, Shelley. It's not your fault.'

She shoved her hands through her hair. 'I'll never work again . . .' she said bleakly.

'Don't be so melodramatic, Shelley, of course you will. Look, there's absolutely nothing you can do about it now, so it's no use getting into such a state.'

But I couldn't help seeing the situation through her eyes. It called into question the whole focus of her act in a way my theoretical arguments had never been able to. The confidence was suddenly whipped from under her like the chair she kicked from under the victims in her audience.

Her head was bowed as she dropped on to the couch beside me, all her earlier nervy energy gone. Suddenly she was my child again, under the frost-tipped hair and made-up face, she was the nine-year-old Shelley, bereft of artifice, needing me for comfort after a nightmare. I did love her, maddening though she'd been with her poses and her wilfulness. I couldn't help but hold this shuddering child against my shoulder and let her weep. To be honest I was surprised. I had thought she had grown a tough shell with her single-minded pursuit of her career. It had made me think her more mature than she really was, but I also felt a stirring of relief that she wasn't so hard as she made out. It made me more proud of her, if anything. I stroked her hair and gradually her crying subsided.

'Thanks Ma,' she said simply as she drew away. 'God, I must look a sight – I'd better get going for the theatre. I meant to wash my hair. That damn policeman drove everything out of my mind. Look I haven't even – would you like some coffee? I haven't eaten since breakfast.'

'Your hair looks fine, it just needs a brush. You go and repair your face while I make some coffee and sandwiches. You can't go on stage on a totally empty stomach.'

She blew me a stage kiss. Over the sandwiches, I broached the idea of seeing Sammy's pictures. I wanted to take her mind off the rapist. She seemed to see through what I was doing, but she went along with it, striving to get back to her normal, insouciant self.

So, I collected Sammy from Greg's house the following afternoon. Skin pale as skimmed milk, he looked even less substantial than before. He climbed into the car, dwarfed by a great portfolio of pictures, and I felt I was carrying a creature fragile as porcelain.

I was hesitant, unsure whether he still resented me over his ordeal at the hands of the police. As I drove along the seafront I suddenly felt aware he was staring at me – and more than that – he seemed to be listening to me, although I was silent. I snatched a glance away from the traffic, and was caught in the full stare of his blue eyes before he closed up on me again, withdrawing like a sea anemone. Eventually, he spoke.

'I don't blame you,' he said, gazing away from me. 'For going to the police about me. I can see it was the right thing for you to do. You're not to blame for the way they treated me. It's not your fault. I don't hold a grudge. I wanted you to know that.'

'Thanks, Sammy,' I responded, grateful to him for clearing the air. 'But tell me one thing: I was right, wasn't I, I did see you with Harry Jansen that night?'

'I don't know what you saw or didn't see. I know I saw you with a copper, a married copper.'

His stare had fastened on me again, and I felt my face suffuse with pink. He knew he needn't say any more. I wondered if he'd seen Tom's hand reach out to stroke my neck, that first betrayal.

'What were you trying to tell me?' I asked. 'When you picked up the glass?'

'It doesn't matter now.'

'Were you trying to warn me off, like Greg had done? Not to get involved?'

'I was a bit jumpy that night. I thought the manager'd seen me. They don't like people like me hanging around. Yours was the only face I knew.'

58

'You were pretending you were with me?'

'I knew you wouldn't turn me away.'

He was right. But how did he know? His face, that angelic child's face, aroused a spurious affection. He had a power to attract, and he knew it and used it, but he would snap it off at will when it suited him. Now he was staring at me again.

'Don't do that, please,' I said. 'You make me uncomfortable.'

'I'm sorry, Anna, I forget sometimes.' And he turned away. He was wearing white flannel trousers, a white open-necked shirt and a striped blazer, like a schoolboy cricketer. I realised that his clothes were consciously chosen as costumes, identities. His accent struck me as put on – a self-tutored refinement of the basic Northern tones in his half-broken boy's voice.

Suddenly he seemed to take a decision to appear friendly.

'My grandfather was a hypnotist – I'm supposed to have inherited his stare,' he said. 'He used to travel with a caravan, he'd follow the fairs and put on a show. He always used to say I had his eyes. He was bedridden by the time I was six or seven, dying, my mother looked after him. He hated it, stuck in bed, unable to move. I'd sit with him, he'd show me his tricks . . . the Great Mesmeroso . . . that's what he called himself. He said my eyes were a gift, but I should be careful, they could bore into someone's soul. I forget sometimes. They're too intense. He made me hypnotise him at the end, so he could cope with the pain. It's just something I have, a way of looking.'

'But you were staring at me.'

'Yes, at your profile. Such a long, lovely line. With your hair sleeked up like that, you could be a ballerina. I'd like to use your profile in one of my pictures. Would you let me?'

For a moment I felt flattered, and I smiled at him. 'Yes,' I said. 'If you really want to.'

But as my attention turned back to the road I felt the

exchange cloying like treacle on my tongue. I still did not trust the boy. I knew I'd seen him with Harry Jansen that night, whatever he or Harry might say. I also knew flattery must be part of his trade, bolstering the egos of his ageing, inadequate or misfit customers.

We arrived at Shelley's apartment block. I hate lifts, and take the stairs wherever possible, but I could not very well toil up seven flights. We manoeuvred the giant portfolio into the mirrored capsule, and the doors closed upon us. I tried not to show my fear of the walls crowding in on me, but he was staring at me again, and I knew he sensed my panic.

I was relieved to see Shelley waiting for us at the top, and I realised I had become more and more uncomfortable in the boy's company.

Shelley was being her bright, brittle, professional self – the brilliant smile, the welcoming arm on both our shoulders, the charming hostess; it all seemed to say, 'I'm fine again now, I'm over that business, now let's get on with the rest of life.'

Sammy seemed silently impressed as he walked into the apartment. Shelley had bought it, furniture and all, after it had been the show-flat for the block. It had been furnished to appeal to as broad a cross-section of the market as possible – and it reminded me of an executive hotel – fashionable and inoffensive. He could obviously see the potential for his pictures on the pale, dove-grey walls.

As the boy opened his portfolio, and bent to lay the pictures out on the carpet, I saw Shelley eye him with fascination, much as I had when I first saw him, struck by that fleeting beauty caught between boy and man. He must be vain, I decided – no other boy I had ever known had hair quite so gleaming or skin so fastidiously washed.

He stood back, and I turned my attention from him to the pictures. They were extraordinary – mostly black and white, with colour in sparing, brilliant flashes giving maximum impact. I stooped to pick up the nearest.

It showed an old man dressed in rags, mouth open in a wail of desolation, a dead bird round his neck, tied to the mast of a skeleton ship, and beset by luminous creatures sliming over a murky ocean. Sammy's technique, merging photographs and distortion, gave a quality of frozen immediacy I had never seen in a painting. The man's agony seemed as real as that of a tramp ranting on a street corner, arresting embarrassed passers-by with his glittering eye.

'The Ancient Mariner,' I said, almost under my breath.

'Yes, it is, Anna,' the boy responded with a smile I'd never seen him give before – one of unalloyed delight. He took the picture from me and placed another in my hands. 'See if you can get this one.'

His own face stared at me from the frame – his face, and yet not his, for the eyes had been etched into caves of ice, and his hair billowed around his head.

In the hair were strange shapes, that as I looked, became apparent as trees, mountains, towers, a river, fading out into a curved heaven pocked with stars. The image was disturbing, an image of him demented, the evocation of his drug-induced dreams.

'No, no . . . I don't know what that is,' I said, passing it back to him, not wanting to look any more.

'Come, it's easy,' he coaxed. 'If you knew the other one you should know this. Try . . . I'll give you a clue.'

He closed those haunting eyes and began to recite in a dramatic voice, which sounded as if it was imitated from someone older, more grandiloquent.

> 'Beware! Beware!
> His flashing eyes, his floating hair!
> Weave a circle round him thrice,
> And close your eyes with holy dread,
> For he on honey-dew hath fed,
> And drunk the milk of Paradise.'

I responded quietly, 'It's from "Kubla Khan".' His enthusiastic smile confirmed I was right.

His choice of subject intrigued me, for I had studied the Romantic poets as part of my English course at university, and I had become immersed in them. As I looked at the rest of Sammy's pictures I realised that each one was a visual evocation of a poem by Coleridge, Keats, Shelley or Wordsworth. I was puzzled. He did not seem a studious boy.

'Why these?' I wanted to ask. What convoluted path led you from falling down in gutters to this lofty summit of poesy?

I had been so distracted I had momentarily forgotten Shelley, kneeling on the carpet with a picture in her hand. To her, poetry – particularly of this antiquity – was dead as dust. I neither expected her to know the source, nor to care.

But I could see that she did care. She was staring with such intensity into the picture, I almost feared for an instant she would tear it in two. Her hands gripped the flimsy cardboard with white-knuckled tension.

'What is it?' she said haltingly.

I saw it was a huge snake, coiled in a sensuous embrace around the legs and body of a naked man. The young man swooned in trusting languor on the reptile's glistening skin, unaware that above him the snake's head – with a beautiful woman's face and utter contempt in her eyes – was about to strike at his vitals. The snake's tongue slithered from its mouth, ready to fasten poisonous fangs on his small and tender manhood.

I found it an evil picture, and a mistaken one too if, as I believed, it was meant to be Keats's Lamia. His snake takes on a woman's form for love, not the hatred I saw in this picture. And yet it had obviously struck a deep chord with Shelley. She scarcely glanced at the other frames.

'Yes, yes,' she said, 'I'll take them.'

'What? All of them?' said the boy, as if unable to believe his luck.

'Yes, of course,' she said irritably. And then, recollecting herself, she smiled at him quickly. 'I'll pay whatever you normally charge. They're good – don't you think so, Ma? This place needs something unusual, and these've really got impact.'

Yes, I thought, they certainly had impact, but I was sure I couldn't live with them comfortably every day.

'I'd like you to get them framed properly – good frames – I'll pay for all that,' Shelley was instructing him. 'Tell them to send me the bill, and then I'd like you to hang them yourself. You've obviously got a good eye, and you'll arrange them well. I haven't the time to do it myself.'

'Fine, fine,' breathed Sammy, somewhat overwhelmed by the unexpected strength of her response.

He began to pack the pictures away, but she stopped him when it came to the snake-woman.

'Can you leave this one with me?' she asked hesitantly. 'I want to look at it again tonight, when I've more time, when I've finished at the theatre.'

'Sure,' he said. 'Anything you want.'

The way he looked at her – sideways – transmitted itself to me. She had resumed her glittery effusiveness as she let us out of the apartment, but we both knew she had a fixation about that picture, and I couldn't help but feel deeply uneasy.

NINE

Tom Irving rang me at work the next day.

'How's Shelley taken the news about the rapist?' he said, as though he'd been worried. I warmed to him for that.

'Badly I think,' I replied. 'It's shaken her up. She's trying to keep it out of her mind. But I really don't know how soon she'll get over it. It's bound to worry her, knowing the court case will be coming up.'

'It's probably going to take months.'

'I know,' I said glumly. 'Anyway, how's your investigation going? Have you found any more clues to who pushed Harry Jansen out of the window?'

'I have found someone else who saw him with Sammy Trickett at the hotel – but not at the crucial time, I'm afraid.'

'So they are both lying about not being together?'

'Yes – well I believed you anyway – so it doesn't get me a lot further.'

I told him about the boy's pictures that Shelley was buying: 'You know, he even says he can hypnotise people. He's a really strange creature, Tom.'

'I have a feeling the more we find out about this kid, the nearer we'll get to what happened that night,' he said. 'I don't suppose . . .'

'You don't suppose what?'

'I don't suppose you'd volunteer to help me, would you?' he asked slowly. 'I mean, you've got a legit reason for talking to him now, haven't you? Perhaps you could just casually drop in the odd question about his background, his friends – anything?'

64

I sighed. I didn't know how to answer. I didn't particularly want to get to know the boy better – he set up such disturbing reactions in me. And apart from that, I didn't know whether I should actively help the police do their probing. What Greg had said about their treatment of him and the boy upset me.

'Tom, you didn't . . . mistreat Sammy Trickett in any way – when you took him in for questioning?'

'Is that what he told you?'

'No . . . not directly. Greg said you gave him a hard time.'

'Listen, we're not here to give people a good time, are we? We're not bloody psychiatrists or social workers. We do what we have to do to get results. But I won't stand for any rough-house stuff, if that's what you mean. I don't get physical, and neither do my men if they know what's good for them. We ask questions and we ask 'em hard if we have to.'

'I see.'

'So will you help me?'

'I'll think about it.'

'Anna . . .?' his voice dropped low and soft. 'Will you think about me, too? I want to see you again. I can't help it, I can hardly think about anything else, it's distracting me from work. Listen – no strings, no complications, no secret meetings in bars – right? Just let me see you, that's all I ask.'

When he said all that in such an urgent rush I quickened. Now he was coming to me the way I wanted. Desire charged through me, blocking out my better judgement.

He arrived at the flat that night. We talked, drank a little wine, and afterwards the inevitable happened. I woke up later, and he was gone. I relaxed, glorying in my lonely bed.

TEN

'Phone for you, Anna!' someone shouted across the busy office.

I hurriedly returned to my desk, wanting it to be Tom.

'Anna! Long time no see.'

'Alys – where the hell have you been?'

Despite my bad-tempered response, I was glad to hear her. She was my dearest, oldest friend: we'd gone through schools, secrets, boyfriends and romantic novels together. She was as much a part of me as I of her, with all the closeness of two only children growing up as friends, closer than most sisters.

'I'll disappear again if that's all the welcome I'm going to get.'

'Don't you dare – I've had enough of your disappearing acts. I've written you two letters and tried to ring you countless times. Where've you been the past six weeks? Why didn't you tell me you were going for so long?'

'I'm sorry, Anna, it was difficult. It's all been a bit hush-hush – I couldn't have told you what I was doing, it's a little delicate, and I honestly didn't know I'd be away so long. Anyway, here I am, back in the land of the living, and restoring full communications with abject apologies.'

'Ay, ay, you're being mysterious are you . . . even with me? Well thanks a bunch.'

'No, not mysterious, merely careful. Telephone lines can have ears which are not yours and mine. Don't worry, ace reporter, I'll reveal all when I see you. Which is why I'm ringing now.'

'You're coming to Northport?'

'Yup, all the way to the Candyfloss Coast – although I'm afraid my visit will not be all pleasure.'

'What d'you mean?'

'We've got a job on. We're picking out some of the major seaside resorts for a survey and one of them's Northport. I could do with your help actually – both professional and private.'

'Go on – I don't suppose you'd let me say no, even if I wanted to.'

'It should give you some good copy – honestly – would I tell you a lie? We'd really appreciate a piece in the paper before we arrive, telling people what we're doing and why, and then you could cover it while we're there.'

'What's this survey all about?'

'Well, it's a load of crap really.'

'What? Why d'you expect me to write about it then?'

'No, I mean it – literally. It's about sewage. We're taking sea-water samples round the coast where people swim, to find out how much contamination there is from sewage discharges. We're also doing some dye tests at Northport – out where Western Water's planning to put that long sewage outfall – to see just how much bacteria will be killed, and how much will be brought back to shore on the tide – quick enough to be still contaminated.'

'You pick yourself some fine jobs, I must say.'

'All for the good of the cause.'

'How long's it going to take you?'

'About ten days – which is where the other side of my humble plea for help comes in.'

'All right, all right, you can get off your knees. You want somewhere to stay, am I right?'

'Please, Ans – I mean I can always rough it in the camper-van if it's inconvenient.'

'Oh we are getting discreet in our old age – you mean if I have a man around.'

'Well, it is a small flat.'

'Don't worry, Alys dearest, I'll give my army of admirers the boot so that you can have my sofa-bed.'

'You're all heart.'

'How many of you will be doing this survey?'

'Myself and two science graduates who're giving some of their free time to help us. They'll be using the camper-van – but it does get a bit cramped for three.'

'I'll bet. Well, you'd better give me more details about the campaign if I'm to write this story for you. Go ahead, my pen is poised.'

Succinctly, using her official voice, Alys reeled off all I needed to know about her group's anti-pollution drive.

She worked for an international environmental organisation called Groundswell, a network wholly supported by voluntary donations which ran high-profile campaigns to save threatened wildlife and fight pollution. Of recent years I had grown used to recognising her on TV, a small, slight figure, always muffled up in great padded jackets of brilliant hue, being interviewed while her colleagues carried out some daring publicity stunt in the background.

I'd seen them in dinghies being nearly drowned by high-pressure hoses from chemical dump-ships, lying in the path of bulldozers preparing to rip up a butterfly sanctuary, and on ice-floes forming a human barrier between men with clubs and the seals who were their target.

I too had backed such high-minded causes in my student days, when we had all condemned capitalism and marched against the Bomb. I had done my share of sit-ins and protests. But all that stopped abruptly when I had a child to keep and a mortgage to pay: other priorities filled my vision, and the extent of my idealistic support had dwindled to the odd stuffing of a charity cheque into an envelope. Not so with Alys. Unencumbered by dependants, she left college to work for Groundswell as an unpaid volunteer, working at night as a waitress or an office-cleaner. She stuck it out, living in near poverty for four years. She committed herself wholeheartedly to their campaigns, parachuting with a protest banner into a nuclear power station, chaining herself to the prow of a whaler, being arrested as she tried to prevent plutonium ships leaving a French port. She spent spells in jail for her actions, and earned the reward of being taken on to the Ground swell payroll. She was now one of their main campaign organisers, but unlike some of her colleagues who stayed safe at headquarters, Alys still went out on the road, leading from the front, getting wet and dirty with the rest of the crew. Looking at her dispassionately, I couldn't help but admire such selfless devotion – she still earned little more than subsistence wages – but sometimes I wondered if she was becoming over-zealous, obsessive. Other times she seemed so strong and right as to put shame in the hearts of the rest of us. But to me she was always Alys, ten inches smaller than me and one month younger, the girl I'd paired up with at school when we were eleven, her teeth full of braces.

She rang off after we'd made arrangements about the following week, and I sat at my desk pondering how to tackle the story. Gradually I became aware I was being glared at by Ellis Clancy, the news editor, over the top of his computer screen. He was looking at me meaningfully, with his 'Why the hell are you sitting on your arse, doing nothing?' expression. Ellis was young, aggressive and nailbitten, with a taste for sarcasm. He had risen hard and fast up the newspaper echelon and now had his sights on a down-market tabloid as his next career move. It was my task to convince him that Alys's campaign story was worth running. I knew he found me difficult to deal with. I wouldn't stand for his malicious sniping, yet he wanted to keep in with me because of Shelley, and her value to the news pages.

We had reached a kind of stand-off, only communicating when necessary to the job. So when I went over to him and started talking, I was taken aback by the enthusiasm that lit up his face.

'When do you say these Groundswell people are coming?'

'A week today – Tuesday,' I answered.

'Great! That'll give us time to really stir it.'

'What d'you mean?' I asked warily.

'Well – you say these people are testing for sewage in the sea, right?'

'Yes, but—'

'D'you think that'll bring our cheery tourist traders out singing the Hallelujah Chorus?'

I saw exactly where his thoughts were leading – he liked nothing better than headline-words like 'slam', 'row', 'clash' and 'uproar'. And he was not averse to prodding potential combatants to produce them.

He was warming to his theme: 'Even if your friend wins, you're talking years, and big bucks, before anything's done at all. Meanwhile Groundswell's made a big play of saying "Ugh, don't paddle in there – it's niffy." Result: holiday-makers go somewhere else and the hoteliers are hit where it hurts: in the wallet.'

'We don't know what the samples'll show yet.'

'Anna, get a grip' (his favourite phrase). 'It's the very fact that they're doing it at all. Draws attention to something nasty, something you'd rather forget soon as you've flashed your fanny in the flusher. Have a look in the files, Anna, we've had all the stats before – all they do round here is take the raw stuff, mash it up, sieve out the big jobbies, and pump it out half a mile or so – something like 50 million gallons a day if my instant Trivia Recall serves me rightly. Troop out a few facts like that, shake 'em up with the news that Groundswell is on its way, and wham bam thank you, Ma'am, you're in *Biz*ness.'

My revulsion must have shown.

'Sorry it has to be you, Anna, don't look down your nose at it – your friend's the shit-stirrer. 'Scuse my Anglo-Saxon

70

but it happens to be appropriate here. Better keep your wellies handy for next Tuesday.

'In the meantime,' he continued, checking over his schedule for the following day, 'We'll take a scene-set for tomorrow – make it sing, we're a bit short on strong local stuff. Tell you what, ring the hoteliers' wallah – what's his name? – Cyril something or other?'

'Cyrus,' I replied with deepening misgiving, 'Cyrus Lander.'

'Right, get him to spout off what he thinks of these people and their survey. See if you can provoke him – we'll get some good mileage out of this one.'

Cyrus Lander, secretary of the Holiday Association of Northport, never needed provoking to 'spout off' about the tourist trade. He seized publicity by the throat and shouted in its face at every opportunity.

'They're doing what!?' came thundering out of the telephone in a tone so loud I had to hold my earpiece away.

'Conducting a beach survey to monitor pollution, Mr Lander.'

'Cranks from the capital, I'll bet,' he roared. 'What's the matter with these people, poking their noses into our business, what right have they got to come and tell us what to do? I bet they've never stuck a toe out of their open sandals to have a paddle on our beach. I know these people, they eat wheatgerm and go rucksacking for their holidays round places like Baluchistan, they don't come here. What do they know? They can't just start kicking up a stink about our beaches – there's nothing wrong. I should know – I've splashed about in that sea since I was a nipper and that's a lot longer than I care to remember. I've never had a day's illness in my life, put that in your paper. They should mind their own business – all they want is to do us down. Well I won't have it. I'm not having it – you'll see.'

I coughed slightly to remind him I was there: 'Do you intend to take any action, Mr Lander?'

'Action – action? You bet you'll see some action. My

association won't take this kind of shenanigans lying down. You'll be hearing from me before the week's out.'

'And in the mean time we can say that you resent this exercise?'

'You can say that and more. My official statement is that we shall oppose these people – what was it you called them? Groundswell? Headswell's more like it, or Ground-nuts. We'll issue a warning: keep out of this town and don't dare try to spoil our image in the tourist trade. We don't need these hotheads.'

'But surely, Mr Lander, if there is a problem, you should be the first to want it cleaned up properly – for the sake of the tourists?'

'There is no problem, darling, that's it, period. How many years has this been the best resort in the North? How many millions come and swim in that sea every year? How many get sick because of it? Come on, if there was a problem they'd be falling sick in droves: find me one, just one person you can prove got sick from that sea. You can't, can you? It's just not true, darling. People come here, let their hair down, drink too much, eat a dodgy hot dog – a change of routine – anything can upset your innards on holiday. Look I know they pump that stuff out, but they've been doing it for years, it just gets washed away, the bugs can't survive; it does not, and never has caused any harm on our beaches, no one can tell me otherwise. And you can tell those folk to stick that in their peace-pipe and smoke it. Do I make myself clear?'

'You do, Mr Lander, perfectly. Thanks very much for your comments.'

'You're welcome. I'll be in touch later in the week when I've talked to my committee. Anna, isn't it?'

'Anna Knight, extension 440. Thanks Mr Lander.'

I did not have to wait for his phone call at the end of the week to find out how much enmity Alys's group had aroused. The beach was the resort's only natural asset, the original source (along with its nearness to smoky factory towns) of its prosperity. Northport tourist traders, never slow to shout the odds where their interests were concerned, took this as a personal attack and prepared for warfare.

The phone started ringing almost as soon as the first article appeared. 'These people should stop meddling in other folk's affairs. They don't realise how it affects us, trying to make a decent living,' said one. 'What's in it for them, anyway?' came the suspicious demand. 'What do they get out of knocking our town, that's what I want to know? Coming here to look down their snooty noses, that's what it is. Why don't they go and pick on Blackpool instead?'

By the time Cyrus Lander came back to me I had more than an inkling of what was afoot.

'Anna,' came the Lander voice booming from the telephone, needing no introduction, 'I want to brief you on our plan of campaign.'

'You want to have a meeting with Groundswell – am I right?'

'It'll be a bit more than a meeting, love, quite a bit more. Listen, can you tell me what time they're going to start this sampling job on Tuesday?'

'Around 8 a.m., so I've been told, off Middle Beach. They'll be doing it four times a day for ten days, in different places, as well as pouring dye out to sea where the outfall pipe's supposed to end.'

'We'll see about that,' he said with a tone of threat in his voice. 'We're going to have a little welcome party waiting for them on Tuesday morning, you'll see. My members are mobilising, Anna, you'll be surprised at our secret army. I tell you what, these Groundnutters'll be lucky to take a sample at all. We're going to stand and fight them on the beaches, we're going to link ourselves a human chain, hundreds of us, they'll never break us, we've fought better foes than them and won!'

*

Sure enough, on Tuesday, as the town bathed in its early-morning miasma of bacon smells from thousands of guest-house kitchens, I watched a multitude massing on the normally placid wakening shore.

Cars pulled up on the promenade from all directions, halting briefly on double yellow lines to disgorge their contingent of the task force. Cackles and raised voices of greeting followed as they gathered in knots along the seafront. Paper-fetching holidaymakers and dog walkers stared in puzzlement as the groups of mainly middle-aged, amply built citizens formed themselves into squadrons at regular intervals.

Darting between them, rallying the troops and issuing orders, I saw the bulky figure of Cyrus Lander, easily identifiable by his mustard-yellow trousers sandwiched between white jacket and white shoes.

He spotted me as I stood waiting for events to develop from a strategic point on the promenade. Puffing with exertion, his cheeks red between bushy, yellowing side-burns, he hailed me.

'Quite a turn-out already, eh? I told you we wouldn't let this go without having our five penn'orth. We'll show 'em who's boss in this town.'

'How many people do you think will be supporting you this morning, Mr Lander?'

'The whole lot, darling. I haven't had a single one of my members say any different – the whole lot are behind us, it's our livelihoods that could be at stake here.'

'He's right you know,' added a woman joining him, whose flame-red, helmet-like coiffure momentarily distracted me. 'It really saddens me. I know these folk mean well, but they're going about it all the wrong way. Why sink to attacking our town?'

Cyrus Lander was checking the gold manacle of a watch on his wrist. He rooted in his jacket pocket to draw forth a large white tea-towel, emblazoned with a gaudy print of

Northport Tower. He raised it above his head and proceeded to flap it up and down, first to his right along the promenade, and then to his left.

At this signal I saw the troops on either side start making movements down the beach. In the distance I saw another flapping tea-towel take up the signal and pass it further down the line. All along the beach as far as I could see, the hoteliers were advancing towards the shoreline, fanning out at equal distances a few yards apart.

Cyrus Lander had now been waylaid by a thin young man from the local radio station, who was visibly quailing as the thunderous voice resounded into his microphone. It all seemed too harsh an intrusion on the morning's wakening calm, and I could not deny a trace of guilt at setting this reaction in train.

'Anna!' I heard a familiar voice shout from behind me. 'Anna – we're here!'

I turned to see Alys with two other women, one of them carrying a large instrument case bearing the wave-and-whale emblem of Groundswell.

I ran over to greet my friend as the little group crossed the promenade towards me. I hugged Alys – but as I did so I glanced up over her shoulder and saw Cyrus giving me a look which went from suspicion to anger.

He was striding over before I could give Alys any warning.

'So you're in this together are you?' he accused. 'I might've known.'

'Not at all, Mr Lander,' I replied, with all the self-control I could muster. 'This is Alys Finestone, who is leading the Groundswell survey team. We happen to have gone to school together but that does not mean I have anything personally to do with Groundswell. I'm here to report both sides.'

He prodded a finger towards my face: 'Yes, well, make sure you do report us fairly, my lady – or there'll be trouble. I'm not without influence as far as your bosses are concerned. You mark my words or you'll never hear the last of it.'

He turned from me to Alys and her two bemused supporters: 'As for you – why are you picking on us, eh? What's this all about? Do you want to ruin us, is that it? Can't stand the idea of people working damned hard to give themselves a decent living? If you people had your way we'd all be grubbing away in some sort of socialist commune. You want to undermine us. Well just let me warn you we're having none of it – none of it, you hear me!'

He had already turned his back on us to stride away when Alys grabbed his arm, her delicate features pink with suppressed anger.

She fixed him with a steely glare: 'I don't know who you are, Mr—'

'*Lander* – secretary, Holiday Association.'

'Very well, Mr Lander. In the interests of fairness I think you ought to hear our side. We are simply here to test whether this sea is in fact a health risk at present, and whether Western Water's proposals to bring it up to European bathing water standards are adequate. Nothing would delight us more than if our samples show your water is completely safe. But if it is not, and if our tests show that the proposed three-mile sewage outfall will still leave it contaminated, then I presume you will thank us for highlighting the hazard facing your paying customers, and join us in compaigning for proper sewage treatment plants all along the coast to render any discharges sterile. I hope you now understand what we are trying to do.'

With that she picked up the instrument case and started to walk towards the promenade rail.

'Understand, understand!' wailed Lander after her. 'I understand you're trying to stir up trouble, my girl.' He strode to keep up with her. 'I've never known anybody get sick from this sea – nobody even thought about it till you lot started muckraking.'

'Mr Lander,' insisted Alys calmly, 'a significant level of

bacterial contamination in sea water can pose a health risk. Gastroenteritis, ear and throat infections, even hepatitis can all result from immersing the head in polluted water.'

'*Not ours!*' He was roaring now. '*Not ours!* Go down to the blooming Costa del Stinko if pollution's what you're after. Go down to the Med. – that's more like a ruddy great cess-pool. It can't get away. *We*'ve got tides here, madam, we've got the ruddy great Atlantic Ocean running round into the Irish Sea – it doesn't bear any comparison.'

'We'll see then, Mr Lander, won't we?'

'Ay, that we shall!' he shouted, departing to rejoin his assembled army. 'That we shall!'

'I am sorry about all this, Alys,' I hurried to try to explain. 'I tried to get in touch, to warn you but—'

'I haven't been at home, I know. Listen, don't worry about it, Anna, we can handle people like him.'

'Yes, but it's not just him, it's—'. I stopped, since further explanations were pointless; Alys had seen what awaited her on the shore.

She and her two friends stood, too stunned to speak, at the prospect before them. All along the shoreline, ankle-deep in the water, stretched the holiday traders' defence force – women with their skirts tucked up into their underwear, men with trousers rolled to expose their knees – paddling back and forth with placards held high above the waves.

Sounds of a tribal chanting reached us above the water's constant surge, the words unintelligible at this distance, heightening the air of menace tainting the sea wind.

For a moment I almost felt that Alys's first thought was to turn and run. Then one of the women put her arm on Alys's shoulder: 'Come on Alys,' she coaxed. 'The sooner we get it over with, the sooner we can get down to the real job.'

'That's right,' said the other. 'They can't keep this up for long – they just want to make a fuss, get their picture in the paper, and then they'll probably leave us in peace.'

Alys smiled. 'I don't know what I'd do without you two. Oh Anna – you've not met Martina Ramczyk and Lynne Hattersley before.'

Both women smiled and shook hands. They were younger than Alys, probably in their early twenties, and Lynne had an American or Canadian accent. Both looked fresh and healthy as farm-girls.

'Martina's a marine biologist, and Lynne's a biochemist,' explained Alys. 'They'll be doing the preliminary analysis.'

'For our sins,' remarked Lynne.

'OK – here goes. If everyone's ready, we'll walk into the lions' den,' said Alys determinedly, picking up the case and leading the way down the beach steps. I watched her go, reflecting with affection that her taste in clothes never changed; always comfortable, usually jeans and sweaters – but always in brilliant colours. Her handknit jumper was hooped in yellow, red, blue and green. She looked like an exotic bird among drab sparrows.

As soon as she stepped on to the sand the local radio reporter was there with his microphone, asking urgently for a statement on what they were doing, and why. He dogged their footsteps as they marched purposefully towards the waiting line. A photographer from my paper was among a posse walking backwards in front of the women, clicking and shouting, 'This way, love! Thank you!', 'Can you lift the case up high, darling? Show the logo – both arms up – that's right. Wonderful, great.'

'Can you tell the listeners what you're going to do with the samples?' queried the radio reporter.

'After analysis we'll decide whether it is necessary to warn the public if there is a health hazard,' replied Alys. 'We shall inform the local authorities, Western Water, the Department of the Environment and the EC of our findings.'

'What have you to say to the members of our tourist trade who feel you're out to destroy their businesses.'

'We say they should await the results of the tests. We

don't want to destroy anyone's business – quite the reverse – but if the beach is polluted they should be demanding efficient clean-up measures for their own sake.'

All the time Alys was talking she was stalking grimly towards the waiting line. I could see she was speaking automatically, like an actress so familiar with her lines she need not think about them. What she was thinking about was the defiant beach patrol up ahead.

Following at a safe distance, I saw the placards – 'Groundswell – Go to Hell' – start moving up and down like war spears to the rhythmic chant: 'Northport sea's a healthy sea – don't you dare to come near me! Northport traders say you're wrong – go and find some other pong!'

Gradually the whole line – some in tight, bright swimming costumes corsetting their girth, others in cardies and jackets above their bunched skirts and rolled pants – were stamping in a static march, the water splashing and foaming round them in a surge of white surf.

The stamping became faster and faster as Alys and her press hangers-on approached, and by the time she halted at the water's edge the whole length of sea was churning, the sand and foam making a brown salt rain spraying everyone in proximity. I suddenly lost sight of Alys in the crowd as she bent down, evidently to take the sampling equipment from its case. She raised the metal object high to show it to the assembled hosts.

'Ladies and gentlemen,' I heard her thin voice against the background of the chanters' thrashing. 'We mean you no harm. Our only aim is to stop the possibility of polluted water harming swimmers. We never wanted a confrontation—'

'Too late – you've bloody got one!' came from somewhere along the line.

'Please – ', persisted Alys. 'Just let us take our samples and go as we came – in peace and goodwill towards the people of Northport.'

'*Go!* That's right,' came the unmistakable fog-horn of

Cyrus Lander. 'You go in peace all right – straight back where you came from. Groundswell, go to Hell! Groundswell, go to Hell!'

'Shame, *shame!*' brayed a crimson-costumed woman close to Alys. '*Shame* on you! Think you know better than us, eh? Who are you, to tell us something's wrong with our sea? There's *Nothing* wrong – nothing, nothing, nothing!'

I gulped as I saw Alys start walking towards the crimson costume. 'Here!' the woman shouted in Alys's face. 'Here – here's your precious sample – take it, take it.'

With that she began kicking the water towards Alys, while beside her, more irate hoteliers took up her lead and began kicking the waves towards Martina and Lynne, who were flanking their leader. Totally drenched by now the three women drove through the water under the rain of spray. Immediately the hoteliers closed ranks to join hands, casting their placards down to add to the obstacles.

Alys made one move to bend and take a sample, and the line all round her contracted as the hoteliers linked arms and shoulders together.

'*Now!*' came the Lander command – and with one surge the tightened army closed in a pincer movement around the three women, beginning their chanting once again: 'Northport sea's a healthy sea – don't you dare to come near me! Northport traders say you're wrong – go and find some other pong!'

Inexorably they were bearing down on the three women, forcing them to turn and flee. Suddenly I saw Alys lose her footing in the thrashing waves. I bit back a cry as my friend fell backwards into the water while all the time the marching feet pressed nearer and nearer. I was gripped with the sudden conviction that they were not going to stop – that Alys would be drowned under the unmindful advance of the mob. Seized with panic I ran into the water and managed to reach Alys as she struggled to regain a grip on the turbulent sea-bed and keep her head above the seething deluge.

'*Alys!* I'm here, hang on to me!' I desperately shouted, grabbing her sodden body before the encroaching legs could reach her. Alys, half stunned, managed to get her arm round my neck and stand up – but, unnerved by the noise and unbalanced by my friend's limp weight, I found myself floundering on the slithering sand. My shoes came adrift and I fell over them, Alys on top of me, both now saturated, with eyes stinging from the salt and grit.

Through the confusion, I realised with infinite relief that the stamping and bellowing had stopped, and all that was now dragging us down was the waves' natural undertow. I felt my arm being lifted by one of Alys's friends while the other assisted Alys, and we all limped towards the shore. As we collapsed on the hard-packed sand I felt beaten and humiliated, clothes hanging in sodden rags, hair flat to my wet head. I looked over at Alys and the others, who appeared similarly defeated, chests heaving, trying to regain their breath. We must have seemed a sorry quartet, for the hoteliers began to disperse quietly, not looking at us, as if they were embarrassed. Even Cyrus Lander was subdued as he walked away. But watching all those retreating backs I saw someone coming towards us, someone bearing blankets and towels and a look of serious concern. It was Sammy, who hurried to wrap one of the rugs round my shoulders before handing towels to Alys and her friends.

'When I knew what Cyrus Lander and his cronies were planning I feared you wouldn't get away without a soaking,' he explained. 'So I thought I'd watch, and I came prepared.'

He delved in his shoulder bag and brought out a flask of hot coffee, pouring out warming draughts with more than a hint of brandy. I was both surprised and deeply grateful for the boy's thoughtfulness – but he seemed to want no thanks, shrugging them off while he saw to our comfort. Soon we were all laughing, sitting in a circle round our

81

cups of laced coffee on the beach, guffawing over our ridiculous ordeal.

ELEVEN

Alys and I talked into the night. We were sitting in my flat, having eaten dinner with her friends who had now gone back to their camper, and we were finishing the remains of the Rioja.

Alys sank among the cushions of my softest chair and stretched her stockinged feet out to a stool.

'You just don't know how much of a luxury this is to me, Ans,' she said.

'What, drinking wine in my humble abode? Lord, we've done that often enough. I wouldn't put it in the luxury bracket.'

'Don't underestimate the pleasures of ordinary life . . . I sometimes think I should jack it all in with Groundswell and become a humble housewife.'

I laughed out loud: 'Now I know you're not serious – who'd have you anyway?'

'Some poor sap would succumb to my charms – as someone's succumbed to yours by the looks of things. I can read the signs – candles by the bed, flowers in the boudoir. You've been going to bed with more than a paperback lately.'

'I like candlelight and flowers – why shouldn't I indulge myself?'

'Can't hide anything from me, Ans. Methinks thou dost protest too much. There's a man around somewhere.'

I gave in. She would keep my confidence, I knew that, and I saw her face take on a slow, amused smile as I told her about my married policeman.

'I have to hand it to you, Ans, all sex and no sock-washing – that's the best kind of arrangement.'

'Oh sure, and how about you? Is Jay still on the scene?'

She smiled: 'Faithful dependable Jay, yes, he's there all right.'

He was a boyfriend she'd had at university, who'd become impatient with her pioneering spirit and married someone else. The marriage, however, had failed a few years later, leaving him a divorced father with custody of the two children. He was a teacher, and had never moved from Lancaster. I suspected that their relationship had simply gone underground for a period of hibernation during his marriage, occasionally surfacing in surreptitious meetings.

'But oh God,' Alys shook her head. 'I'm not the stepmother type, now am I? I just sometimes think I'd like to be, I'm tempted to hearth and home.'

'What's brought all this on?'

I looked at her closely for the first time since she came, and I saw that she was drawn and tired, with an exhaustion not merely temporary, but persistent and profound. She raked her fingers through her short dark hair.

'I'm shattered Ans,' she said frankly. 'This last project has really taken it out of me, and I don't know if it's worth holding the candle any more.'

'What's been going on, Alys? I'm worried about you.'

She gave a heavy sigh, 'Oh, it's a combination – one damn thing after another. I used to be able to take any amount of hassle – water off a duck's back – I even found it exciting. Now it's just become a constant battle. I'm war weary – perhaps it's my age.'

'Come on,' I eyed her suspiciously, 'I know you – you can't fob me off with vague talk. Only six months ago you were full of enthusiasm – the expanding movement, more funds, campaign successes – so what's happened to change your attitude?'

'Well, you're right,' she admitted tensely. 'Things have been happening. It's the project I've been doing these last few months. Look, I've said I'd tell you about it, and I will – but this is strictly between us, OK? Not for publication in the blessed *Evening News* or anywhere else. Publicity could land us in greater danger than we are now.'

'You have my solemn word – but what do you mean by danger?'

'OK. Six months ago I was really pleased with myself; Groundswell had at last given me the go-ahead to set up a task force for research around British shores.'

'Yes, you told me about it at the time. It was after all those seals were washed up on the beach, dying of distemper?'

'That's right. It gave me the trigger to persuade Groundswell to release the funds. I'd felt for some time that our seas were getting sicker. All the pollution over the years was mounting up, and the marine ecology couldn't cope with it any more. I saw the seals and their lowered immunity as a warning signal – if we weren't careful we wouldn't only have dying seals but a dying sea. But we needed the research data to launch a campaign. Luckily the rest of the Groundswell executive agreed with me. They made a boat available and ten helpers on a shift basis. As it happens they were all women, which I rather welcomed. I think we work together better as a single-sex team. We called ourselves the Women's Action Research Nucleus – WARN for short – and some bright spark rechristened the boat the *No Man's Land*. We stripped the Groundswell logo from it: we wanted to get on with our research quietly, and sometimes Groundswell attracts harassment.'

'Being economical with the truth?'

'Sometimes it's more practical. Anyway, we started work in the Irish Sea, planning to go round the coast. We began to track discharges – nuclear, chemical, even soap and sewage sludge – it's a real soup out there. We ran tests on seals, fish, shellfish, seabirds, seaweed. We took sea-water samples. It's a huge job, but it was going well. Then along came Harry, and that was when the trouble started.'

My senses sharpened: 'Harry – Harry who?'

'Jansen I'm afraid – yes, the same Harry who leaps from windows.'

'But . . . what has he got to do with you? Why didn't you say anything when I told you how I got to know Sammy?'

'I wanted to wait until I had time to tell you the whole story, which I'm doing now if you'll be patient. From what you've said, it's hard to know whether Sammy had a hand in Harry's fall or not. But someone did, someone who wasn't a common-or-garden thief, of that I'm sure. And I'm also sure that that someone could be after us next.'

I looked at her, speechless.

'Look, I'd better tell you about Harry,' she went on rapidly. 'He has a lot to do with us as it happens. He's one of our major supporters – financially I mean. He's a wealthy man – family money – and he gives us a hell of a lot of cash and equipment. He doesn't make a song and dance of it – perhaps he thinks it might put off some of his voters, I don't know. Anyway, he gives us serious money: serious enough for him to pull a few strings when he wants to.'

'And he pulled yours?'

'That's right. He'd found out about the work we were doing, and he asked us to do some work for him at the same time. Well, I agreed – I mean, not only does he give us money, he's also been useful to us in the past as part of the political machine. He asks us for research data, then he trots it out on TV or in the European Parliament, and people take notice – the same people who'd dismiss Ground-swell as a load of scaremongers.'

'So what did he ask you to do?'

She took a deep drink of her wine, tensing her mouth into a grimace before she went on.

'He wanted us to analyse the sediments in certain areas,

85

and he gave us some extra equipment to take on board the *No Man's Land*, to carry out a seismic survey.'

'A what?'

'It's a kind of echo-sounding system: he wanted us to take measurements of the layers under the sea-bed by sending out sounds and recording their reverberations. All within a specific area.'

'But why?'

'Exactly. He told us it was for two reasons. One, he wanted to compare the Irish Sea sedimentation with that in the North Sea, to see if we could predict any common patterns that may cause environmental crises – well, that suited our purpose anyway, especially as he was giving us better equipment than we could afford. And two, he wanted to find out if any pollution was coming up from under the sea, from layers disturbed by drilling for gas or oil. The seismic survey, he said, would show him what was down there – from a source other than the gas and oil people who have a vested interest.'

'You sound as if you don't believe him.'

'Oh I did at the time, it sounded plausible enough, and he was paying for it after all. You know how he works, you'll've seen him on TV – all charm and manipulation. He puts his arm round your shoulder and convinces you that this is the greatest thing you could do for him in his whole life.'

'So what happened?'

'Well, I first suspected he might be mixed up in something more dubious when he swore us to absolute secrecy about the research, to a degree that seemed totally out of proportion. We had to get the data to him personally, not through the post, and we hadn't to mention the seismic equipment to anyone. He seemed paranoid about security. Then strange things began to happen to us – worrying, threatening things – and it's culminated in this – this murder attempt on Harry.'

'Murder?'

She nodded: 'I'm convinced someone is trying to shut Harry up for good. There've been other things too . . .' She paused, looking pensive. 'The reason I haven't been in touch, the reason I haven't been home. Every time I've come ashore I've had this awful feeling someone's watching me. I even had a – an accident that really scared me. I was driving down a back lane from the port to Jay's late one night. There was a car behind me, so close it was almost on my bumper, and I couldn't shake it off. Then it suddenly glared its headlights on full-beam, straight into my mirror. I was blinded, and the next thing I knew, this car was alongside me, trying to make me swerve. I came off the road and ended up in a ditch. Luckily a motorbike came along just then and the car shot off. The motorcyclist came to help me, and I realised I'd stopped just inches short of a huge tree – I could well have been wrapped round it if I'd been made to swerve just a second later.'

'When did this happen?'

'About a month after we started doing the work for Harry. I had a roll of computer data ready to give him in my car at the time, and that was when I began to link the work we were doing for him with these frightening incidents. I felt there was a third ear listening to my telephone conversations, there were clicks on the line, some of my mail looked to have been steamed open and stuck down again. Jay was worried – said I was screwing up, being neurotic – but eventually I had to stay away from him, to keep *them*, whoever they are, away from him and the kids.'

'That's why I haven't been able to get in touch with you anywhere.'

'That's right. Someone is trying to stop us doing this work, Anna, they're trying to intimidate us, and if all else fails, I'm convinced they'll try to kill us like they tried with Harry. So . . . you know me when somebody wants to stop me doing anything—'

'You just become more stubborn.'

'Determined at any rate. As a result, I haven't been

anywhere but that damn ship – and the Irish Sea's anything but a painted ocean. Me, with my weak stomach, I throw up on a millpond, never mind a Force 8. It was the seasickness that eventually ground me down. I had to come away, to try to decide if all the hassle was worth while. I told Groundswell I wanted a break from the project. So they put me on the seaside sewage trail for a few weeks.'

'Has the work stopped then?'

'No, the other women are still out there, carrying on. Harry sent word from his hospital bed to headquarters, for goodness' sake, telling us he wanted more data from a different area.'

'And what about you – are you going to go back?'

She sighed, 'I think I have to, Ans. There's too much at stake, I do want the work to go on.'

'But why, Alys? What's it for? Surely it's ridiculous to go on when it's putting you at risk and you don't even know why?'

She paused before speaking again, sombrely: 'But I think I do know.'

Then she was silent. 'Well, come on, Alys,' I said, leaning forward, 'you've told me this much, you can't stop now. It must be important if you're prepared to lay yourself on the line.'

'Obviously we talked about it on the boat, and from the kind of analysis he'd asked us to do, we came up with some theories.'

'Which were?'

'We think Harry has got wind of a serious accident – probably involving toxic waste – and someone is trying to cover it up. There's a hell of a lot of traffic in the Irish Sea, including ships stacked to the gunwales with chemical or industrial waste. There's ships carrying spent nuclear fuel too, highly radioactive, deadly stuff, going to Sellafield for reprocessing. Below the surface there's submarines – NATO and Soviet – nuclear powered, blundering about, dragging down trawlers periodically. We believe Harry has heard of some sort of collision involving one of these poison ships and possibly a submarine. If they've lost cargo overboard, and it leaks into the Irish Sea, it would mean an environmental catastrophe. It stands to reason a company would want to hush it up and so would a government if one of their subs were involved. The prospect is really frightening, Ans. I mean, it may take years for a container of the stuff to rust or rupture, but that doesn't mean to say it'll never happen. We think Harry is using our survey to try to track down that lost cargo.'

'But if that is the case, why didn't Harry come clean with you?'

She shrugged worriedly: 'I don't know, Ans. It could be a number of things. Maybe for our own protection. It's obvious from what's happened to him and to us, we're dealing with some ruthless people. Perhaps he thought the pretence of a genuine ecological survey would shield us. But it's plain they're on to what we're doing. Maybe he simply wanted enough evidence that the accident had happened before he made it public. On the other hand, he could want to keep his name out of the whole mess. Perhaps he thought if he pointed us in the right direction we'd make the discovery ourselves. He may have a source in the industry he needs to protect, you see. I just don't know.'

'Have you told him you were being followed? Did you ask him why?'

'Of course. He said he knew nothing about it, I couldn't prise anything out of him.'

Her eyes narrowed, and anger seemed to well up inside her.

'Darn it, Anna – I resent having my research threatened like this, after I worked so hard to get it going. All right, I can take Harry Jansen hijacking my project to some extent – but how dare his enemies try to put the frighteners on us? Well, they won't stop us, I can tell you that – the work's too important to me. I'm going to finish this project if it's the last thing I do.'

'Alys, for God's sake, be sensible – you said yourself these are ruthless people.'

'I'm not giving in to them, Anna, they'll not stop me, they'll not stop my work.'

'But what use is your work if it makes you a martyr? They tried to crash your car into a tree – and next time they might succeed.'

But I saw my entreaties were fruitless. Her anger had charged her with renewed energy, and I recognised a stubborn look in her eyes.

'Just be careful, then,' I sighed. 'I do care what happens to you, you know.'

TWELVE

Nine days later I got a worrying telephone call from Shelley's agent in London. Alma Ransome was a powerfully built American woman in her forties who had been on the boards herself and brooked no nonsense either from poverty-pleading theatre managements or petulant performers.

As usual, she came straight to the point: 'What the hell's the matter with your daughter?' she said. 'She rang in sick three days ago, told the theatre she'd got a headache, and no one's heard a squeak out of her since. She's got the phone switched permanently to the answering machine and she doesn't return our calls. What's up with her?'

I did not know. The last time I'd seen her, four days before, she hadn't looked ill. Nevertheless, I was convinced she was stricken by the claim that she had triggered a rapist's rampage. She had been much more withdrawn than normal, with jittery bouts of exaggerated cheerfulness that failed to fool me. I knew she was deeply upset, but she refused to admit it. She had dismissed my queries with an irritated, 'I'm fine, Ma, stop worrying.'

But I did not know she had been off work. I'd never known her cry off before – she'd worked through colds, ankle sprains and even gastric flu, against my arguments.

The agent was going on: 'Look, I've got the Vegas Theatre screaming down the phone at me every half-hour – when's she coming back? And I can't tell them because she's playing Greta Garbo. If she's really ill, fine, let her stay off till she's better, but the theatre needs to know for goodness' sake. They have to book stand-ins and—'

'All right, all right, Alma, I understand,' I broke in. 'I'll be in touch just as soon as I know what's the matter.'

'Well it'd better be soon, I tell you – Riverside TV's on to me to fix a time for her to do that comedy pilot. Now if I don't hear from her pronto, they're gonna quit hanging around and hire someone else. I'm warning you, Anna, this is serious. If she misses this pilot just because she's fannying around, she can get the hell off my books. I worked damn hard to get her that TV interview. I have a right to know what's going on.'

'Sure,' I said, picking up the American twang unconsciously. 'I realise it's important, and I'm worried about her. I'll get round there and find out – I'll ring you back this afternoon, I promise you, Alma.'

'OK,' said the agent abruptly, and put the phone down without even a farewell.

I had hardly moved from my desk when the phone rang again. I snapped into the mouthpiece: 'Editorial.'

'Oh, is that Mrs Knight?' came a hesitant woman's voice.

'Yes.'

'It's Carol Macready here – I'm your daughter's cleaner, you know?'

'Oh yes, yes of course, how are you?'

'I'm fine thanks. But it's Shelley. I hope I'm doing the right thing. But I thought you ought to know – when I went to do my usual couple of hours this morning – I let myself in, you know, she gave me a key for when she was out. Well, I thought the flat was empty, so I did my work in the living room and kitchen, you know, but when I went to the bedroom – it was locked. And then I listened, and I could hear her crying inside. I called out, to see if she was all right, to see if she wanted anything. When she opened the door to me, aw, Mrs Knight, I've never seen her looking so pitiful – she's such a lovely girl – and her hair all over and her face puffed up from the crying, fair broke my heart to see her.

'Her night-dress was all crumpled like she'd had it on for days, and she had this – this – picture in her hand. Well I tried to make her more comfortable. I ran her a bath and changed the bed and brought her a clean night-dress. But she wouldn't let me phone the doctor – kept saying there was nothing a doctor could do. And she wouldn't let me do anything with that picture, wouldn't let me touch it . . . I don't know, Mrs Knight. I'm concerned for her, you know. I think she might be sick. That's why I rang, I hope you don't mind.'

'No, no, Carol – of course you've done the right thing. I'm very grateful to you. I'll get round there straight away.'

The flat was quiet as I let myself in with the key Shelley had given me for checking the premises while she was away. I knocked tentatively on the bedroom door.

'Shelley . . . Shelley . . . are you in there?'

I heard a shuffling, as of bedclothes moving. Then her voice came, flat and dull.

'Yes, Ma. But I'm not coming out. You can't make me.'

'I don't want to make you do anything, darling. But if you're ill I want to help.'

'I'm contagious.'

'What? What do you mean, Shelley? Look, can I come in, please?'

'All right,' she said with a long sigh. 'It's not locked.'

She was stretched full-length on the bed, draped in a chrysanthemum-yellow kimono which made her skin look wan and pasty. She had her head buried in a pillow, but she looked up as I came round. 'I'm not ill, Mama,' she said, her eyes sticky. 'I'm just dying.'

'Don't play around, Shelley, people are very concerned about you. Now I want to know if you're really sick.'

I held my palm to her forehead, but there was no high temperature, only a cool clamminess.

'People? What people?' she asked scornfully. 'The people who make money out of me? Huh? I'll bet they're concerned . . . well, I'm sorry, the milk-cow's dried up. I can't do it any more.'

'You can't do what?'

'Work! Work! I can't work any more. See what my work's done! It's made some poor sap flip his lid and near-on batter the life out of women. How can I go on working, knowing that? How can I even live with myself?'

'But of course you can work, Shelley. Change the act, do something different.'

'The act is me – that's what people want me for – they don't want me to sing and dance like some Miss Goody Two-Shoes, they want sass, they want balls on a plate, pricks with everything, and the more I make the punters look like wankers, the better they like it.'

I stared at her, hating to hear the obscenities. Self-loathing filled her face. Suddenly she reached out towards the picture leaning on her bedside cabinet – Sammy's picture of the youth and the snake-woman – and she hurled it face down on to the floor.

'This is the end of Shelley Chantelle, Mama. I'm not going to do it any more. I'll have to get a job in Woolworth's – if they'll have me.'

I hardly knew whether she was serious or not. She had a

tendency to over-react – she was a performer. I could not believe she would give up everything she'd worked for – in essence, her whole life – on the strength of one setback like this.

I tried to talk her round.

'Woolworth's?' I said. 'Of course they'll have you. They'll fall over themselves to have a smart girl like you on the checkout. You could help keep the customers entertained. Is that what you want?'

'I'd be contributing more to society than I am now, wouldn't I?'

'Well, whatever you're going to do, you'd better choose quickly. I've had Alma on the phone to me today, saying if she doesn't hear from you soon, you'll lose that TV pilot show.'

'How can I do it, Mama?' she turned to me tearfully. 'I can't even drag myself out of here to take rubbish to the dustbins, never mind do a show. I've lost it, Mama. I can't hack it any more. The minute I stepped on a stage I'd be paralysed – scared of talking to the audience, petrified to pick somebody out in case it was another bloody psychotic. I can't make my living like that any more. I'm like that snake-woman, I'm dangerous, I'm poisonous.'

I sighed and sat on the bed, taking her hand.

'You need a holiday, love. You've been working too hard, putting too much pressure on yourself. This rapist business must just have been the last straw. I should have seen you were getting over-tired. Look, how about coming with me somewhere hot, sunny and away from telephones for a couple of weeks. Then you can decide what you want to do. *I'll* phone Alma, and I'll phone the theatre and tell them you need a break, you're suffering from exhaustion, and I'll fix things at work.'

'I'm not over-tired,' she said bleakly. 'Honestly Mama, that's not the trouble. A holiday wouldn't make any difference. I may as well tell them all now as in two weeks' time

. . . Shelley Chantelle has made her farewell performance, thank you and goodnight.'

The doorbell rang. I looked at her, convinced she wouldn't want to see anybody.

'Oh God, that's probably Sammy,' she said. 'I'd forgotten he was coming this afternoon. He's supposed to be bringing the pictures now they've been framed.'

'Shall I let him in?'

'Yes, let him come,' she said. 'He'll have had to struggle up here with them. I wouldn't like to disappoint him. But if it's not him, I don't want to see anyone else.'

It was. He was weighed down with two heavy flat parcels which I presumed must be the pictures. His smile of greeting turned to a frown as I told him Shelley was not feeling very well. As I helped him carry the parcels to the living room I noticed he seemed somehow more mature and composed, less adolescent than previously. His hair was trimmed shorter, and he wore a workaday white shirt and striped tie with plain grey trousers.

As he began to unfold the pictures from their wrappings he asked what was wrong with Shelley. I told him. I didn't see any point in being coy about it. She'd had a crisis of confidence and was threatening to finish her career.

'But she can't do that,' he said earnestly, stopping fiddling with the picture-hooks and cord. 'She mustn't stop working, not when she's got so far. It would be a criminal waste.'

I heard Shelley's laugh from behind us in the doorway. She had been listening, barefoot and silent.

'It may be a criminal waste but it's better than baiting a criminal, isn't it?' she demanded, half hysterically.

Sammy was staring at her, the yellow kimono knotted tightly round her waist, hair tangled, face blotched and her hand gripping the doorknob so hard I thought she would wrench it away.

'I can help you, you know, if you'll let me,' the boy said calmly.

'It isn't anything that can be helped, Sammy. I've made up my mind. I'm going to phone my agent now.'

She started to walk across the room to the telephone.

'Shelley, don't,' I said. 'Don't say anything you might regret. Let me ring her and tell her you're sick. You need more time to—'

Sammy had grabbed her arm as she passed him.

'Give me an hour,' he said. 'Just one hour and we'll see if you still feel the same way then.'

Alarm bells began to ring in my head. What was he proposing? According to Greg, this boy was well versed in the alchemy of mood-changing drugs. I was damned if I was going to let him introduce her to that iniquity. Surely he couldn't, he wouldn't suggest that – not in front of me – would he? I still couldn't judge just how trustworthy he was, with his mask of innocence, his facial charm.

He was stroking her arm now, his voice dropped lower and gentler. 'You're so tense,' he was saying, 'I can ease that tension away if only you'll let me. Let me do it, Shelley, let me try. You've nothing to lose.'

I saw her shoulders drop as she looked down at him. 'You're right,' she said, sighing. 'I've got nothing left to lose. Do what you want . . . I don't care any more.'

He gave a half-smile and turned to me.

'Anna,' he said. 'I'm going to take her to the bedroom, make her lie down, lower the lights and close the curtains. Then I'm going to massage her neck and her shoulders and back. I'm going to talk to her . . . to make her relax. That's all. She'll feel much better, I can almost guarantee it. I know what I'm doing, I promise you.'

'No, Shelley,' I glared at her, anxious to shield her from his persuasive charm. 'Perhaps this wouldn't be such a good idea. What you need is a doctor, it's obvious you're ill. I'll phone now, he'll give you something to help you sleep—'

'No!' she turned on me with over-sensitive ferocity. 'I'm not taking sleeping pills, I'm not starting that kick, stuffed full of pills and potions, uppers for this, downers for that. I've seen that happen in showbusiness. They mess you up and burn you out.'

'But surely just for a short—' I started, but Sammy interrupted.

'I can help her without pills or potions, that's the whole point. Believe me, Anna, the mind can heal itself given time and encouragement. Just give me a chance – if it doesn't work, then you can fetch a doctor.'

Shelley didn't wait for me to respond, she was already going towards her bedroom, and Sammy followed her. I felt miserably torn.

'I shall be here, Shelley, I'll be here all the time,' I called after her. 'Just call if you want anything . . .'

Perhaps I was being over-suspicious, I told myself. Shelley had been so adamant about not wanting drugs from the doctor, she wouldn't take them from Sammy either. Of course not. Unless he did it surreptitiously – relaxed her then slid in the needle. But why should he do that? No, he must be genuine. I made myself some tea to calm my fluttering thoughts, but found myself so anxious, I couldn't drink it.

Half an hour later, I peeped into the dim bedroom and saw the boy bent over Shelley, who was lying on her front with the kimono dropped from her shoulders. He was gently massaging her bare back and murmuring low into her ear, rhythmically and slowly.

I tiptoed away again, and waited another half-hour. This time I ventured into the bedroom, and he looked up from his work as I came in, putting his finger to his lips and then going back to the rhythmical rubbing.

'She's sleeping now,' he whispered. 'I put her into a deeply relaxed state, it was what she needed, it's a hypnosis technique.'

He must have noted the sceptical expression on my face.

'She'll feel much better, I know it,' he said firmly. 'Actually I was surprised just how suggestible she was.

She must have been very weak, emotionally. She needed her self-confidence restoring. I've tried to do that, but it will take a few more sessions to complete.'

Shelley stirred, and her eyes lazily opened, as if rousing from deep slumber.

'Mmmmmm . . . oh that's wonderful . . . mmmm, Sammy, I could have you do that for ever, just lie here for ever being stroked.'

'How do you feel, Shelley?' asked the boy.

'Blissful, oh this is so sweet, they should put you on the National Health.'

'And how do you feel now about giving up your job?' he went on, still stroking, lightly now.

She turned over, unselfconscious about her naked breasts.

'No . . . that would be wrong,' she said, the words long and low. 'That would be giving in to the monster . . . I see that now. He mustn't win, I can't let a lunatic destroy Shelley Chantelle.'

I smiled and took her hand: 'No, my love, you're too good for that.'

'You think I am, Mama? Do you really?' she asked, needing my support.

'Of course I do. I'm proud of you, Shelley . . . but you know I've never liked the material you chose for that act.'

She closed her eyes: 'You were right too. At least this nightmare's taught me that. But I've got other material in me . . . all I need is time to work on it . . . it'll come good, just as good as my man-eater act. If I can't take knocks I shouldn't be on the stage at all, right?'

'Good, Shelley,' said Sammy soothingly. 'You're getting stronger, but take it slowly, slow and calm, slow and calm, gather your strength.'

She lay back again in utter relaxation.

'So, Shelley,' I asked, 'what about Alma? What shall I tell her?'

'Tell her I'm sorry . . . I've been ill. But I will do the TV pilot . . . I'll speak to her tomorrow . . . thank you, Sammy, you've been a marvel.'

I looked at the boy. I was impressed. She was chastened, but confident – he'd put the fight back in her. And she was willing to listen, open to suggestion. As far as I could see, this was no drug-wrought transition, Shelley's eyes were clear and bright. Perhaps he really did have hypnotic skills, and had used them for Shelley's good quite voluntarily. Perhaps I should trust the boy a little more.

THIRTEEN

The Groundswell sea survey found, as we thought it would, that Northport's bathing water was way below European health standards. And sure enough, during the ten-day survey, the purple dye appeared back on our shore in far less time than it would take harmful bacteria to perish. A considerable tide of public opinion swung behind the Groundswell campaign, despite the enmity of the hoteliers' home guard. But the hoteliers and the other holiday traders had a powerful influence on the council's ruling party. And when Alys staged her end-of-survey press-call on the beach, the ruling party took up the notion of staging a counter-blast. So it wasn't just a collection of reporters, photographers and curious bystanders who gathered on the seafront. As Greg and I drew up we groaned to see a large and cheerfully rancorous band of councillors, together with a retinue of officers and functionaries, waiting on the promenade as if on a seaside outing.

Alys had left the flat early to join Lynne and Martina in

preparing signs to put up on the beach, signs which read 'HAZARD – contaminated water' in line with their findings. The signs were not meant to be permanent – a propaganda ploy to make sure the point got over through the media before they were removed by the offended local authority, as inevitably happened.

The council contingent was led by the worthy Councillor Irene Millichop, first lady of the resort's leisure and tourism committee, who despite her sex was always referred to as 'Mr Chairman'. She was a former Mayor and a wealthy undertaker's wife who devoted herself to numerous voluntary fund-raising bodies. A councillor for seventeen years, she was a ruddy, well-built force of a woman who exuded an aura of compassion. No one, not even her political opponents, was immune from the flood-tide of her motherly concern. That morning, for instance, she had no sooner seen me than she clucked over my unsuitable footwear and offered her own 'flatties' from the car.

A hapless local radio reporter who tripped on the beach steps found himself subject to an embarrassing fuss as she gave her lace handkerchief to bind his grazed wrist. 'I do hope it doesn't swell too much Mr Nicholas. I feel almost responsible as you were recording me when you missed your footing, but really I'd far rather you took care and waited. Dear me, that's a nasty graze.' The young man himself – far more concerned about his battered recording equipment – had to submit himself to her ministering care.

Her devotion to people's welfare was so all-embracing that she was readily accused of sham by her critics. Her own side would huff in indignation, but they all used the nickname endowed by her penchant for floaty, flowery chiffon dresses: she was known to one and all as 'Frilly Milly' behind her ample back.

The sun was obscured, that morning, by a swathe of sallow, yellowy cloud. The expectant bunch on the promenade shuffled and entertained themselves with idle jibes and back-chat. The Groundswell women were late, and

Frilly Milly rechecked her watch worriedly. She had a presentation of her own to perform for the media – to rebut the Groundswell campaign – and if the women were not there it might lose its impact. Nevertheless she could see that her brood was getting impatient.

Milly had a simple outlook on her job: to her the resort was the brightest and best in the country and she would hear no criticism without springing to its defence. I knew that her belief in Northport's sea quality was utterly genuine. She had been told for years by the council's environmental health officers that it presented no significant health hazard, and this was what she wanted to hear. The fact that they could say so while admitting it failed to come up to European standards made no jot of difference. To her, the standards were wrong or, rather, unrealistically high and therefore she viewed any attempt to achieve them as costly and unnecessary. Today she wanted, she had told Ellis Clancy on the newsdesk phone, 'to prove to the millions of Northport's loyal visitors that their health is safe on our sands'.

'How do you intend to prove that, Councillor Millichop?' asked Ellis, who, to give him his due, had given a good show to the Groundswell campaign.

'Oh, Mr Clancy,' she had twittered coyly, 'let that be a surprise for you and your readers – but let me just tell you that it will be a convincing one!'

No wonder Alys was late, I thought. The prospect of more antagonism after that first bitter confrontation was hardly heartening. I knew, from her subdued demeanour during her ten-day stay with me, that she had been anxious about it, though she would not admit it.

Just as the waiting councillors were beginning to lose patience and demand to go down on the beach without further ado, I saw a taxi draw up on the promenade, and Alys flusteredly tumbling out of it, weighted with unwieldy placards, a toolbag and a large holdall. Where were Lynne and Martina, and the camper-van? Was something wrong? I hurried over to help Alys with her burdens.

As soon as I saw her face I could tell she had been crying. Her eyes were puffy and bloodshot, her cheeks raw and vulnerable.

'Anna – the bastards!' was her greeting.

'What's happened, quickly, tell me.'

'Someone set fire to the camper.'

'God – were the women in it? Are they hurt?'

'Yes they were in it – they were sleeping – it happened about 6.30 a.m. They managed to get out before it really took hold, thank goodness, but they've both got smoke in their lungs and shock – and Lynne's hands are a mess.'

'Where are they now?'

'At the hospital, that's where I've just come from. Dear God, what bastards these people must be.'

'You know who did it?'

'Not exactly, but it's obvious isn't it? It must be the same people who're trying to stop us finding out what's happened out there.' She indicated the Irish Sea. 'We had a call from the WARN ship yesterday. They'd come into port with some more results for Harry, so Lynne and Martina went up there to collect them last night. The data were in the van with them this morning when it went up in smoke. Someone must have followed them. Anyway Lynne managed to grab her holdall from the flames, with Harry's data in it, so at least that was saved. But Christ, Anna, I'm reaching the end of my tether. I don't know how long I can go on. I mean, it's my project and I'm putting people in danger for it. It's my fault.'

A harsh look came across her face, leaching the vitality from her skin, frightening me with its bleakness.

'Nonsense, Alys,' I said hurriedly. 'You haven't forced anybody to do anything. They do it of their own free will, how can it be your fault? It's Harry's, if anything.'

She sighed as she looked at the waiting throng. 'Yes,

you're right I suppose. Come on, I'd better get this over with, then I can wrap up and get out of this town.'

I hoisted her holdall on to my shoulder while she lifted the toolbag and placards. I noticed a couple of latecomers walking across the promenade to join the party. One was the bulky figure of Cyrus Lander, the wide shoulder-pads of his checked jacket lending him a swagger as he rubbed his hands together, relishing the business in hand. But it was the other who drew the attention of the crowd. A sound went up, familiar to my ears at least, a 'Shhh – Shhh' sibilance as people repeated her name: 'It's Shelley Chantelle – Shelley Chantelle – from the pier show. Wonder what she's doing here?'

I watched with astonishment as my daughter, who yesterday had seemed a mere shadow of her former self, strode out with confidence across the promenade dressed in a striking emerald-green leotard and leggings with matching canvas boots and jacket. She came over to greet Alys and me, kissing Alys on both cheeks and beaming: 'How's my favourite godmother? I've come to help the good cause.' Alys would normally have been pleased to see her, but now she could only muster a weak smile and a thank you. She looked a worn-out dishevelled figure under the embracing arm of the vibrant Shelley. I could hardly believe the change. I hoped it would last.

I hurriedly drew Shelley aside to tell her of Alys's shock that morning, attributing the fire to vandals.

'My goodness, I'm glad I came,' said Shelley. 'I felt so much better when I got up this morning, like a great weight had shifted, Mama.'

'Good, well I'm glad you came too,' I said. 'Alys is going to need all the help she can get with this lot lined up against her.'

The council crowd was now beginning to move in a slow surge down the beach steps. Cyrus Lander had already forged through to align himself firmly by the side of Frilly Milly, who had welcomed him like an old friend.

103

'Come on,' said Shelley. 'I know what we should do – take the initiative from them. We can't have Alys being a sideshow to their efforts.'

She trotted over to the photographers, who had gathered in a hunch-shouldered knot near the sea rail. They needed no prompting to focus their attention on Shelley; their perking up at her approach was almost palpable. She had a few words with them, they nodded and grinned at each other, and then she came running back to us.

'Right Alys,' she said. 'We've got to try and overtake the council mob, get down there before them. Look I'll take these.' She picked up the placards. 'Can you two manage the rest?'

'Look, Alys—' I said worriedly, 'I – I'd better not. I'm not supposed to be here to help. I'm supposed to be reporting. They've accused me of bias enough as it is. I'm sorry.'

'Go on – it's all right – you go,' said Alys, still with her weak smile. 'Do your job, it's what you're paid for, and I'll do mine.'

'Come on, Queen Canute,' said Shelley, 'we can manage on our own. We'd better get a move on though.'

They moved off with their equipment, the photographers following in their wake.

I joined the back of the council party, watching as Shelley and Alys, hampered though they were, quickly overtook the slow march led by Frilly Milly and her faithful vice-chairman, the gullible Councillor Repton Armitage. I saw among the entourage the council's sleek-suited chief executive, Giles Hurt.

Giles seemed to catch my eye, and he made a point of side-slipping from the main stream to join me as I struggled to keep up on the soft sand in my high heels.

'Need help, Anna?' he asked solicitously. 'You know you only have to ask: my manly arm is available.'

'Thanks, but I can manage quite well,' I replied, trying to overcome my momentary embarrassment. Giles smiled and shrugged, but maintained his position beside me. He was in his mid thirties – young for a chief executive – a high achiever brought in for his flair in getting big business and local authorities working together on projects of mutual benefit. It was an approach which found great favour with the ruling party at the moment, although one such project had proved a financial catastrophe lately, and Giles was very much on trial.

He was a perfectionist, a tall, dark-haired man who paid meticulous attention to his appearance, alternating his extensive range of suits each day, matching the colour of his socks to his tie and pocket handkerchief, and wearing a daily renewed, colour co-ordinated carnation in his buttonhole.

That day the suit was navy, the carnation yellow with a red-edged tinge, echoing his red and yellow spotted tie and canary socks. He smelt powerfully of a citrus-noted after-shave as I lumbered along downwind of him feeling untidy in comparison. His features were refined, his tastes artistically highbrow; an avid follower of opera and ballet, he was also given to poetic quotations which were a sure method of stunning raw-educated, recalcitrant councillors into dumb submission.

'You've brought some mischief on our heads lately, Anna, I must say.'

'Have I really?' I enquired, in mock-innocence, hating the headmasterly admonishment in his tone. I could not say I disliked Giles, but I did mistrust him, and when he spoke to me as if I were a naughty schoolgirl, I wanted to screw his dapper carnation up his aquiline nose.

'She's a friend of yours isn't she?' he motioned towards Alys, who with Shelley's assistance had now found an appropriate spot for her notice and was hammering with vigour, as though venting her anger on the inanimate stake.

'Yes – why?' I asked guardedly.

'You didn't put her up to all this by any chance, did you?

Come on, you can tell me, Anna, surely,' he said in a low voice.

I was too affronted to give his question the dignity of a reply, but he must have taken my silence for culpability. He went on: 'Perhaps you dreamt it up together – no? – one dark winter's evening with nothing better to do – let's test the water, give Northport a poke in the eye?'

I snapped with indignation: 'No, Giles, no, I most certainly did not. Alys is an old schoolfriend. I admit it, but I have nothing to do with Groundswell, and this is their campaign.'

He was silent for several seconds, before saying, with nonchalance, 'Don't you agree with what she's doing then?'

'It doesn't matter whether I agree or disagree, does it? I'm here to do a job – a non-partisan reporting job.'

'I do,' he said suddenly, facing away from me so that I could not be sure I had heard aright.

'What?'

'I said I do.'

'You do what?'

'Agree with her,' he replied, holding his hand up to shield his words from the councillors and utter a feigned cough. I stopped in astonishment and looked at him. He saw that the official party were out of earshot before turning to me. 'She's right – you know she must be right. You've seen the sewage pumping station, you've seen the outfall pipe. It pains me that such primitive methods exist – here, and in my remit – but what we're doing is barely better than the Middle Ages, swilling out the chamber-pots not in the street but in the sea, and then swimming in it!'

'But Giles,' I could not hide my surprise, not just at his support for Alys but also at his uncharacteristic indiscretion. 'Your own officers say it's safe for swimmers. They've repeatedly maintained that any harmful organisms quickly die in the sea. That's what the water company's whole policy towards sea disposal is based on. It's supposed to be a giant, natural disinfectant tank.'

'Supposed to be . . . supposed to be . . . one so-called expert tells us one thing, another says the opposite. And what are we poor non-scientists to believe when even the experts don't agree?'

I shook my head to egg him on.

'We follow our artistic noses in my view,' he pursed his mouth fastidiously, sniffing the wind, 'and mine tells me there's something rotten in the state of Northport – or rotten in its sea – for I certainly would not want to paddle in the dilute contents of piss-pots, however "disinfected" they may be.'

'Nor I,' I had to admit. 'But what do you think we should do?'

'Common decency would prescribe a proper treatment plant, where the stuff can be filtered and purified to the highest possible standard.'

'Aren't you in a strong position to argue for that? The authorities listen to you where they might dismiss Alys and her organisation.'

'Oh, they might listen, certainly they'd listen,' he said with a world-weary expression, 'but I'm afraid something else has a louder voice than me, Anna, and always will have.' He rubbed the thumb of his right hand against his fingers in explanation.

'Money?'

'Money. It would cost "too much" in their view – in other words, more than they want to spend. And for lack of filthy lucre we may never again see "the moving waters at their priestlike task of pure ablution round earth's human shores".' He paused, for dramatic effect.

I saw Councillor Millichop look round to see where her chief executive was, but he seemed too engrossed in his theme to notice.

'It's paradoxical, isn't it? Just a few miles up the coast the atomic people are trying to find a safe disposal site for nuclear waste. What do the good councillors say? "No thank you – not in our back yard – no way." Yet some of them are quite prepared to accept that their back yard – the sea – is used as a dump for human waste that laps right on to the doorstep.'

He was right. A campaign was still being waged further up the coast against an underground nuclear waste dump – despite the nuclear industry's arguments that it would be as secure as Fort Knox and a danger to no one.

By now Giles had realised that he was in danger of being peremptorily admonished by Councillor Millichop as she pierced him with X-ray eyes to indicate he should be by her side.

He left me, trailing an apology: 'And, needless to say, Anna, this *was* all off the record, wasn't it?' He had gone before I could reply, joining Mrs Millichop with an ingratiating smile.

As the rest of the media party was congregated round Alys and Shelley, the councillors had little choice but to wait for them to finish their work.

Finally Alys stood with her hand on the placard, a serious expression on her face, while Shelley retreated into the background. She began to declaim from a prepared statement: 'The Groundswell organisation is erecting this warning notice after careful monitoring over the past ten days. The results of our survey will be published in a report in due course. In the mean time we want to make it clear to the public that swimming in this water presents a possible risk of infection, and children may be particularly vulnerable.'

Her voice was tired, her tone flat, and the assembled crowd was beginning to shuffle and mumble. A bark of '*Rubbish!*' went up in the inimitable Cyrus Lander style.

Alys ignored him, pressing on: 'We would like to point out that according to our analysis, pollution levels of certain samples were more than three times the limit permitted for bathing beaches by the EC. None of the resort's beaches met EC standards, and we would therefore urge its citizens to join us in campaigning for a treatment system which would prevent raw sewage being pumped out to sea and improve water quality as soon as possible. Your health and that of your visitors is at stake . . .' Her speech stumbled and petered out as she realised everyone's attention was being drawn elsewhere. The photographers were pushing round her, cameras beginning to click and squeal. She looked round to see what was happening, and turned back to me, biting her lip with a look of consternation.

Shelley had stripped off to a strapless white swimsuit and was standing poised with one foot over the water's edge, ostentatiously holding her nose. The noise of the cameras pierced the air with frantic rapidity, masking a couple of long, under-breath whistles from the photographers themselves. I saw Greg disengage himself, and with a glance at me, run back to where Alys was standing in bemusement.

''Scuse me, love,' he said. 'You don't mind if I take this a minute.' And he uprooted her placard and took it over to Shelley, who accepted it readily as her prop, standing with it at the sea's edge like Aphrodite rising from the waves, her gold hair tumbling over her bare shoulders.

I saw Cyrus Lander give one of his council cronies a dig in the ribs, saying in what passed for him as an undertone, 'You know what happens to white cozzies when they're wet?' The councillor chortled gleefully, nodding. Cyrus Lander took this as encouragement. 'Go on in, love – the water's lovely!' he shouted.

Shelley looked at him disdainfully. 'Much as you'd love the pleasure of seeing my costume transparent, Mr Lander, I'm afraid I draw the line at dirty pictures. However, I'm sure you don't – why don't you go in and show us the colour of your Y-fronts – they'll be anything but see-through in this filthy sea I can assure you. Perhaps in your case that'd be no bad thing!'

Cyrus, his hide horny as a rhino's, simply laughed as loud as the rest of them: 'She's got spirit – eh? Cheeky madam.' I saw his wide shoulder-pads levering their way to the front as he made for the shallows in front of Shelley. Regardless of the waves soaking his golfing loafers, he scooped a handful of foam and tossed it at her, hitting her square in the stomach. She squealed in shock and indignation and kicked a wave back at him, splashing his face as he bent once more towards the water. Droplets hung off his yellowing whiskers and he bared his teeth in challenging laughter. 'Come on!' he shouted. 'The water's great! Admit it – you love it, you love it!' The photographers were in turmoil, wanting to catch the action while anxious to shield their precious lenses from salt water.

'Give us a smile, Shelley, love – jump in the air when he splashes it to you – that is really great, wonderful!'

But abruptly Shelley seemed to collect herself.

'No, no,' she said. 'This is ridiculous. Alys – Alys.' She waved her over and positioned her on the other side of the placard while they linked arms together. Alys put on a brave face, posing for the cameras, but I knew which pictures would make the bigger splash in the papers that evening, and so did the grinning, dripping Cyrus.

As soon as the photographers had taken their fill, Alys extracted herself from Shelley's arm and ran back to her belongings. The councillors were distracted by a haranguing match which had now developed between Shelley and Cyrus, with their respective supporters among the council party determined to have their say.

I rushed to rejoin Alys.

'I can't – I'm not going to take any more,' she said as she stuffed documents and mallets back in her bags.

'Alys, I'm sorry – about Shelley, I mean. I'd no idea she was going to pull a stunt like that.'

'Oh, that's all right,' said Alys. 'I'm sure she never expected the water-fight. She didn't start it. To tell the truth I was grateful to be stage-managed today. It's just—'

'Just what, Alys?'

'I've had enough. One thing after another – the harassment, and then the fire this morning. And now this three-ring circus. I can't stand any more. I'm going – now.'

'Alys, is there anything I can do to – can I help? I want to help.'

'You do? Really help? Are you sure it won't compromise your position?'

'I want to help you,' I said emphatically.

'OK.' She looked around, but everyone's attention was still focused on the argument in the water. 'Here, quickly,' she said, unzipping her holdall. She withdrew a roll of documents, tightly bound with string and secured with sealing wax. 'Put them in your bag,' she said urgently. Obediently I opened my roomy shoulder-bag, which doubled as a briefcase, and she shoved the papers in. 'It's the latest results from the seismic survey. The ones Lynne and Martina collected last night from the *No Man's Land*. The one way you can really help me at this moment is to deliver them to Harry Jansen so I can get away.'

'To Harry? Where is he?'

'He's convalescing in the Muirfield Nursing Home – it's in Stainsby Avenue. Look, I could go, I could do it—'

'Nonsense,' I said. 'It's too risky for you now to go and see him. It's obvious someone's really on your tail. Look, it'll be easy for me, honestly. No problem.'

She leaned forward and kissed me on the cheek. 'Thanks, Ans.'

'Where are you going now?'

'I'm going to collect Martina and Lynne from the hospital. They're being discharged shortly. Then I'll make sure they get home safely. I feel responsible – they're not even part of the organisation, they were doing this out of the goodness of their hearts. Then I'm going to get down to work, find out what's at the bottom of all this if it kills me.'

The unspoken thought that it might hung between us.

'I'll be in touch just as soon as I can, Ans,' she said.

'Take care, Alys. Don't worry about the papers.' I

watched her retreating figure until she disappeared from sight behind the promenade.

Turning back to the council party, I noticed Giles Hurt standing at the back of them, watching me rather than his masters, and I wondered how long he'd been there. He darted away as he was brought to heel by Councillor Millichop, clapping her hands to bring her unruly audience to order. She beckoned to her loyal subordinate, Repton Armitage. They both took off their shoes and stockings and waded out into the water, Milly delicately holding her skirts above the wavelets while Repton's furled trouser-legs exposed his knees.

Shelley had put her clothes back on over her wet costume, and she came over to join me, shivering.

'Has Alys gone already?'

'Yes, she was in a hurry. She wanted to get back and see how her friends were. But she was grateful for your help, love.'

'What an oaf that man Lander is. Still it made for some good publicity shots for Alys, didn't it?' Her teeth were chattering.

'Look, Shelley, there's no need for you to stay for this – you're freezing – you'll catch your death.'

'Of cold, or waterborne diseases?' she grinned. 'Hey, I'm getting into this ecology business, aren't I? Well, you're right though, I'll go home and dry off. Actually I feel quite invigorated. Salt water's supposed to be good for the skin.'

She jogged away, back up the beach and I couldn't help but wonder how much of this had been for Alys's publicity and how much for her own. I turned back to the goings-on among the council party.

'Now,' called Mr Chairman Milly in as commanding a voice as she could muster, 'I want you all to look at this beach, this stretch of sea, very carefully, and tell me if you see any sign of this so-called contamination.'

The pack looked. The beach presented itself in all its flat, bland seeming-innocence, unbesmirched even by bits of litter. The sea, commonly a drab brown-grey, was blessed by a cessation of cloud, reflecting back the sky's blue for Milly in a mood of Mediterranean azure. There was silence from the crowd, and a look of serene satisfaction overcame Milly.

'Now, Councillor Repton Armitage and I intend to demonstrate our faith in the cleanliness of our sea. I am sorry that the Groundswell representative has seen fit to leave before our demonstration despite the fact that we have listened to her argument. Nevertheless I am sure the people will listen to us – and that is what counts, ladies and gentlemen.'

Repton Armitage, meanwhile, had begun to look very uncomfortable as he stood in the water at Milly's side. A man who had risen to local prominence on the strength of a chain of fish and chip shops ('Fresh Fish our Forte'), he went red to the roots of his thinning white hair. Milly gestured towards him and he followed her into the deeper water, until the predatory waves were snapping at the hem of her multi-hued froth of a dress.

She motioned to a bag she had left on the beach, and Giles Hurt snapped to attention, smartly, handing it to Mrs Millichop. Holding it up like a magician's hat she drew forth two sparkling cut-crystal whisky tumblers, and as Giles removed the bag she raised them into the air, displaying them to the audience.

That done, Milly delicately lifted her hem, and bent down to scoop up first one glass of foaming brine, and then another, which she presented to Repton Armitage.

Then, both turning to beam at the cameras, they shouted 'Cheers!' in rehearsed unison, and gazing hard into each other's eyes, they put the glasses to their lips and gulped the lot. I could hardly believe what I was seeing. The cameras were clicking madly and young Nicholas the radio reporter went splashing out in excitement to record the gulps on tape.

Gasping for breath, the duo finished their libation, and

Councillor Millichop, her voice distinctly hoarse, suddenly fastened her gaze directly on me.

'Now Mrs Knight,' she eyed me penetratingly, 'do you suppose we would have done that had we not known for certain that it is perfectly harmless?'

This was greeted with a loud cheer from her supporters and a smattering of applause, which effectively relieved me of the need to reply. The performance finished to her satisfaction, Milly held her vice-chairman's hand as they paddled back to shore, urging him to use her talc to dry between his toes.

I was again joined by Giles Hurt as everyone returned up the beach. I felt he had detected my discomfiture. 'See what you've done to these good people, Anna. Drinking that vile stuff – for your benefit.'

Amusement was scarcely masked in his voice, and I looked at him cynically: 'To echo a question you put to me earlier, Giles, are you sure you didn't put her up to it?'

'What me? Perish the thought!'

His eyes glinted and he made a graceful wave-like gesture with his hand through the air. I sensed a quotation was coming on: '"The very deep did rot: O Christ! That ever this should be! Yea, slimy things did crawl with legs Upon the slimy sea."' He bent towards me. 'Mrs Millichop's a simple woman. Perhaps unlike you and me she's never heard of such things.'

I knew the quotation. It was from 'The Rime of the Ancient Mariner'. And suddenly I looked at Giles with an edge of suspicion. Had he anything to do with Sammy? Was Giles the source of the boy's flights of artistic fancy? I tried to look back over my dealings with Giles. He had always seemed condescending about the resort, as though its people were beneath him, as though it were the means to an end for him. But could he have a sinister other life? One with Sammy and his like? It seemed scarcely credible.

My thoughts were interrupted by a call, 'Mrs Knight!

Mrs Knight!' It was a puffing Milly, body bouncing as she sought me out. 'I do hope we have proved our point to you.'

She stopped to regain her breath before, rosy-faced and radiating smiles, she pressed my hand: 'You see, this is nothing new. It's what they used to do in the last century. Sea water was said to be most conducive to health. Not only did they bathe in it, they drank it, like we've just done, by the pint – followed by dark stout and oysters!' she laughed. 'It's true dear, I do assure you – Mr Giles Hurt showed me in the historical records. They found it most salubrious, and there is no reason why we should not do the same.'

Giles suddenly found he had something most urgent to tell one of his officers, and fled my reach. Sea water had dried on Milly's top lip, which glistened with a salty moustache. I wondered whether, as woman to woman, I should discreetly draw it to her attention. But Milly wafted away too quickly, anxious to have a personal word with another reporter. A now distinctly green-tinged Repton Armitage manfully followed in her trail.

Greg lumbered over with his camera-load. 'Come on, Anna, we've got a deadline to make. With a bit of luck I can flog these pics round for the nationals later on.'

'Want some words to go with them?' I asked, knowing his unsure touch with any caption more complicated than identifying a flower show.

'You're a mate, Anon. Split the readies?'

'It's a deal.'

I had to smarten my pace to keep up with him as he strode away. 'Greg, Greg, hang on just a minute. I want to ask you something.'

He turned round impatiently.

'Do you know if Giles Hurt is one of Sammy's so-called friends?'

He darted a glance over to the chief executive as if assessing him in a new light. 'Lord knows, Anon,' he said, shaking his head. ' Sammy doesn't tell me everything, you know. I gotta go, I've a film to process.' And he sprinted away towards his car.

That night's paper carried huge pictures of splashed Shelley opposite a spread of the grinning sea-drinkers under the bold headline:

'YOUR VERY GOOD HEALTH, SIR! –
IN NORTHPORT BRINY.'

Towards the bottom of the page they used a small picture of Alys and Shelley under the hazard placard, cropped to a minimum. In my copy I had tried to bring out the drama of Alys's determination to go on with the exercise, despite the shock of her friends' near-immolation. But the copy-taster liked the water-fight and Milly's stunt better, and the worrying results of the Groundswell survey were dwarfed into obscurity.

FOURTEEN

By mid-afternoon that day I was flagging. After an interview with a mud-wrestler for the women's supplement I felt too whacked to go back to the office immediately, and realised I hadn't had any lunch. I called into one of my favourite cafés in the town centre – a chic little place, aromatic with coffee beans and fresh pastries. But when I sat down, I realised I had little appetite. I ordered coffee instead, and succumbed to the allure of nicotine, pulling out my cigarettes.

They were at the bottom of my bag, underneath the roll of computer print-out that Alys had given me for Harry.

As I smoked, I turned it over and over in my hands. What could be in there that was worth all this trouble? Was it for this he had been thrust out of the window? A few measly bits of paper? Was there a connection between the attack on Harry, and Dr Jefferson's death – apart from Sammy?

The answerless questions hammered in my head. I hadn't yet made arrangements to see Harry. I decided to do it as soon as I got back to the office. Then when I saw him perhaps I'd get the chance to ask him a few questions myself – like what the hell did he think he was playing at, putting Alys in danger? If he was well enough to receive documents, he was well enough to hear that.

I let the roll of papers drop to the table, and against my best intentions, lit another cigarette. But as I blew out the match, something made me gasp.

A shadow had been cast over my hands as I held the document, a shadow too dark and close for comfort. I looked up, and there was no one there. I was in a window-seat, so I looked out into the precinct. By then the shadow had gone. I was certain someone had been staring hard at my package – and indeed at me – but for how long before a shifting cloud had exposed the sun and cast that shadow?

I hastily put the papers back in my shoulder-bag and made my way outside, crossing the street and plunging into the innards of the shopping mall.

The usual cluster of buskers were begging for coinage in the entrance, a clown vying for the most lucrative spot with a singing monk. The cacophony grated in my ears, but it was not the noise that made me shudder. It was something in the clown's eyes – a look at me, a glance at someone behind, and then back at me, as though there was someone the clown had seen watching me. A chill bristled up my back. I walked, quick, brisk, weaving through the crowd. Twice I stopped dead and swivelled to see if I could catch someone in the act, but the continuous jostle of shoppers camouflaged any follower. Nerves brittle, eyes darting, I suddenly felt utterly self-conscious.

Then I saw one man, static like a boulder in the swirl. I felt his eyes pierce into me. He was tall and thick-set, wearing jeans which looked too tight. He stood feet planted apart, hands thrust deep into the pockets of his red bomber jacket. He looked about thirty, clean-shaven, with gingery hair short-razored above his ears, erasing to baldness on the crown. And he was staring straight at me, so hard that I stiffened rigid.

I looked away, and looked back, and he was still there, about twenty yards away, watching me watching him. I turned to walk away, not knowing where I was going, just wanting to get away from him. I tried to measure my pace, control my flight, not wanting to indicate my alarm. But I stole a glance over my shoulder, and I could see the bald head coming closer. My steps quickened, I spilled out into the glare of daylight on the other side of the precinct, forcing my way past dawdling chip-eaters who congregated, greasy bags in hand, outside one of Repton Armitage's fish-and-chip emporiums. Turning round to check again on my pursuer, I stumbled into one of the street-grazers – a woman who roundly cursed me as her chips fell to the ground. I could not stop. I could not apologise, for I had seen the bald head gaining on me. I realised I was hopelessly outpaced, with my heels and close-fitting skirt. I turned a corner, and looked desperately for somewhere to hide until he'd gone by.

A dark doorway beckoned. It was the rear entrance to the Tower. The founding fathers of Northport had tried to emulate Blackpool's success in many particulars. One of them was this Tower, a blatant copy, but one about which the rival resort was powerless to complain, since it had stolen the idea from Eiffel in the first place. With no time to think further, I headed straight for that dark entrance, flinging money from my purse at the cashier and snatching the ticket from her hand.

I pushed through a door and almost fell into the interior darkness. As my eyes became accustomed to the gloom I leaned against a wall to quiet my fluttering heart. The place I was in felt warm, wet and enveloping. It was an aquarium, tricked out to resemble an undersea grotto, and the vacant stares of fish eyes surrounded me from the tanks. I waited, safe in a corner of the darkness, fervently hoping I had lost him. He must be after the information I had for Harry, there could be no other reason for such sudden stalking. But how on earth did he know Alys had given it to me? Minutes went by, people passed in and out of the door, but I saw no sign of the bald head and red bomber jacket. Gradually I began to feel safer, and edged away from my corner. I paused by one of the tanks in the centre, which had viewing windows on each side. Its inhabitants were gigantic black fish from South America, huge, dense and meaty-looking, with gentle, cow-like faces. I stared at one head-on, while it stared back at me, its jaw dropping and shutting. In my state of heightened nerves I almost felt it was trying to warn me. Slowly it heaved its black bulk of a body round in the water and swished away, tail receding through the green-lit murk. My gaze followed it across the tank to the other side, to the opposite window. Another face was looking back at me, a human face, with human eyes. The red bomber jacket was below it, the bullet head above. He was here, he had found me.

I staggered back, stumbling into a mother with a push-chair. Its toddler cargo set up a wail like a siren. I saw an exit and fled, straight into the foyer at the front of the Tower building. I had two choices: to go out again, on to the seafront, or up, towards the Tower itself. I took a gamble. Guessing he would assume I'd gone outside, I raced up the staircase. But at the top, I glanced down, over the banister, and there I saw him. He was at the base of the stairs, staring upwards, head to one side as he craned to get a better view. I could see what I thought was a massive bruise on the side of his neck. But as my eyes focused, I realised it was a tattoo, a bluebird, imprinted on the most vulnerable part of his neck, between his ear-lobe and Adam's apple. As he saw me he broke into a malicious grin, and I saw the bluebird's tail lift as if in flight. I turned and ran, not knowing where I was going, shoving people from my path. Swing doors beckoned me through, and I found myself in a vast, ornate hall, a great cavern of golden and scarlet opulence. It was the ballroom. Couples were mincing across a floor smooth as satin.

A male voice grated close to my ear: 'Fancy a dance, do you?' I started, and turned, to see the bluebird tattoo so close I could touch it, so close I could see the spit bubbling on his grinning teeth and smell his breath. I sprang away, but was yanked back again by a sharp pull on the strap of my bag. Turning round, I saw with embarrassment that it had caught on the back of a chair – and he was leaning on it and laughing at me.

'Listen,' I said sharply – the dancing couples looked round – 'I don't know who you are, or what you want, but please stop following me.'

I saw the laughter extinguished in his eyes – lashless, milky blue eyes that fixed me coldly, as if with strengthened resolution. I pulled my bag away from the chair and stalked off dismissively towards the door. I hated this man with all my being. 'How dare he?' kept ringing through my head, 'How dare he do this to me?'

I looked back, but could not see him. I realised I was walking erratically, confused by all the neurotic yammering from banks of gobbling slot machines on either side.

'You lost or summin'?' a boy's voice said, seemingly addressed to me.

'Yes, yes I am actually,' I looked at him, almost gratefully.

'You looking for the lift up the Tower? That's where we're goin'. It's just through 'ere. Follow us.'

It seemed to offer my only chance of respite. There was no other way out. Perhaps, by going up the Tower, I could evade Mr Bluebird long enough to lose him.

The lift arrived, and a clanking metal gate concertinaed

open. I was propelled forward with a crowd of others into the cramped confines.

Too late I realised just how oppressive it was. Claustrophobia rose within me as I stood, compressed against the wall, bodies crammed all around. Some of the children panicked, scrabbling at the windows, trying to get a grip on the walls with their fingers and feet. One of them missed his footing and his shoe scraped painfully down from my shin to ankle.

I cried out, eyes blinking in an involuntary start of tears, and I saw through the blur the lift-man beckoning for one more passenger before the doors clamped shut.

My vision cleared, and I found myself transfixed, biting my lip to prevent the terror screaming out. Mr Bluebird was there, in the lift with me, his blank, lashless eyes giving no indication he had seen me, staring straight ahead of him. But his lips parted to expose his teeth in a mirthless grin.

The cabin jolted, and the lift started its shaky ascent. It juddered upwards, and all I could see were the giant, brutal iron struts, criss-crossing and flashing in front of me.

I shut my eyes, feeling the blood throb in my temples. The car abruptly jarred and I realised we had clung to a halt at the Tower top, 500 feet in the sky. The lift-man drew back the gate to let out his load, and I spilled out with the rest of the crowd on to the viewing platform.

Daring to look neither behind nor down, I pressed as close as I could to the wall. Through the windows I could see the sea, fading into the horizon, looking like a viscous, brown-grey sludge. Remote on the skyline, far away, were the ghostly hulks of gas rigs pumping riches from the depths. Across my vision came the red bomber jacket. He stood, rooted, simply looking at me. I could see the razor burn on his cheek, the fleshiness of his ear. I never felt so repulsed by a man. And yet . . . what had he done? Nothing. Merely followed me, intimidated me when he saw my flaring reaction. I should have ignored the creep in the first place: I was being neurotic, ridiculous.

I retraced my steps, studiously ignoring him, hoping that the lift would be ready to go back down – but the doors were firmly shut. A narrow staircase led upwards, and I followed it, leaving the crowds to find myself expelled into the full blast of the high, open air. I listened for a following tread on the stair, but the wind was gusting round the railings in a rushing stream of sound.

I heard noises on the stairway. I didn't stay to see if it was him. Another staircase led upwards and I took it, hitching my skirt up and tripping out on to a much smaller tier, no bigger than a good-sized bedroom, bare of adornment save scabby paint scratched with graffiti. As long as I kept moving, I thought, I could evade him until I could rejoin the lift and go down. Breathless by now, I burst out on to the top level, and a spit of rain hit me in the face.

I stopped, holding my breath, listening, hearing only the pumping of my heart. I was quite alone up here, right at the pinnacle. The staircase downwards was on the other side. I started towards it, but suddenly my ears were filled with a frightening roar. I stopped, looking round in panic. The throbbing, predatory sound was rising louder and louder, deafening towards its crescendo, and a shadow fell. It was a helicopter, only a helicopter, but it swooped so near I could almost distinguish the face of the pilot. Hands pressed to my ears I turned round to avoid its down-draught – and cried out.

For now I was looking straight into the face of my shadow, the slowly grinning face lifting the tail of the bluebird tattoo. I ran for the staircase, but he anticipated me, leaping round to stand in my way. A decrepit iron stair spiralled up out of the centre, an access to the highest point, used only by workmen. It was barred half-way by a padlocked iron gate. Nevertheless I ran at it, pulling at the padlock, hoping the rusty chain would give way so that I could slam the gate on him and call for help. But it held fast. I shouted, but my cry was whipped away in the wind, and I heard his throaty laughter.

'You can't get away from me any more,' came the low, slow voice. 'You know what I want, and you're going to give it to me.'

In my mind's eye the horror of the bleeding Harry Jansen flashed before me, bones shattered, his life saved only by a bit of canvas. I had no hope left, should this seeming automaton throw me from here. I sank down in utter defeat half-way up the spiral staircase. What else could I do? I cupped my hands together . . . stopped panicking . . . and lit a cigarette. I looked down at my hunter. The shiny head was bowed. He seemed to be searching in his pockets, fumbling in front of him. So this was it. A weapon of some sort? Would he pull a knife on me? With a new surge of energy I stood up to defend myself with all my strength. I could throw him off, kick him down, run to get help. He looked at me again, with a slyness in his face, and then looked down.

I saw what he was holding – not a weapon, not a knife, but something even more repulsive – his own male member, and he was rubbing it up and down as its bulbous head rose towards me. The shock of it made me laugh out loud: that here, at the top of this tower, I should be confronted with a sordid flasher, rubbing his phallus for all he was worth.

Was it just for this I had suffered the humiliating chase up here? He wasn't interested in Harry Jansen's research papers at all – he was just a pathetic, frustrated oaf. I laughed in sheer relief – for this was easy to deal with, easy to report – and the louder I laughed, the faster he rubbed, until in anger he lunged towards me, blocking the foot of the staircase with his bulk.

'Come on, come on,' he was urging through his teeth. 'You want it, you want it. You've been giving me the come-on ever since I saw you. I know your sort.'

'Yes, and I know yours,' I said. 'I know yours, thank

123

God.' I continued to laugh, knowing that mockery was the best deflator, but he grinned back at me.

'You're enjoying this, aren't you?' he snarled. 'Come on, say you're enjoying it. Look at it. You want it. Come on down.'

In a wave of revulsion I kicked out at him. He ducked and my foot missed, overbalancing me. I fell from the stairs on to my knees and he grabbed the strap of my bag to haul me up. I pulled back, gripping it by the flap. He gave a violent yank and the fastening broke, spilling the contents of the bag all over the floor.

'Curse you!' I shouted. 'You're an imbecile!'

I scrabbled on my hands and knees to retrieve my possessions, struggling to shove everything back in. There seemed so much – old bills, wage slips, notebook, credit cards, make-up bag, purse, cheques. I was so furious I failed to see what he was doing behind me – until I heard an inane giggle. I looked round to see him pumping away at his member with one hand – while in the other he brandished Harry's roll of data, aiming to strike it at my hitched skirt and exposed knickers. I flung out at it but he whipped it back out of my reach. In an access of rage I picked up my lighted cigarette, which had rolled to the floor, and with one swift thrust I pierced the burning ember straight into the bobbing bluebird on his neck.

The pumping hand stopped its motion as he keeled over in pain. Clasping his neck, he fell to the ground, Harry's papers underneath him. The way was free for me to escape. I hesitated only one second before leaping down the stairs, leaving him rolling in agony.

'You *bitch*!' I heard as I stumbled down the stairways. 'You *sow*! You *cow*!' And his howls followed me all the way down.

Mercifully the lift doors were open, and I saw a rabble of boys already inside. It was a relief to join them, and I felt almost comforted by the closeness of their bodies as the doors closed, excluding my tormentor.

Their noise washed over me as the full enormity of what had happened gradually weighed on my consciousness. I'd lost more than my dignity on the Tower top, I'd lost the papers. And I still didn't know whether he'd been after them all along, or only my body.

The doors opened. I was free. I fairly ran away from the building, pathetically grateful for the solid ground and honest faces. I retrieved my car and drove straight home, ripping my clothes off as soon as I got through the door, and plunging under the shower, not caring that the water was practically cold, only wanting to wash away the grubbiness of the experience. Later, still wrapped in towels, I rang the Tower to ask if anyone had found the papers and handed them in. They gave the answer I feared and half expected: no. They even asked me to ring back in half an hour when they'd sent someone to check where I'd lost them. The answer was still negative. I had to face it: they'd been stolen. Mr Bluebird had won.

FIFTEEN

'Hello, this is Groundswell. How can I help you?' said a woman's voice.

'I'd like to speak to Alys Finestone, please.'

'Alys? I'm afraid she's not here at present. Can anyone else help?'

'It's a personal matter,' I said. 'I'm a friend of hers. Could you possibly tell me where I might find her – it's important.'

'Oh, a personal call, I see,' said the woman, pausing a

little. 'Tell you what, I'll put you through to Reg Johnson in her section. He'll probably be able to help you.'

Reg was one of Alys's oldest colleagues – a hearty, well-meaning chap, I'd met him at a couple of parties with Alys. But he seemed as perplexed as I was: 'The truth is, I'm afraid, I don't know exactly where she is.'

'Didn't she come back to the office after finishing the survey in Northport?'

'She was supposed to. I'm a bit miffed actually – I wanted to get to work on those results. Anyway she rang in to say she'd taken the two research assistants back home but she'd had a change of plan. She wouldn't be coming in to the office – there was something she had to investigate urgently, something to do with the WARN survey in the Irish Sea, and it couldn't wait. Well, I mean, I know the WARN stuff's important, but so's my sea-discharge analysis – she could at least've put the results in the post. Actually, that's really not like her, she's usually pretty conscientious about things like that.'

'What about Lynne and Martina – did she tell them about her change of plan?'

'Nope, I've been in touch with them. It was the first they'd heard of it. They thought she was coming back here, and the women on the WARN ship are equally in the dark. I really don't know what she's playing at. She has been distracted by the WARN work lately I must say, and the sewage trail was supposed to be a break for her, a bit of a breather. Doesn't seem to have worked though, does it?'

'No, you're right. Look, if she does contact you, can you ask her to ring me, urgently?'

'Yup. You'd better give me your number.'

But there was no call from Alys that night or the following day. I called Reg Johnson again.

'I'm sorry, Anna, still no joy. Is it anything I can deal with perhaps?'

'No, no it's OK, thanks.' I didn't know whether Alys had told anyone else about the secret survey work for Harry, and I was loath to blunder about, raising alarms that might rebound on her.

I rang Jay, Alys's friend in Lancaster. He was a gentle man, not likely to panic unnecessarily, but I could sense that he was concerned.

'No, I don't know where she is, Anna, I'm afraid. I'm glad you've rung actually. I've been worrying about her lately. She's become sort of . . . secretive, distracted. It's not like her.' He gave an embarrassed laugh. 'I – I'd begun to wonder whether she'd taken up with someone else – found a rich sugar daddy or something. I thought she might have been more open with you, Anna.'

'Oh, Jay . . . no, it's nothing like that at all. It's all to do with this project she's been involved with – the one in the Irish Sea – she's gone in too deep, I think. Way above her head. She's been upsetting people by what she's doing—'

'That's not unusual.'

'No – but this is different, Jay. It's undercover, underhand, and it strikes me as really sinister. I'm worried about her.'

'How long is it since you saw her?'

'Only a couple of days – but she said she'd get in touch, and she hasn't, not even with Groundswell. She's just disappeared. And I have to speak to her. Something's happened, some data of hers have been stolen from me, and I just don't know what to do.'

'Well – just a couple of days. It's nothing really, is it? Not for Alys. You know what she's like when she gets her teeth into something – she won't let go. She forgets the niceties of keeping in touch. Sometimes she's been out of circulation so long I've been on the point of registering her as a missing person, and then she'll just walk through the door. I wouldn't panic yet, Anna. But if she does contact me, I'll get her to ring you straight away.'

'Thanks, Jay.'

'Anna, will you do the same for me?'

'Of course.'

127

I rang the Muirfield Nursing Home, thinking that at least I could tell Harry Jansen about the theft if no one else. But the matron said he'd suffered 'a bit of a relapse', and he wasn't taking phone calls or receiving visitors except for immediate family.

I was utterly torn when it came to Tom. I wanted desperately to tell him the fix I was in, to ask him to help me – but the barrier of his job prevented me. I had officially reported the indecent exposure, but I stopped short of telling the police about the theft. I was hamstrung by the nature of the document – what if they questioned me more closely about what it was, and why anyone else would want it? Alys could have broken the law with that surveillance for all I knew, and I had given her my promise of secrecy about the whole affair. It was her property that had gone, it should be her decision what to do about it. But how could I tell her when I couldn't find her?

Tom felt my tension when he came to my flat late that night, having finished his shift. Instead of the spontaneous embrace he'd come to expect I could muster only a tense kiss and a strained smile. It was obvious I was in no mood to go to bed with him, and though he didn't say anything, I sensed he accepted it with ill grace. He resigned himself to stroking my head while we drank wine on the sofa. Gradually I began to relax.

'Tom?' I said, at length.

'Mmmm.'

'Do you keep any tabs on an organisation like Groundswell?'

'Like Groundswell, you mean?' he asked, emphasising the first word. 'Or actually Groundswell?'

'Actually Groundswell.'

'Hm,' he said, twisting a wisp of my hair. 'Why do you want to know that?'

'Well,' I tried to sound casual, 'they have been known to break the law, there have been rumours of sinister subversives in their midst.'

He laughed: 'You want to know if we bug them, you mean? You want to know if we've got a tail on them? Just so you can warn your little friend? I'm sorry Anna, I'm not exactly in Special Branch – and even if I knew, d'you think I could tell you? You can use my body all you like, but not my job, my sweet. There are limits.'

'Indeed there are.'

Having tried the indirect approach I realised there was nothing for it but to tell him, direct.

'It's my little friend, as you call her, that I'm worried about, Tom. Alys is missing. I have not heard anything from her for two and a half days. Neither has her boyfriend, or Groundswell. She seems to have disappeared.'

'I thought you were still upset after that idiot on the Tower. I might've known it was someone else you were worrying about, never yourself. You're too good, Anna.' He kissed the tip of my ear. 'I've never known anyone like you,' and his kisses were growing stronger. This was not what I wanted.

'But I am worried about her, Tom,' I said firmly.

'All right, all right,' he said with a note of irritation. 'If it's Alys that's keeping me out of your bed I'd better hear all about it.'

I told him the skeleton of the story – that she'd been upset by the van fire when I'd last seen her, just before she left, and that since then she'd phoned Groundswell only once, telling them of a change of plan.

'Look,' he said. 'It sounds to me like you've nothing to worry about. She's been out of touch before, hasn't she? You've told me so – so why the big worry now? If she's phoned in with a change of plan I don't see why you're so concerned. Listen Anna, you really should think of yourself more. That business with the flasher probably affected you more than you think.'

So, he thought I was over-reacting, being neurotic. I got up to get a cigarette.

'Hey, if you really are worried,' he said as I came back,

'call in and put her on the missing persons register. That'll make you feel better, won't it?'

I supposed it would. After all, it was all he really could do. He wasn't about to drop everything and help me try to find Alys, whom he'd never met. He was a policeman. What I needed was a friend. I thought of Greg.

I called at Greg's house the next day, after work. It had been his day off, and he came to the door in an old track suit, his bits of beard ruffled this way and that.

'Glad it's only you,' he said, waving me in. 'Wouldn't let just anyone see me in my scruffs, you know.'

He brought me a cup of strong tea, and we sat in his living room, where, among the photographs crowding the walls, Greg's monochrome images of Sammy's naked body stood out in striking simplicity.

I liked them, and said so, but I was surprised when my remark brought a hurt look to Greg's face.

'I'm losing him, Anon,' he said into his cup. 'When I asked you to introduce him to Shelley, I didn't think she'd take him as well as his pictures. He's always going to see her, I hardly get a look in. I know I don't score much in the celebrity stakes compared to Shelley, and he's probably a bit starry eyed. But I don't like to see him used like that, just showing off for the newspapers.'

It was true, Shelley had taken him up, and they'd been photographed in restaurants and nightclubs together, the picture captions making much of Shelley Chantelle's pretty boy companion. But though they both enjoyed this attention, and indeed deliberately courted it, Sammy's hypnosis was the key to the attachment. Once caught by the lure of what hypnosis could do for her, Shelley wanted more. Hypnotherapy relaxed her, she told me, and Sammy was helping her over the mental trauma of being blamed by the rapist. I counted it as one of her fads and judged that if it made her feel better, let it run its course. But I did feel that Sammy was exploiting her publicity value to feed his own vanity.

Greg got up and stared into Sammy's monochrome eyes in a picture on the wall. 'Look at that,' he said. 'The boy's got dignity, see the way he disdains the camera. And then he lets Shelley tote him about on her arm like the latest bloomin' designer accessory, like a lap-dog. D'you know what she calls him? Trinket – Trinket, I ask you. Just like a lap-dog.'

I couldn't help but feel sympathy for Greg.

'He'll be back to you before long, Greg. I know Shelley. She wants him for this hypnotherapy kick she's on at the moment. She'll tire of Sammy when the novelty wears off.'

'He's been with her all week, I just know he has. He told me he was going to see his father for a few days, but that's not true – his father rang here yesterday wanting to speak to him, saying he hadn't been in touch for months. I suppose Sammy wanted to spare my feelings – but when I see him flaunting himself all over the papers with Shelley, it screws me up, Anon.'

It struck me that in actual fact there hadn't been any pictures of them together for the last few days – and indeed Shelley had mentioned that she wasn't seeing Sammy this week, he'd gone away to see his father. I told Greg, and his face tightened.

'Oh God . . . don't say he's at it again. Why else would he lie about what he was doing? He must be back on the game – some rich bastard'll've taken him away, showered him with money. He's a sucker for all that, y'know? Swanky cars, flash suits . . . and I'm a sucker for thinking I could change him.'

'No, you're not Greg. You've done a hell of a lot for him, and I've seen him with those pictures, I know what they mean for him. You're jumping to conclusions.'

'Hm – I hope you're right,' he shrugged.

So did I, but I still mistrusted Sammy. Why had he lied to Greg and Shelley, what was he doing? It was fruitless to speculate on the boy's duplicity, and besides, I hadn't come to talk about Sammy.

'Greg, the reason I'm here—'

'There had to be a reason, Anon, I know I'm not wanted for the pleasure of my company.'

'Don't be ridiculous, you idiot. Alys is missing, I'm afraid something might have happened to her. I need help, to try and find her.'

I told him what had happened, mentioning the harassment she'd been suffering.

'So you've sent for Super-Greg. How can I help you, you poor distressed maiden?'

'You could run off a set of photographs of her for me. I was thinking of trying to retrace her journey, at the same time, same day of the week she was last seen. I could show people photos. They may remember seeing her.'

'No problem. I'll come with you if you like – greater love hath no man than to give up his day off for a friend.'

I smiled genuinely for the first time in days. 'Thanks, Greg. I knew you'd help me.'

Before I left, a half-finished picture on a draughtsman's drawing board caught my eye. It was at the other end of the room – a dining area which Greg had converted into a study – and beside it were piles of photographs, some of them cut up, and a scattering of books.

I went over to look at the picture more closely.

'That's Sammy's work in progress,' said Greg. 'That's where he produces his masterpieces.' Though he meant to sound sarcastic, he could not mask a tinge of pride.

The picture was tinted a rich sepia, and showed a brown bird soaring out of an open grave, piercing its own brilliant path towards a burst of light in the night sky. I felt I knew immediately which poem it represented, for it was one that my husband, Ralph, had recited in the depths of his drunken depressions:

Now more than ever seems it rich to die,
To cease upon the midnight with no pain,

While thou art pouring forth thy soul abroad
  In such an ecstasy!
Still wouldst thou sing, and I have ears in vain –
To thy high requiem become a sod.

I looked down at the book beside the drawing board, and there it was, an old, worn volume of Keats, open at the 'Ode to a Nightingale', here translated into a single graphic image. It pained me to see the words and hear Ralph's guttering hymn to death in my head. I picked up the book only to turn it over, to hide the hated phrases, but as I did so I saw an inscription written on the flyleaf in ink. 'Giles Hurt,' it read. 'University College, Cambridge. Oct 1972.'

I stared and stared at the signature, familiar to me from countless council documents, as the enormity of the words rendered me dumb. Here was proof that Giles Hurt, the chief executive, Giles Hurt, Mr Scrupulous, had a relationship with a low-life rent-boy. Here was proof that Giles, with his orotund quotations from antique poetry, had been the inspiration behind Sammy's incongruous choice of subject for his pictures. It was Giles he'd been trying to impress.

I stood with the book trembling in my hand. Suddenly all my earlier misgivings about the boy seemed to gather force. Perhaps it was the influence of that mordant verse, but I found myself no longer giving Sammy the benefit of my doubts. He had taken everything Greg offered, then lied to him. Despite his services to Shelley, he was using her for his own self-seeking ends. Two men – Jefferson and Jansen – had already come to physical grief over a relationship with him. Was anyone really safe around this slippery little creature? Greg and Shelley? I would urge them to keep him at arm's length. But Giles Hurt – how could I tackle the subject with him? Especially if, as I suspected, sex was the real key to Sammy's dark malevolence. If Giles Hurt was using him as a rent-boy, what fate awaited him?

SIXTEEN

Despite the turmoil in which I found myself, I still had to work, fretting between jobs, living largely on my nerves, caffeine and biscuits. A couple of days later I arrived too early at an assignment and sighed when I realised I had time on my hands to brood.

I was in the resort's recently-built 'splash centre', an effort to defy the North-West's windy blasts by recreating an indoor tropical paradise. It had been an expensive venture – all waves and waterfalls, fountains and foliage – and it had cost the council dear, not only in cash but in criticism. For this had been one of the joint efforts between private enterprise and local authorities, much vaunted as both progressive and desirable. What had happened, however, was that private enterprise had found itself deep in debt after building the thing, and the council, as guarantor, found itself carrying the financial can. The reaction of the town's residents, on whose doormats the bill eventually fell, was predictably enraged – and the splash centre now sat heavily in the council's burden of care.

In an effort to bolster takings the centre was now being marketed as a venue for conferences and meetings, and it was for one of these that I was here. Giles Hurt had called to say he would be presenting a press briefing with a company called Amphitrite.

'It's a subject I can guarantee you'll be interested in, Anna,' he said. 'Very important for the town, I can assure you. I can't tell you what it's about until the briefing, but I know you'll find it newsworthy.' I hoped it might also give me a little more insight into Giles himself. I knew he had taken much of the blame over the splash centre fiasco, for he had been instrumental in arranging the deal on what were now seen as disastrously misconceived terms, and he usually avoided being seen around the place for that reason. If he were prepared to show his face there publicly, then Amphitrite's press briefing must be important.

I found a seat on what was called the 'piazza' which gave me a view of the 'fun' pool below – a diversion for my thoughts while I waited. The water was full of pale bodies in fluorescent costumes, spotty backs and fleshy folds exposed in the merciless white light. A continuous cacophony of shouts and screams bounced off the clinical white walls and echoed under the roof.

Here, away from the threat of rain and the mess of sand in their shoes, families picnicked in sanitised splendour at tables round the edge of the pool. They bought drinks at a mock Greek taverna and drank them under redundant umbrellas. Up above, the innards of the building's support systems were exposed in yards of industrial tubing, and children sluiced down water-chutes as if on a production line.

Strung from the ceiling, a flock of plastic parrots flapped their hinged wings, going nowhere. I looked at them, and felt as useless as those strung-up birds. I thought of the vibrant nightingale in Sammy's picture, and wondered what to do. I had borrowed the Keats book from Greg with the half-formed idea that if Giles saw me with it he might suspect I knew of his relationship with Sammy, and that might be enough to stop him seeing the boy. I was, after all, a reporter, with the malicious weapon of publicity in my power – though that, in fact, was the furthest idea from my mind.

I drew the book out of my bag. I had impressed on Greg my mistrust of Sammy, and, hurt as he'd been by the boy's fickleness, he had taken it to heart. Shelley . . . as I'd predicted, she had begun to tire of him already. His absence had broken her dependence on his hypnotherapy, and she demurred little when I asked her to see less of him. All her attention was now concentrated on creating new material for her act, and she had little time for anything else. But the conundrum of the boy still plagued me. I sought to merge his bright and talented face with his sinister shadow, but it eluded me. Could he really have brought a doctor to suicide, and stood by while he committed it? Could he have tried to murder a politician? Or was my overactive imagination playing on circumstantial evidence, and was there no harm in the boy at all?

A tangy smell of citrus-scented aftershave cut through the chemical atmosphere and a voice made me start, addressing me out of the background racket.

'Ah, the admirable Anna. Punctual as ever – and, I see, "complete and ready for the revels rude when dreadful guests would come to spoil her solitude".'

Such a perfume, such a greeting, could only herald one man.

'Giles, how are you? You startled me, I was in a dream.'

'Yes, I could see you were engrossed.'

He looked down at my lap, and I realised with a thump that I still had his volume of poetry in my hand. He opened his mouth as if to say something, but his gullet seemed to strangle the words and he coughed explosively.

'Poetry and the press – a pretty mix,' his voice rasped. 'What next – the news in iambic pentameter?'

He must have recognised the book, he must have known where I had found it. The shock-waves still reverberated in the air as I watched him hurry away, hunched in his finely tailored pale grey suit, coughing discreetly into the pink lawn handkerchief that matched his pink carnation.

'What on earth have you done to Giles, Anna?' came a cheerful voice behind my shoulder. It was Deanna Duncan, a reporter from one of our rival papers, who dumped her bags and files around her as she sat down. 'He was huffing fit to burst.'

'Coughing fit,' I explained, folding the poems back in my bag.

'Oh, is that all?' she moaned mockingly, 'I'd hoped someone had managed to prick his pride at last. Jeez, but isn't it hot in here?'

'It's meant for near-naked bodies, Deanna.'

'Well I'm game for a strip if you are – let's get down to the bare essentials for Mr Smug and his precious briefing.' She laughed heartily. 'That *would* bring his eyes out on stalks!'

Deanna was invariably laughing, her chins folding like dough into her ample body. 'What's this all about anyway, Anna? I just got some garbled info from newsdesk – something about a company called Amphitrite and "sanitary sanity".'

'Sanitary sanity? Is that what Giles said?'

'So I'm told. It's not the sort of term my news editor'd forget even with his benighted brain. Ha! Perhaps they make tampons and they've just stitched up a deal for the Town Hall supplies.'

'You could be right,' I laughed with her.

'If they'd asked me I could've recommended my own particular brand on the tampon front – it's called "Up Yours", and like me it expands widthways to absorb all the bloody rubbish!'

Both of us were chortling at this when I looked up into a frigid glare from Giles Hurt.

'If you'd like to come this way, ladies,' he said, ushering us towards a side room, set up with a large table at one end and neatly arranged chairs in front. The doors shut out the ambient noise. 'The party will be arriving shortly,' he said, disappearing again.

Other journalists began to filter in, and I realised Giles had cast his net far and wide – not just to gather in the local media, but regional, and one Northern correspondent for a national. He must have felt this press briefing, whatever it was, was of importance, and been able to persuade some hardened hacks too.

I was surprised to hear a familiar trill behind me, and

looked round to see Councillor Irene Millichop slipping in at the back. She was fluttering her eyelashes like an abashed maiden at her companion, who, though he was hidden behind someone else, I could hear quite plainly. It was Cyrus Lander's fog-horn voice, broadcasting his thoughts over her head.

'I always say I'll give any man a fair hearing,' he was saying. 'It's no use wearing blinkers, you've got to move with the times.'

'I think you'll be very interested in what they have to say, Cyrus,' twittered Milly. 'I certainly was – and I think you ought to hear it right from the gift horse's mouth, as it were.'

Giles re-entered the room, followed by half a dozen men in suits, and a hush fell as they took their seats behind the table at the front.

'Ladies and gentlemen, thank you for coming here today,' said Giles. 'I'd like to introduce you to the representatives of Amphitrite, the company that, if I may say so, will be seen in future years as the saviour of our bathing beaches *if* the community is far-sighted enough to give its backing.'

One of the men got up to uncover a large map of the coast, accompanied by a series of diagrams, and proceeded in a well-mannered tone to explain their purpose.

The privatisation of the water industry figured largely in his introduction, a subject which evoked an ill-smothered yawn from Deanna. However, he became much more animated as he outlined the opportunity this presented to his company. What they were proposing was to solve the coast's sea pollution problem at a stroke by building an advanced inland sewage treatment plant and operating it as subcontractors to the water company.

This, he glowed, would be the answer to all the resort's worries over threats to the tourist industry from contaminated bathing water. And, he emphasised, it was a solution that Western Water alone could never afford on its own. It would placate not only those who criticised the present sewage outpourings, but also those with misgivings about the water company's future plans. These involved cursory treatment and sending the resultant broth down a long pipeline out to sea. The comparison, said the Amphitrite man, was like that between a Rolls-Royce and a Morris Minor.

Western Water was currently deliberating over Amphitrite's proposals, he said, but his company wanted to put its plans to the people in the belief that public support would help its case.

'The water that leaves our plant will be pure enough to drink,' he beamed, and eyeing Frilly Milly at the back, he added, 'I'm sure Councillor Millichop will be only too happy to prove it by drinking the first glass.'

'May I ask, sir,' responded Milly – never one to let an opportunity to speak slip by – 'what benefit your company hopes to get out of this scheme? It is an enormous outlay – £100 million I think was your estimate – I hardly think the water company would pay anything like enough to recoup that amount, even over a very long period.'

'You're very right, madam,' he answered, with a salesman's polish, 'and of course, as you suggest, our motives cannot be entirely philanthropic. No indeed, we do plan to profit from the enterprise in a number of ways. The processing of sewage generates a range of by-products which, with the latest technology available, we will be able to exploit to the full. The gas, for example, can be tapped off as an endlessly renewable source of energy, the solids can be processed into fuel or agricultural fertiliser. We see enormous potential in this field, and we are willing to invest a considerable amount of cash and expertise in seeing our treatment plant come to fruition as a model of modern technology. We have a vested interest in ensuring it succeeds, not just for its own sake, but for the sake of spreading such Amphitrite plants all over the country.'

'These are fine words, sir, but will it work?' persisted Milly.

'Yes. That's my simple answer. It will work. It does work already in countries more enlightened about recycling than our own, and I have documentation here to prove it,' he said, waving a sheaf of papers.

'Well,' said Milly, 'I know I've gone on record defending the quality of our bathing water, but I have listened to your arguments over the last few days, and I must say I've found them convincing. One must not forget that environmental concerns are coming increasingly to the fore nowadays, and perhaps there comes a time when one must eat – or rather drink in this case – one's words. I think, ladies and gentlemen of the press, you may say that on this occasion this lady is for turning. I am not immune to the turn in the tide of opinion about environmental issues, and I'd like to add my support to Amphitrite's proposals. Let Northport sail forth into a brighter future, aboard the good ship *Private Enterprise*.'

'Jay-sus,' muttered Deanna under her breath, 'do we have to quote that garbage?'

'It's what we're here for,' I whispered.

'If I may have a word, Mr Chairman,' boomed Cyrus, addressing Giles, who gestured graciously. 'I like to call a spade a spade, and I think we in the tourist trade have to start looking to the future. Now, while I've said our sea's a healthy sea – and I stick by that – I can see the time is coming when people will look askance at resorts that still pump their sewage out. You've got to move with the times in this game. If people want a fancy new treatment plant then that's what we'll have to give 'em, just like they all want *en suite* baths in hotels nowadays. It's all marketing, it's all psychology or whatever you like to call it. But I say, if this company wants to build us a treatment plant then I don't see what we've got to lose. I'm sure my members'll think the same – even though we don't accept there's anything wrong with our sea at present – we're not ones to stick our heads in the sand where business is concerned. Thank you, I've said my piece, and I don't want any of you reporters saying I've done a U-turn, because I haven't, all right? I'll be watching you.'

'We hear and obey, Big Brother,' came Deanna's undertone.

Giles thanked both Cyrus and Milly for their endorsements, before introducing the other Amphitrite men, who explained details of their revolutionary technology in terms which could only excite a sewage engineer. The reporters began to shuffle and check their watches. We'd heard the essence of it, and there were deadlines to meet, other jobs to go to. Giles sensed the time was ripe to wrap up the meeting, which he did speedily, though with tact and aplomb.

As the press filed out, I saw Milly and Cyrus move forward towards Giles and the Amphitrite cohort and, helping Deanna collect her bags and files together, I overheard some of their conversation.

'We really have Mr Hurt to thank for this, you know,' Milly was saying to Cyrus. 'It was he who sought out the company and interested them in coming to the resort, and it was he who introduced them to the water company. He's put in a great deal of hard work – but then he always does. Such a pity he was let down over the splash centre business, but you know, I believe he's been made a scapegoat on that one. I'll say no more, but I do think there was a measure of blame-shifting on the part of some of my colleagues. Still, perhaps he can redeem the situation if this Amphitrite scheme comes off.'

'Hmph,' responded Cyrus, growling low so as not to be overheard by Giles, who was in any case talking to one of the Amphitrite men, 'no flies on him, I'm sure. Drop him in the shit and he'll come up smelling of roses every time.'

The rose-scented one looked up as Deanna and I left the room, and I was struck by the cold, bleak stare which momentarily masked his polite face, as though for a few seconds he was overcome with bitterness.

Deanna and I hurriedly escaped, and I said goodbye to

her outside in the car park. I looked back at the splash centre, an unlovely piece of modern architecture which but for its coat of larky colours would squat on the shoreline like an air-raid bunker. I suddenly felt as hollow as that place, wishing Alys could have seen the hasty back-pedalling of Milly and Cyrus, wishing I could tell her about Amphitrite and the victory it represented for her campaign, wishing I could find her. She was the one missing, but it was I who felt lost and alone.

SEVENTEEN

A phone warbled shrilly under a heap of old newspapers and court sheets on the desk next to mine at work. It was the crime reporter's desk, but I knew he was out, attending a court case in Liverpool. I wrenched my thoughts away from the train journey I was planning with Greg tomorrow, retracing Alys's movements. Greg had done the photographs and I was studying railway timetables. But the phone did not shut up. It had to be answered.

I reached under the paper mountain and found the receiver.

'Anna,' came a thin, faint voice. 'Is that you? . . . Couldn't remember your extension.'

'Wha – who – *yes* it's me. My God, Alys – where the hell have you been?'

'Hell – ha – that's right . . . nor am I out of it.'

She sounded very strange. Her voice was sliding, slurring away, almost as if she were drunk.

'What do you mean, Alys, for goodness' sake? I've been

going crazy trying to find you. Are you all right? What's happened to you?'

'It's like I said, Anna, it isn't worth the bloody candle any more . . . I'm going, going away . . . I'm going to float away where no one can find me any more.'

'Alys!' I shouted, seriously alarmed. 'Just tell me where you are, I'll come and get you. Listen, Alys, I have to talk to you – the package you left me – it was stolen before I could deliver it. I don't—'

'Doesn't matter, Ans. Doesn't matter a damn. Nothing matters . . . all a sham. Ha-ha-ha – I rhymed.'

She really was drunk – or worse. I had to try to get through to her.

'Alys – Jay's almost demented with worry. Phone him, tell him where you are, then he can come and get you.'

'Jay, jay, fly away . . . no Anna . . .,' and she gave an uncharacteristic sob. 'I can't. That would be too much. I've caused him enough worry and trouble. Everything I do seems to drag other people into my mess. Well, I'm not going to do it any more. We . . . we were happy here. The happiest times, the picnics. Tell – tell him I'm sorry. That's all I ask, Anna, tell him I'm sorry. You understand, don't you?'

'No! No! I don't understand, Alys. Please, please tell me where you are!'

'I'm going . . . I'm going.' Her voice was singsonging lightly away – and then I heard a clatter as though the phone had been dropped.

'Alys. Alys!'

No response. All I could hear were gulls screaming, and I imagined the receiver left swinging free in some call-box – where? Could I hear the sea, or was it just the wind? Then abruptly the line clicked dead, as though someone had replaced the handset.

I had to find her, and there was no time to lose. Whatever had happened, I was convinced she was in a suicidal state – mentally disjointed enough to do herself real harm.

Whether it was drug- or drink-induced at that moment did not matter. I had to find her before she did anything drastic.

I phoned Jay's school and they dragged him out of class when I told them how urgent it was.

'Picnics, Jay, she said you'd had picnics wherever she was – and I heard seagulls.'

'Christ – we had dozens of picnics, all over the Lake District and down the coast. It was a treat for the kids whenever she was home, we'd have picnic lunches at the weekend.'

'Try and remember the ones that seemed happiest, the ones you went back to.'

He gave me a list of names, and told me he would go to some of the places himself, though he would have to get back for the kids after school as he had no one who could look after them.

Armed with the larger part of the list, I quickly took Ellis Clancy on one side and told him what had happened.

'You'd better go find her then, hadn't you?' he said, biting a stub of fingernail. 'Hey, but Anna, if you're going to play heroine we want the story – OK?'

I went to the photographers' department to track down Greg, but was told he was out on a job, unlikely to be back for an hour or more, so I left a hastily scrawled message.

Within an hour my black Metro was plunging into the edge of the Lake District, heading for Grange and Barrow. The locals looked in alarm as I screeched up to the harbourside, ejected from my seat-belt, scanned the surroundings with and without my binoculars before hurling myself back in the driving seat and powering out again.

Millom went by, and Ravenglass, its serene expanses unappreciated by my distracted eyes. By the time I got to Whitehaven I was desperate. She could be way over in another direction. Jay said they'd even had picnics in North Wales and once they'd gone on a day trip to the Isle of Man. But now I'd come this far I had to persist, even though both I and the car were tiring rapidly, neither of us young enough to be dashing about like this any more. I rang Tom from a phonebox, and between pips managed to tell him what had happened. He sounded reassuring, saying he'd put out an alert for me, they'd do their best to find her, but somehow it didn't make me feel any better, I couldn't be comforted by him.

Workington was next, then Maryport – a grim, stone-built town which seemed to drag down my own incipient despair. I decided I would go as far north as Carlisle and then turn back. Sometimes, when I saw a distant, slight figure, alone – walking or waiting – a spark of hope still flared, but each time I raced up to see a strange and startled face the spark grew dimmer and dimmer.

By the time I got back on the motorway at Carlisle I was exhausted, and it was getting dark. I pulled into a service station to refuel the car. I rang Jay, who was by now at home. But he too had had no success. He had also told the police, but as yet they'd come up with nothing. I rang off and went to try and refresh my tired eyes with a cold-water splash in the Ladies.

As I looked up into the mirror, the water dripping down my face, the reflection of defeat looking back at me was more than I could bear. Tears joined the drips clinging to the dark rings round my eyes. Damn it, Alys, if she really believed she had caused people too much trouble, why do this and cause more? Did she think after a phone call like that I wouldn't come looking for her? Of course she didn't. It had been the classic cry for help. Alys, Alys, how can I help if I don't know where you are? I railed at myself in the mirror, and then in sheer frustration I thrust my hands into the water-filled bowl, splashing myself, the floor and the woman powdering her face next to me. She cast an injured look in my direction and ignored my apologies, dabbing at her soaked sleeve with a handkerchief. Her disapproval broke a strained nerve within me.

I ran out of the washroom and slammed myself back into

the cocoon of my car. I drove, and kept driving with the radio on at full blast to drown out the thought that it was too late, that Alys by now could be lying somewhere beyond help, alone.

As I neared the turn-off for Lancaster, I wondered whether I had the strength left to visit Jay, so that we could keep each other company while we waited for news. I took the turn-off, but when it came to the roundabout where I should have sheered off to Lancaster, I simply could not bring myself to go down that road. I could not give up, I could not admit defeat. I went round and round the roundabout and finally came to a halt in a side road that ran off it.

I ran over and over what she'd said: 'We were happy here. The happiest times, the picnics . . .' And I knew a glimmer of memory was hovering within reach, a tissue-thin recollection of Alys telling me about a picnic . . . a couple of picnics. Yes, it was coming nearer. She had been striving hard, so hard, to overcome the initial animosity of Jay's children towards her. They'd missed their mother, they resented her intermittent intrusion. And she'd wanted to give them an adventure. She'd borrowed an old butcher's bike, put their dog in the pannier, and shepherded them on their own bikes around the country lanes, leaving Jay behind. And I remembered her telling me about watching the boats as they ate their picnic – and the sudden triumph of a first hug from Jay's daughter as they played tug-of-war with a seagull scavenging their French loaf, and the laughter with his son as they tumbled on the grass. And, yes, she'd told me later, she'd never felt so happy in her life before, laughing with these children at . . . where, where?

I peered through the windscreen, looking for road signs, a spur to drag the name out of obscurity. It could not be far from where I was now, within a bike ride of the town. But it was not a road sign that finally gave me the clue, it was a small sticker on the windscreen that caught my eye

– 'Shatterproof glass'. Glass . . . glass . . . through a glass darkly . . . glass – Glasson. Glasson Dock. That was it. Glasson Dock.

Immediately I was in reverse, swinging the car round and heading down the lanes to the little port. Darkness had fallen as I pulled up on the quay. The place was quiet as the grave, the only movement that of ships shifting heavily above the lapping water. I grabbed a torch from my car boot, and walked along the harbourside slowly, hope ebbing and flowing like the sea in this last little sailor's knot of civilisation. Dinghies, yachts and pleasure cruisers nudged alongside the larger commercial vessels. All seemed bereft of life. Only the water gulped and swallowed eerily in the harbour basin. I walked along, peering into the darkness, helped only by my weak torchlight. I read the names of the boats like a litany. *Iolanthe, Lady Day, Jack's Folly, Lollipop . . . Libra, Castle Maine, Sandpiper, Sirius . . . Minotaur, No Man's Land* – WHAT! I looked again, and yes, there it was, the WARN women's ship, *No Man's Land*. I stared and stared at it, a solid, workaday ship, the size of a medium trawler, no frills. Nothing stirred on its decks, no lights glowed within. The gang-plank was still in place, and I ventured up it warily. I knocked on one door, then another. I tried them both. They were locked. I called 'Hello', with no reply, and I shone my torch through the windows and along the deck. It seemed empty and lifeless. Slowly I walked back down to the quayside, reached the end of the harbour, and turned back to the *No Man's Land*, hoping for inspiration.

I sat exhaustedly on one of the capstans to which the boat was tied, and contemplated my isolation. There seemed nowhere else I could go now but back to Jay, tell him I'd found the *No Man's Land*, but no Alys. I slumped, dispirited. But then something on the edge of my vision made me stare. Out of the corner of my eye I thought I saw an abrupt movement on the ship's deck. It seemed to come from a crumpled tarpaulin or pile of rope. Perhaps it had lifted in the wind. But the air was almost still. What little wind there was seemed too slight to shift heavy canvas or rope. Perhaps it had been a cat, pouncing after a night insect. I went to the harbour edge to look closer.

Straining into the dimness I was sure I saw it move again – a slight shuffle across the deck – in the opposite direction to the ship's gentle sway. Then I saw a white hand briefly illuminated in my torchlight, a palm emerging from the pile, grasping the air.

Filled with alarm I ran the few steps to the gang-plank, raced up it and leapt on to the deck. I approached the shape slowly, warily, fearful of what I might find. It was slumped against a metal hatch-cover, and it was shivering. I moved towards it, and froze as it started to move again, shuffling against the obstacle in its path. My tongue clogged my mouth, strangling speech. Then I saw it start to rise, a head lifting out of the shroud and looking at me. Eyes bleared, skin bleach-white, mouth dragged down in agony. I could hardly recognise her – but it was Alys. Dear God, I was there with my arms about her before I could think. Whispering urgently as I lifted her towards me, I could only utter nursery soothings, 'Shhh . . . Alys, Alys, I've found you, you're all right now, you'll be safe, I'm with you . . . ssshhhh . . . don't worry.'

But for all my reassurances I could see that she was not all right: she was half conscious, and she was squinting at me as though she could barely recognise who I was.

'It's Anna, Alys – Alys, it's me,' I urged. The only reply she gave me was a grunt, and I felt her body contract in a dry paroxysm as she retched.

'What's happened to you? Alys, please, you have to tell me what's happened to you.'

She groaned, and brought her knees up sharply as if pain shot through her abdomen. As she did so something hard and light fell from her trouser pocket. I picked it up. It was a small empty plastic tablet bottle. And as the boat moved on the swell I saw an empty quarter-bottle of whisky slide across the deck. She had done it. She had tried to kill herself. My first reaction was rage – first against her, and then against the forces that had driven her to it. I saw, with some relief, that she had already been sick and brought a lot of the poison back up. But I had to get her off the boat, I had to get her to a hospital.

Gently as I could, I lifted her to her feet, hooking her arm round my shoulders and clamping her body tight to my side. Her feet slithered along the deck beside me, and I dared not think how I was going to get her safely across the flimsy gang-plank.

I was startled by a sharp shout from the quayside, followed by the flash of a blinding light in my eyes. 'Here – what are you up to?' came the male voice behind the light. 'What d'you think you're playing at on there?'

I wasn't about to reveal to a complete stranger what had really happened.

'I – I'm terribly sorry,' I shouted back. 'I'm afraid my friend's rather drunk. She had a row with her boyfriend and ran out on him, we've been looking for her everywhere. I found her collapsed on this boat. She's in a bit of a state I'm afraid.'

'You're not joking – women – I dunno,' came the response, along with a muttered oath. 'All right, all right, I'm coming. I'll help you down with her.'

'Thanks,' I shouted in gratitude as I saw him approaching up the narrow walkway.

'I'm Jim Bentley, by the way, in case you're wondering – from the Harbour Office,' he said, a stocky man who took Alys's waiflike weight with ease.

He eyed her slumped head dubiously, 'She doesn't look well at all, does she?' he said, softening. 'Better get her home, out of harm's way love, if I were you.'

'I will, I will.'

By means of shuffles and heaves we managed to get Alys safely on to dry land, and Jim Bentley helped me to load her into the car. Almost crying with relief I strapped her

149

in and drove for the casualty department at Lancaster hospital as though my own life depended on it.

I did not know what to expect when I visited the hospital the next day. I tentatively scanned the shapes lying in the women's ward – and then I saw her turn towards me, her face almost as white as the pillow behind her head, but awake and alert.

I sat at her bedside, not knowing what to say – but then she groped for my hand, pulling me towards her and hugging my neck.

'Thanks,' she whispered. 'They said you brought me in. I don't know how you found me. I'm just thankful.'

'So am I,' I replied, beaming behind the flowers I'd brought her. 'After your phone call I spent all day looking for you. I—'

'What?' she interrupted. 'What phone call?'

'The call you made to me yesterday, at work, when you said to tell Jay you were sorry . . .'

'Phone call . . . I don't remember . . . I don't remember ringing you at all. Oh Jesus, what's happened to me?'

'You sounded very strange, Alys. I thought at first you were drunk.'

'I've been trying, trying to remember . . . but it's all a mist . . . I woke up here this morning. I didn't know where I was or how I got here. I thought I'd had the most dreadful nightmare, and somehow it was still going on. I screamed and shouted, and nurses came running to hold me down. And then I realised I wasn't dreaming, I was really awake.'

'And did they tell you I'd found you after you'd taken an overdose?'

'Yes,' she said, a spark of panic in her eyes.

'What made you do it, Alys? What's happened to you since you left me on the beach that day?'

'That's just it, Anna – that's what's frightening me so . . . I can't remember, I just can't remember. The last memory I have is of being at a railway station – London it must have been – I know I'd taken Lynne and Martina home earlier. It was night-time, but I remember thinking I still had to go to Groundswell headquarters.'

'But you never got there.'

'Didn't I?'

'I rang them, trying to find out where on earth you were. They said you'd rung to tell them you were diverting elsewhere, on one of the WARN projects.'

'You see . . . I don't remember making any such phone call. I do remember the crowds at the station – there was terrible jostling going down to the Tube. And then . . . and then . . .'

'What?' I urged as she seemed to trail away.

'I do remember something else . . . a sharp pain at the top of my leg, at the back. So sharp I thought it was a bee sting, or a hat pin, or a . . .'

'A needle . . . it could have been a needle. Someone pumping a syringe.'

'It must have been – yes, it must have been – that's my last clear memory until I woke up here.'

'It's been six days.'

'I know . . . some bad trip, huh?' she smiled weakly. 'Look – look at my arm.'

I saw where she was pointing, a scattering of tiny brown scabs on swollen skin.

'They must be needle marks,' she said. 'Someone's kept me drugged the whole time. No wonder the doctor assumed I was an addict when she came to see me this morning. That was the first time I noticed them.'

'But don't you recall anything at all in the past few days – nothing?'

She shook her head worriedly. 'I think I remember things, and then I don't know whether they were reality or dreams.'

'What do you think you remember?'

'Voices mainly, it's all voices in a fog.'

151

'Shouting? Screaming?'

'No, no. It's one voice in particular, it's calm and steady, but it's making me feel dreadful – making me feel I'm totally worthless and everything I'm doing is futile. I can't remember the words, only the feeling of being dragged down, and seeing the future like a bottomless grave – just totally hopeless and depressing . . . I . . . when I think about it now, that whole feeling's coming back to me. That's how I must have been when I took the pills . . . I really did want to die . . .'

She looked at me with an expression of horror.

'Look,' I said, 'don't you think it's about time you let the police in on this? Before anyone else gets hurt.'

She paused. 'Yes,' her voice was barely audible. 'Tell them, tell your friend the detective. It's gone far enough. I didn't want PC Plods wading into our research, I didn't want to break my promise of secrecy to Harry, but it can't go on like this. We need help.'

I told Tom that night – about Alys's research, about Harry's involvement, and about the stolen papers. His warmth at seeing me quickly cooled as I sat and told him all I knew. By the end of it his eyes were cold and steely.

'Is that it?' he said finally. 'Or is there anything else you've been keeping from me, you and your friend?'

'Tom,' I said. 'I wanted to tell you before, but I promised Alys I'd keep quiet about it, and I keep my promises.'

'I thought you trusted me,' he said, looking at his hands, looking anywhere but at me. 'How can I trust you now?'

That was rich, I thought, coming from a man who was even now betraying the trust of his wife. I looked at him with detachment, and began to wonder what I saw in him. He was insensitive, and he and I had little in common besides work – his work – for he had paltry conversation apart from that. Only my body had desired his, and that was beginning to pall. He sat there, his face full of turbulent emotion, yet I knew he would not talk about it, and I wasn't going to help him.

He stood up: 'I'm going, Anna. I've got work to do.'

I said nothing. He walked to the door and paused. If he was waiting for me to beg his forgiveness he'd wait for ever.

'Bye, Tom,' I said sharply.

He turned as if hurt, then went out, slamming the door behind him.

I had little time to ruminate over Tom. The phone rang, and it was Shelley in an emotional state. She'd heard from the TV company that day – the pilot show had not gone down well, there'd be no series. The problem was her new material had been too raw, her performance lacking its former verve. I had to soothe her: she'd tried to do too much, too soon – it had just been bad timing, the new act needed audience input before it would be ready for TV, she'd get another chance. But at nineteen every setback seemed to threaten her whole future. And despite what I was saying, I was unsure myself whether she could poke jokes at other targets with the same conviction she'd lampooned men. She'd fed on her father's unhappy example for that comic tirade. But she hadn't lived long enough or seen enough for general wise-cracking observation. Men had been easy – a narrow subject, easy laughs – life was harder. It would take more than a few hypnotherapy sessions with Sammy to put that glossy smile back on her face and keep it there.

EIGHTEEN

'He won't play. I can't get through to him.'

It was Tom again, speaking to me on the phone at work as he would speak to a minion – irritated, short. He was talking about Harry Jansen.

'Can't get past his blasted medics,' he went on. 'They won't let me speak to him. Say he's too ill. If he's so ill why've they released him? Why've they let him go home?'

'To die?' I said simply. I hated this. 'What is it you want, Tom?'

The silence was too long, as if there were something he wanted to say, but couldn't.

'I want you . . .' he said more softly, 'to tell me honestly if there's anything more you or Alys haven't told us. We're groping in the dark without Jansen. His wife calls up the doctors every time we go near.'

'Honestly, Tom, you have all we know, I give you my promise.'

'I know, you don't break promises, right?'

We were jarring against each other.

'Look,' I said, 'Alys knows Harry pretty well. We may be able to get past the medics on the pretext of a get-well visit. I'm sure Alys wants to confront him anyway. If he is well enough, we'll try our damnedest to drag out of him what's behind this.'

'All right,' he said. 'Guess I'll just have to trust you, won't I?'

'Don't force yourself.'

The next day I claimed time off owing to me and drove to pick up Alys as she was being discharged from hospital. I was more than glad to get away. Ellis Clancy had written a melodramatic story about me after I had refused to do it myself. 'Death Race Against Time' was the headline, depicting me as the heroic Samaritan rescuing my depressed friend from the brink of suicide. The whole business had left a bitter taste. Alys too was anxious to get away. She'd heard from Groundswell that the *No Man's Land* had been laid up at Glasson Dock after limping back to port. Sabotage was suspected, and it needed extensive repairs. It was another blow, and it had made her angry. Still frail, she was nevertheless determined to try to get to see Harry.

He lived just outside Pemberley, a small country market town which had turned its efforts towards tourism in recent years. On the way we acquired a great sheaf of flowers and an expensive basket of fruit, and with these bribes we turned into the gravel driveway of Harry's imposing residence, Pemberley Towers. A glowering Victorian edifice of russet sandstone, it presented a daunting face to the world, built to withstand the gales of its commanding situation, high on a hillside.

The driveway was lined with tall, handsome trees, but the garden seemed cheerless and flowerless, bounded by sandstone walls. I pressed the bouquet tight to my chest as we approached the door. Shadowed by the trees, the entrance seemed dim and gloomy, flanked on each side by stone lions mounting cannon-balls.

Alys, the basket of fruit hanging from her arm, looked at me apprehensively before pressing the brass doorbell. Its clangour sounded somewhere far away. There seemed no sign of life, no movement of curtains, no voices, no music from radios.

So when the door opened without warning, it almost seemed as if someone had been standing behind it, waiting for us to call. The girl who stood before us looked no more than sixteen. She wore a sloppy sweatshirt with leggings, and her hair was tied up in a sprig atop her gum-chewing face. I assumed she must be Jansen's daughter.

'You come to see a resident?' she asked, looking at our fruit and flowers.

'We've come to see Mr—'

'You expected?' she interrupted. "Cos they're at lunch.' This seemed to present an insurmountable barrier.

I tried again: 'We've come to see Mr Jansen. But if he's having lunch then we'll come back in an hour or so.'

'Oh, Mr Jansen . . . I see,' she replied, looking at us doubtfully. She was obviously not his daughter. 'I'd better fetch Mrs Jansen. Wait here.'

The thick oak door shut on us once more.

'What's going on?' asked Alys. 'Residents? Is she the latest equivalent of the parlour-maid?'

'Search me,' I answered unhelpfully.

'Perhaps this is how Jansen salves his socialist conscience – employing local teenagers in the service industry.'

Alys, still looking wan, shuddered in a gust of wind: 'This place gives me the creeps already.'

We heard footsteps approaching – high heels on a tile floor? The door opened to reveal a small but elegant, fine-boned woman in her fifties. Her clothes spoke of expensive thrift – good classics bought to look decent over many years. A double rope of pearls wound round her throat, and she looked worried.

'I believe you've come to call on my husband,' she said. 'I'm so sorry. He's really not well enough to see constituents just now. It's kind of you to bring flowers, but—'

'But we're not constituents, Mrs Jansen,' Alys interjected. 'We're – I'm a friend of Harry's.'

'We really would like to see him if we possibly could,' I carried on, seeing her wavering. 'We've come a long way, you see, and Alys – I'm sorry, we haven't introduced ourselves: this is Alys Finestone and I'm Anna Knight – Alys has done some research work for your husband recently.'

'I'd like to give him a progress report,' finished Alys as I began to hesitate. 'I'd like to let him know what's been happening. I'm sure he'll want to be updated – it seemed important to him. I promise it won't take long.'

Mrs Jansen's eyelids seemed to flicker in indecision. 'Research, you say? Perhaps . . .', she started, and then something seemed to strike a chord within her. 'Perhaps it might stimulate him to see some new faces. Your names again? I don't think he's mentioned them to me . . . but then he doesn't tell me everything . . .' Her voice trailed off as though she were addressing the last statement to herself.

'Alys Finestone and Anna Knight.'

'Thank you. Wait here, would you mind?'

And the door shut again.

'So this is Pemberley Towers,' grumbled Alys. 'What a pile, what a mansion – it must have cost him a mint. Some socialist, huh?'

'Hmmmm . . . d'you think she's going to let us in?'

'It sounded like it,' she said, though she didn't sound sure. 'We should've rung first, not just dropped in on them.'

'I did try, Alys. The operator said they'd just changed the number and gone ex-directory.'

'Sounds like he's been getting paranoid about the phone too.' We heard footsteps approaching again. 'Hark,' said Alys, 'Methinks I hear the mistress returning.'

Once more the door swung back and once more Mrs Jansen's refined little figure greeted us.

'Come in,' she said at last.

We passed through a dark vestibule into a vast entrance hall, lit from above by a glass-domed cupola. A wide staircase led up to a gallery from which many doors led off. But what took our attention was a log fire, roaring fiercely up a canopied chimney, and round the fire a dozen pairs of eyes, pointed in our direction.

In contrast with the lively blaze, the eyes were dull and unwelcoming. They belonged to faces that ranged between youth and late middle age, with one common factor – they looked worn out. They had an unhealthy pallor I had come to know well, their eyes had a yellow tinge, and their expressions a grim edginess. I knew those symptoms: they were recovering addicts – of alcohol, prescribed tranquillisers or illegal drugs. I remembered seeing them all round me in the clinic where my husband tried to wean himself off the bottle.

'The residents are just resting after lunch,' said Mrs Jansen over her shoulder as she led us towards the stairs. 'They'll be going in for their group therapies shortly. Do come this way.'

As we climbed the mahogany staircase, trying to keep up with her light, nervous steps, I addressed her retreating back.

'Mrs Jansen, I didn't realise – am I right in thinking you run a rehabilitation centre?'

She stopped abruptly. 'My goodness, yes. You didn't know? Well I don't suppose you would if you don't live in the neighbourhood. We try to keep it as discreet as possible. The clients prefer it that way, particularly as quite a few of them are of some social standing. Dependence can afflict anyone in any social stratum given the circumstances, and there is so much stress in society nowadays. But we accept anyone who asks for help, whatever their means. We have a trust fund to subsidise those who could not otherwise afford it. Harry would not have it any other way.'

She turned to lead us along a corridor and up a further flight of stairs, talking as she went.

'We started it a couple of years ago after the children flew the coop and went off to university. Harry and I were positively rattling around in this old place. I'd never had a proper job of my own since we were married, although I'd done a lot of voluntary work with recovering alcoholics – counselling and so on. Harry said it seemed a natural progression, and I had to agree, it was something of my own, something I wanted to do. So we took on trained staff and here we are . . . as you can see, we're not short of customers.'

And I reckoned it must be a lucrative sideline to supplement Harry's political stipend. He was no fool.

'We have our own suite of rooms at the top,' said Mrs Jansen, opening a door which led into a large living room with views across the valley where the old market town was cupped in a sweep of the river. It was an enviable view, and the room was richly furnished in country manor style. One wall was panelled and hung with old horse-racing prints, and models of racehorses stood on walnut cabinets and tables. A large framed photograph of an exuberant wedding couple was prominent.

'That's my daughter,' said Mrs Jansen, seeing my glance. 'She got married last year. The boys are still . . . what do they say? Young, free and single? – and likely to remain so for some time.'

'Not that I mind – you're only young once, after all. Best to get all the high jinks out of their systems before they settle down, eh?' she asked, seeming nervous. 'I sometimes wish Harry had – got it out of his system when he was young, I mean. My life would've been easier. He's always worked too hard and played too hard. I somehow knew it would end catastrophically – I expected a heart attack every day. His blood pressure was high but he wouldn't let up. It got worse if anything. Just before this happened I hardly saw him for weeks. He seemed driven, as if frightened something would run away from him if he didn't work hard enough. I did a lot of his routine secretarial work at home, you see – just constituency business – but I sometimes despaired at the deluge of paper and dictation tapes. I – I was glad at least that this meant he had to stop. That's one consolation – perhaps the only . . . although I suppose you – ', looking at Alys, 'have brought some papers for him. I . . . I'd better come in with you. This way.'

Her face was drawn as she turned to lead us through a door which opened into a spacious bedroom.

A tall wing chair stood before the window, and as Mrs Jansen brought us forward I saw Harry in profile, his figure seemingly shrunk against the cushions on the chair. A rug lay over his knees, and he stared out through the window, a long, undistanced stare as though seeing nothing except the visions in his own head.

'Harry?' said Mrs Jansen, evoking no response. 'Harry?' This brought a flicker of movement from an eye. She touched his chin, and moved his head round so that we were in his field of vision – and then we both saw the other side of his face. His mouth sagged down on his right side like a clown's grimace of misery; his right eye similarly drooped and ran and I saw his right hand, loose and nerveless, flop from his lap.

Seeing our obvious speechlessness, Mrs Jansen, accustomed hostess that she was, filled in the silence. 'He is doing rather well now, considering the stroke happened so recently. It was a serious setback as you can imagine – he seemed to be making a good recovery from his injuries. Still, we've got him up in the chair now for a little more time each day, he's managing to eat – only soft food, soups and purées, you know – and we're learning how to communicate, aren't we darling?'

She kissed his forehead. A kind of exhaled grunt came from his slackened mouth. Alys and I looked at each other, both shocked. We had not expected to see Harry either so ill or so unable to help us. My feelings softened towards him, seeing his wounded head cushioned on his wife's arm.

'I – I'm sorry Mrs Jansen . . .', I started. 'We didn't realise – we hadn't heard about the stroke.'

'No – I know. We only told a few people. After the hullaballoo over his . . . fall . . . I really did not want any more media fuss. That's why I brought him home. Journalists can be heartless beasts – they were practically writing his obituary as he lay in hospital. They pumped up such morbid glee from every little report on his condition. I wanted to keep those scavengers at bay. Look at him . . .'

An expression of infinite tenderness came over her face, and she caressed his helpless head. 'He's like a baby – defenceless.'

'Does he understand what's going on?' asked Alys.

'Oh, I'm sure he does. That's the awful thing. I am perfectly certain that inside this maimed head his thinking is still as acute as ever. Sometimes I can really sense his brain trying to break through to speech again – it's a superhuman effort. A long process I'm afraid, so the doctors tell me. He's having to relearn almost everything, like a newborn baby. To be honest – ', she turned to look at us directly, 'I greatly appreciate the chance to look after him like this. His work . . . meant we were apart a lot . . . It's just so nice to have him near.'

And I suddenly felt terribly sorry for this constrained little woman, having had what I supposed was a lonely marriage, denied her husband's companionship – and now grateful for it when he was little more than a doll.

'Harry, Harry.' She crouched in front of him, looking straight into his eyes. 'Harry, look. These ladies have come to see you. Here's Anna Knight and Alys Finestone. Alys has brought you news on one of your projects. What is your work, Alys?'

Alys stepped forward and bent to engage his sight. 'I work for Groundswell,' she told Mrs Jansen. 'I've been gathering data for Harry by carrying out seismic surveys in the Irish Sea.'

His left eye looked alert, the eyelid flickering rapidly.

Alys glanced at me quizzically, as if asking whether she should go on. I nodded to encourage her.

'The problem is, Harry,' she went on, 'someone has been trying to sabotage our efforts; the latest survey results were stolen from my friend here before she could deliver them to you, and the lives of me and my colleagues have been put in serious danger. Now I—'

She stopped as Mrs Jansen rushed towards her now agitated husband. 'My goodness, you didn't tell me any of this was going to be upsetting. He's not ready for such – '. But Harry was flailing his left arm as if trying to stop his wife. His left eyeball was so animated it was swivelling up inside his head. Mucus rattled in his throat as his breath became fitful, and the side of his mouth writhed back and forth.

I was convinced he had understood every word of what Alys had said, and was exerting himself to get a word out. His chest heaved with effort, his complexion had reddened and a pulse was visible in his temple.

'Haaa-aaa----ffff,' he spluttered.

'Harry, Harry – he's trying to say something,' said Mrs Jansen, encouraged by the attempt and forgetting her admonishment of Alys. 'What is it, Harry? Try again, darling.'

'Haaa-aa-mmmm.'

The struggle seemed too much. His body collapsed. I began to feel we should take this no further. Our presence seemed to be distressing him so much I feared we might cause a relapse. But Alys was focused on his face, which had begun to strain for speech again.

'Hhhhhhaaam-ffff. Aaaaammmmmffff-t-t.'

'He is definitely trying to tell us something,' said Alys determinedly. 'It's not random sounds. He's repeating something.'

'I haven't seen him so animated since the stroke,' said Mrs Jansen. 'You girls are good for him – look at that concentration. I'd begun to fear he was giving up. He'd been so despondent the last few days – he hates this so much. Now look, there's fire in him again.'

'Amfft, amft,' went Harry, and then a long trailing breath.

'That's wonderful, darling,' enthused Mrs Jansen. 'You're really trying. I shall tell the physiotherapist tomorrow how well you've done.'

'If only we knew what he meant,' said Alys.

I looked at Harry, and could sense his frustration, the

veins standing out on his throbbing temple. He changed tack, producing a different sound.

'Huuu-hhh . . . Huuu-hhh-t.'

Mrs Jansen stroked his head. 'What hurts, Harry, where does it hurt? We've probably given you a headache, haven't we, with all this hard work.' She tucked the rug more securely round his legs. 'Perhaps he's tiring now. Excitement enough for one day, I feel.'

'Haaa-hhh-t,' intoned Harry.

'Of course, Mrs Jansen,' I replied, somewhat relieved the stress would soon be over. 'We'll leave you both in peace – we wouldn't want to overtax him.'

'Try to rest now, Harry,' said Mrs Jansen gently, laying his head back on a pillow. 'Try to sleep.'

But as the three of us left the room I could hear Harry was having none of it.

'HuuuuuHHHT,' he raged. 'Amft, hut, hut . . .', the sounds pursued us.

Mrs Jansen shut the door and smiled at us. 'That must have been quite an ordeal for you, so unprepared for it. Please don't rush off unless you really have to. At least stay and have some tea with me. You've given Harry such a boost – I'm grateful you came.' Her manner was almost pleading, and Alys and I looked at each other in mutual agreement.

The young girl in the leggings was summoned and Mrs Jansen asked her to prepare us a tray. She brought it forth and disappeared once more. Prettily laid out with china cups, an embroidered tray cloth, tiny fairy cakes and a small pot of flowers, it displayed a delicacy of taste which, I was sure, was Mrs Jansen's own. She must have found it difficult dealing with the rough cut and thrust of Harry's type of politics.

'Actually,' said Mrs Jansen as she poured the tea, 'I'm more than glad you came. Perhaps you can be of help to me as well as Harry.'

She gave us our tea, with plates and napkins to avoid spillage of a fairy crumb.

'I really don't know the purpose of the work you did for my husband,' she said to Alys, 'but from what you said to him it has obviously been perilous. He must have trusted you, and you've shown your loyalty by coming here today. I can tell you were affected by his condition.'

That was an understatement.

She went on: 'That's why I feel I can trust you too. Something has worried me very deeply . . . and . . . and I really don't have anyone else I can turn to.'

We both looked at her questioningly.

She looked down at her fingers as she twisted and untwisted a napkin: 'You see . . . I have a feeling that what happened to Harry was not just out of the blue, as he tried to make out. I think someone was actually trying to harm him, not just steal his money. Someone was trying to get him out of the way.'

'What makes you think that, Mrs Jansen?' asked Alys.

The veins stood out on the backs of her hands as she willed herself to go on. 'It may be sheer silliness on my part, of course. When something like this happens to your husband you rack your brains for someone to blame. But I told you before how driven he'd become in those last few weeks, like he was obsessed with something. He was involved in something out of his depth, that's what I think. He was probably trying to expose some injustice and someone didn't like it.'

'And you've no idea what?' I asked. 'Could it have been something to do with this place, for instance, the rehabilitation centre? Could a former drug addict have told him where he obtained his supplies, and Harry was trying to pin down a pusher?'

She looked at me interestedly. 'It's possible, I suppose . . . although I doubt it. We respect the confidentiality of our clients unless of course they want us to pass information to the police.'

'What else could it be then? When did this "driven" behaviour start?'

'I've tried to think back, and as far as I can recall the first time I really noticed a change in him was with Iain's death. When was that? May, I think.'

'Iain?'

'Yes, Dr Iain Jefferson. He was a consultant at the hospital in Northport. He drowned himself in the sea – it was such a shock. You see, he and Harry had been pals since their student days in Edinburgh, that's where they met.'

I sat, tensed, at this revelation. So there had been more linking Dr Jefferson and Harry than the connection with young Sammy.

'Everyone was absolutely stunned when they heard about Iain,' Mrs Jansen went on. 'He had a wide circle of friends, and we were all devastated. It was so unexpected. But Harry . . . Harry seemed to take it worse than anyone . . . He raged about the house, finding fault with everything, and then he'd be morose and depressed. I almost began to think he was blaming himself. One night he drank more whisky than usual, and I overheard him talking to himself – he didn't realise I'd come into the room. He was muttering over his whisky glass: "I shouldn't've asked him to do it, I shouldn't've put him in that position." I don't know what made me immediately think he was talking about Iain, but I did. He had a piece of paper on the table beside him, on which he must've been writing. When he noticed I was in the room, he scribbled something out furiously. The next morning I noticed scraps of the same paper half burnt in the hearth. He must've meant to throw it on the fire, and been too drunk to aim it properly. Out of curiosity I unscrewed one of the scraps, and I saw Iain's name underneath the scribbling. Above it was an arrow pointing downwards, and above that I could only make out three letters – H, U, R. Then there was another arrow, and at the top, where it was most burnt, I could just see a word

165

which seemed to begin with T. I couldn't imagine what it all meant.'

'Did you ask him?'

'I tried – I tried to talk to him about Iain's death – what he thought led poor Iain to do it. But he wouldn't open up to me, he clammed up as if it was too painful. He was never a man to talk about emotional things anyway. It seemed to embarrass him.'

She smiled ruefully, and then, as if shrugging off her loss, said, 'But it didn't stop me storing away that piece of paper, and thinking about it.'

'And then, when all this happened to Harry, I suppose you began to wonder if it might be significant?' I asked.

'Well, yes . . . it's been worrying me so. That's why I wanted to talk about it to you, to see what you think.'

'But haven't you told the police?'

'Well no, no – it would be like telling them I didn't believe my own husband. I mean, he told them he was pushed from the window by a common thief, after his money. He was so adamant about that . . . and he must have had his reasons. I do trust him, you see. I couldn't betray him now, it would be like going behind his back. But I would like to find out if there's anything more sinister behind all this. It's only his behaviour before the fall, and that screwed-up scrap of paper, that's all I've got to go on. It isn't much.'

'Could you show us the paper?' asked Alys.

'Of course.'

She bent to the handbag beside her chair, unlocked the gilt clasp with a tiny key, and drew out an envelope, which she handed to Alys.

'It's in there,' she said.

It was just as she said, half burnt and crumpled, but underneath the heavy scoring I could make out Jefferson's name, with a T at the top, and in the middle, H, U and R.

Alys and I looked at each other in the same moment, and I voiced what I knew must be in her head: 'D'you think he means Giles?'

She frowned and slowly nodded: 'But why on earth – ?'

'Giles?' queried Mrs Jansen.

'It's the letters H, U, R, Mrs Jansen. We think it could mean the surname of the chief executive of Northport Council. He's called Giles Hurt. Did Harry know him, or have any dealings with him, as far as you know?'

She looked puzzled, frowning. 'No, no, I don't recall the name. But then he meets so many people in the course of his . . . wait a minute . . . could that be the name he was trying to tell us just now, when I thought he was saying his head hurt? Could it be the name Hurt?'

Of course she was right.

I strove to understand the other of Harry's stricken utterings. As well as Hurt he'd been saying what? 'Aft – ? Amt – ? Half?' I pondered out loud. 'Half-finished? Ham-fisted? . . . Armitage!'

Alys snorted: 'Repton Armitage? Frilly Milly's deputy? He's frightened of his own shadow. What could he have to do with all this?'

I tried to picture him as yet another of Sammy's band of customers, but it didn't fit. Armitage was so dull and conventional, I doubted he'd even acknowledge creatures such as Sammy existed.

I thought again, trying to widen the possibilities. A seed of an idea germinated, and then blossomed with sudden energy: 'Perhaps it's not a person at all, but a thing.'

'Thing?' came at me from both sides.

'Or rather . . . Well, remember the name of the company I told you about, Alys, the one that wants to build a sewage treatment plant in Northport?'

'Amphitrite!' she exclaimed. 'Of course, Amphitrite. It fits. Those were the sounds – and Giles is connected with them, isn't he?'

'He's supposed to have set up the contact between them and the resort, yes.'

'You've lost me,' said Mrs Jansen. 'If you're right, what can Harry mean?'

I gritted my teeth, and said candidly, 'I don't know myself, Mrs Jansen. But I think Harry was trying to point us in the right direction. It's all he can do in the state he's in. It's up to us to follow his signposts and see what we find at the other end.'

'We'd better find out if we are on the right track first,' said Alys. 'Let's ask him.'

We went back in to Harry, softly in case he was sleeping. But he was not. It was as if he'd been waiting for us, straining to stay alert. Alys took his good hand.

'Harry, we think we know what you were trying to tell us: Amphitrite and Giles Hurt. Is that right?'

I saw him grip Alys's fingers in his own claw, squeezing till her knuckles were white. His face contorted and I could see he was trying to smile.

'Y-y-ya,' came the noise. 'Amft-t . . . Hahht . . . ya-ya.'

And then he relaxed completely, as if his work was done, he could manage no more. His eyes closed, and while Mrs Jansen soothed and settled him, Alys and I looked at each other. We were right.

As we returned to the living room Mrs Jansen said, 'I'm so glad you came. I haven't known what to do these past few days. My life has been turned inside out since Harry's injury – now at least I feel I've got someone on my side. I've felt so alone at times.'

'We'll do what we can, Mrs Jansen,' I said. She came outside to see us off, seeming genuinely sorry that we must go. She stood in front of the huge oak door, and we left her, waving, a lone, birdlike figure looking lost in the shadow of the gaunt house.

NINETEEN

Alys was livelier on the way back, as if Harry's efforts had recharged her with energy. I, on the other hand, felt weighed down, not just with trying to make sense of Harry's sketchy clues, but with worries about Shelley and my strained relations with Tom. Alys noticed.

'What's up, Ans?' she asked. 'You're very quiet. Did that place remind you of Ralph?'

It had, of course . . . and such memories always had a depressive effect. I decided to share at least part of my anxieties with Alys. I told her about Shelley – how the TV pilot had flopped, and how her new act continued to fall flat in the pier show. Shelley had told me some of the jokes, and I wasn't surprised. Weight problems, fat farms and acne figured largely – somewhat stale female comics' fare in any case – but when delivered by someone as slim and spotless as Shelley, it sounded vain and mean. Her agent was displeased, and now she was dwelling on the coming court case, when she would feel as much in the dock as the rapist. I'd urged her to find a writer, someone young with a fresh approach, so as not to have the double burden of both writing the gags and performing them. This had hurt her pride a little, and I didn't know whether she was taking my advice or not.

'She needs a break,' said Alys. 'She's been on stage since she was in short socks, she's been plugging so hard at the great career, she's never given herself time to relax.'

'I've tried to persuade her to take a holiday,' I said. 'She regards them as a waste of time.'

'Mmmm,' pondered Alys. 'I've had that attitude myself in my time. But I really feel she needs to broaden her experience a bit before she can come up with a good new line of patter. I'll give it some thought, Ans.' She squeezed my shoulder, and I took my gaze off the road to smile at her. She would help if she could, I knew that.

'Now,' she said. 'We need a plan of action if we're to investigate both Giles Hurt and Amphitrite. Take your pick.'

I knew she was changing the subject to stop me brooding about Shelley, but I didn't mind. Giles Hurt was easiest for me to take up, so Alys agreed to explore the Amphitrite angle.

It was possible, she mused, that Amphitrite could be involved in industrial waste as well as sewage. If so, it could be Amphitrite whose toxic cargo was lost in the Irish Sea – her theoretical accident that was hushed up.

'Hang on, Alys,' I said. 'You still don't know if there was an accident, remember.'

'Listen, I'll stick to my theories, you come up with yours. At least it gives me an angle to work on, something to be confirmed or eliminated.'

I wished I had a theory of my own when it came to Giles. I ruminated over the punctilious chief executive and the Northport netherworld in which Sammy moved. The link between Hurt and Amphitrite had seemed strong in Harry's maimed mind. Was he receiving back-handers from the company? And what had been the burnt word above Giles's name on that piece of paper? It was obviously significant, but it began, not with an A for Amphitrite, but with a T – for what? The only T I could think of at the moment was Tom . . . heaven forbid.

The phone was ringing as we entered my flat.

'I'll get it – d'you mind?' asked Alys. 'It's just – it might be Jay.'

'Of course, go ahead. Go on before he rings off,' I replied, knowing she was probably missing him.

But she soon came back to me, unable to shade the disappointment in her voice.

'It's for you. It's Tom Irving.'

I left her in the kitchen searching for something to make us a meal.

'Any joy?' was all Tom's greeting.

'Yes and no,' I replied guardedly. 'We did manage to speak to Harry, after a fashion. He is extremely ill, though, Tom. That is genuine. He's had a stroke, he can barely utter a sound – you wouldn't have been able to interview him at all.'

'A stroke? So did you manage to get anything out of him?'

'Nothing useful, no, not for your purposes,' I lied. I was not prepared to confide in him any further, not now.

He sighed. 'At least you tried. Anyway, forget that for now, I've got some news for you.'

'Good or bad?'

'That depends . . . What are you doing tonight?'

'Oh Tom, I can't. Alys is with me and I—'

'All right, all right, you needn't go on. As it happens I didn't mean you and me.'

'What do you mean then?'

'I mean your blessed Mr Bluebird. We think we've got a suspect. I need you to give us a positive ID.'

'You've caught the flasher?'

'No I didn't say we'd caught him. We haven't got enough on this guy just yet, and I don't want to run the risk of him turning tail as soon as we start sniffing round. It would save a hell of a lot of balls-ache if you could identify him first, before we haul him in.'

I didn't relish the thought of confronting that bullet-head again on my own. 'Will you be with me?' I asked.

'I'll be in the background, put it that way, but I can't actually accompany you. It'll have to be a woman officer. See, this bloke's what's known as an exotic dancer.'

'A dancer? Are you joking, Tom?'

'Not really, but I think he must be. In more common parlance, he's a dangler, a male stripper, m'dear,' he said delicately, as if talking to a maiden aunt. 'He happens to be revealing all at Pharaoh's Club in town tonight – it's their monthly hen night. So you see, I'd look a little out of place.'

'You want me to go along there?' It sounded ridiculous. I couldn't help but laugh.

'That's the idea. If he's your Mr Bluebird we'll give him a hell of a finale. He won't be doing any encores, put it that way.'

He made arrangements for me to meet the woman officer, and with my mind full of that, I hardly took notice of his next few sentences, until I realised, with slowly dawning dismay, what he was saying. 'I'm sorry I walked out on you like that. It'd been a long day, I was tired. Listen, can we forget it? If you knew how much I missed you . . .' I was silent. He went on: 'I think I love you, Anna.'

That was the worst point. The hollow words, meant to let him back in, simply rebounded on him as I refused to respond. I knew he did not love me, any more than I loved him, and I saw such pressure as emotional bribery. He was using me as an outlet from his stale marriage, and I had let my body rule my head. We were both guilty, and the sooner it ended, the better. Yet we still had to work together.

'Perhaps I'll see you soon, Tom,' I said, to gain time.

'I live in hope,' he sighed, and rang off.

I was surprised when Alys said she would come with me that night – I knew it could hardly be her choice of entertainment – but I was glad of the moral support, and realised she probably did not want to stay in alone.

She and I and WPC Marian Eames – in her twenties, she seemed a good sport – peered through the dim lighting of the crowded club, looking for a vacant table. Rigged out in sparkle and glitter – Alys in one of my dresses hastily pinned to fit – we felt self-conscious and artificial.

A touch of the same brittle vivacity seemed to affect the

rest of the women there, who hooted and giggled at the smallest provocation, downing their drinks at a smart pace amid a heavy aura of cigarettes, perfume and hair-spray.

The club's décor fitted the Pharaoh's theme. Above the small stage there was a huge, fiery disc, representing Ra, the Egyptian sun god. The walls looked like slabs from the pyramids, and a frieze of hieroglyphics was painted round them. The furniture was gold-painted and claw-footed, and the lighting was a wavering glow.

The show had not yet started, but a small trio of dicky-bowed musicians played background music – an over-ripe mix of jazz and blues. 'Over there,' shouted Marian above the din, and she pointed to a vacant table under the head of a crumble-faced sphinx. The waiters snaked between the tables, back and forth to the bar, seemingly oblivious to our gestures, tucked away in the sphinx's shadow. They were scantily dressed like Egyptian slaves – smooth-skinned golden boys, who must have shaved their body hair all over. Their stony aloofness was undoubtedly due to the fact that the women – the majority of whom seemed to be in large groups who probably worked together – egged each other on to tweak the boys' bottoms as they bent to serve the drinks, or made suggestive remarks about what they wore beneath their 'kilts'.

The trio finished their set and a mellow-voiced black man stepped forward to introduce the main entertainment: 'Here it is, what you've all been waiting for on Pharaoh's Ladies Night – exclusive, sexclusive, and totally *yours*! Please welcome . . . Miss Mary-lynne Munro!!!' He went off, clapping loudly, and the women, ready to applaud almost anything tonight, enthusiastically joined in. Their claps subsided into oohs and aahs as the lights dipped into ultra-violet and I craned to see the figure on centre stage.

Only the breadth of the shoulders and the knotty calves gave away the fact that this was, in fact, a drag queen – a man dressed, bewigged and made up so winningly to emulate Marilyn Monroe, it almost seemed idolatry. From the platinum hair to the red-lipped smile, this man had her gestures and body language perfectly. He wore a full-skirted white halter-neck dress and teetered on spiky white sandals. Balloon bosoms bulged under the white material.

He came forward to address the audience more intimately, 'Hello girls,' he said, in her breathless, little-girl tones. 'Boy, are we going to have some fun tonight!' His mimicry brought more applause, and he launched into a flirting, flaunting rendition of 'I'm Just A Girl Who Can't Say No', which had the women joining vociferously in the chorus.

I looked questioningly at our policewoman escort, but Marian simply looked back at me with an amused expression in her dark eyes. I was certain this couldn't be Mr Bluebird – he was surely incapable of such feminine subtlety. All the same I stared carefully at the length of neck between Adam's Apple and ear-lobe, but saw no sign of a bluebird tattoo. Mary-lynne stopped singing and started a comedy patter, lewd and crude, delivered with a mixture of coy shock and sisterly gossip. The women loved it, shouting, clapping, urging him on. I looked at Alys, and saw that she was astonished – not at Mary-lynne, but at the reaction of the audience.

Mary-lynne wound up his ribaldry, and finished with another song, 'I Wanna Be Loved By You', in which he stood centre stage like Marilyn over the New York subway grating in *The Seven Year Itch*, his skirts billowing high and wide, revelling in his ersatz femininity. As the song faded he again came to the front of the stage, leaning over the audience, caressing the microphone as he repeated the refrain, 'I wanna be loved by you alo-o-one, goo-goo-ga-joob', and smiling his scarlet smile. Suddenly one of the women in front of him nudged her friend, waved her cigarette in one hand and grabbed her friend's cigarette with the other. Then she stood up as Mary-lynne arched over them and popped each of his balloon breasts with her glowing fag-ends.

Screeching with laughter, the woman called, 'Now we see what you're made of – you're just a fella like all the rest!' The deflated Mary-lynne took his bows, clutching his chest, and disappeared into the wings to mixed clapping and mockery.

Mr Mellow-voice returned, endeavouring to arouse tension for the next act, though the women at the front were still giggling. 'This man, ladies, is all man – a real Action Man!'

'I 'ope not,' taunted a frizzy blonde below him. 'My little Terry's got an Action Man and he ain't got nothing in 'is combat trousers – not even a plastic one. I call 'im No Satisf-Action Man!'

'Ladies, ladies,' persisted the presenter. 'Prepare to take cover – to see him is to desire him, to watch him is to want him – you've heard of Rambo . . . contain yourselves – for here is his bigger brother – *Bambo!!!!*'

Several women around the club put their fingers in their mouths and issued derisive whistles. Deep bass-throbbing music came out of the speakers, like the background score to a war movie. We were plunged into total darkness and a spotlight focused on the centre of the stage. Suddenly a muscular man in camouflage gear leapt into the centre of the light. Grenades hung from his waist and two bullet-filled ammunition belts criss-crossed over his chest. He had a machine gun aimed at the audience, and with a snarling grin he raked it over our heads, its muzzle blazing, blasting out an ear-splitting 'ACK-ACK-ACK-ACK'.

He wore a thick leather studded collar round his neck, and as I strained to see him from our darkened corner, I was sure I recognised that repulsive grin. The hair too, close shaven over the ears, baldness half hidden by a rakish bandanna, seemed the same gingery shade as my Tower-top flasher.

He threw down the gun, moving his body rhythmically to the music and began to unbuckle his ammunition belts. These he proffered as trophies to some of the women nearest the stage. Then he turned his back on the audience, threw a lascivious leer over his shoulder, and tore open the front of his combat jacket, whipping it from his gym-hardened shoulders. His torso bare, he whirled the jacket over his head and flung it at another victim. Obscene lurches of his hips followed as he whipped out his trouser belt and sent it scuttering across the stage. Much muscle-flexing went on before he turned his attention to his fly buttons, unfastening them slowly, one by one, to the steadily mounting chorus of the audience. As the trousers finally eased away down his oiled shanks he turned his back towards us, displaying a hard bottom painfully split by a black G-string.

'Come on, show us what you're made of!' shouted the women. 'Don't keep us in suspense! Come on, Action Man, show us your plastic plonker!'

He kicked away his boots savagely, back still towards us, and left the trousers in a heap as he stepped away. Then he raised his arms to the back of his neck and unbuckled his collar, using it as a prop to play between his legs. Still the jeers came, but he soldiered on, twirling on a climax of the music to reveal what he'd been hiding – a swollen leopard-skin pouch held in place by the G-string. I saw his face inflamed and pulsing at the humiliation he was enduring – and I saw on his neck the exposed bluebird.

"Bout time, you great big tease,' called one of the hecklers. 'Come over here and give us a stroke of your leopard skin.'

Hand still holding his G-string in place, Bambo responded to this bid, sidling over to the woman – whose friends raucously pushed her towards him.

'*Ooooooh*, Carole,' she exclaimed to her neighbour as she touched the codpiece, 'it's just like our hamster, all soft and furry. Here – pass me a peanut, I'll give it a nibble!'

Bambo positively stamped away in indignation. A drum roll heralded the finale of his act. He stood, feet apart in the centre of the stage and, as the drums reached their peak, ripped away his final covering – revealing all too clearly the quantity of padding in the leopard-skin pouch.

'Aaaah, poor darling,' was one response. 'I should take it home and put it to bed, petal, it looks tired out!'

I looked at Marian, she looked at me, and as the women applauded themselves, I nodded. 'That's him,' I said. 'That's definitely Mr Bluebird.'

'That's all I needed to know,' she said, getting up. I rose to follow her, but Alys pulled me back.

'Would you mind hanging on a minute while I go to the Ladies?'

I looked at Marian. 'It's all right,' she said, 'there's no need for you to come with me now. We'll pick him up, and we'll be in touch when we need you. I'd better go.'

I finished my drink while I waited for Alys. I stood up as I saw her returning, but as she approached she shook her head. 'No,' she said, with a look of urgency. 'We can't go yet. Sit down, we've something more to see.'

'What?' But she was already grabbing a waiter and ordering more drinks.

'What on earth – ? What's this all about, Alys?' I demanded as she resumed her seat beside me. 'Have you become a sudden fan of this stuff?'

'Don't be an idiot, there's a reason, and you'll see it soon, I hope. I just saw something when I went to the Ladies that astonished me. The passageway where the loos are, it must lead to the dressing rooms backstage. I lost my way when I came out and went through the wrong door. I found myself in a corridor, and you'll never believe what I saw. Coming out of one of the dressing rooms was this . . . this vision.'

'Are you sure the alcohol isn't having a bad effect on you, Alys?'

'Believe me, Anna, you'll see it. It's all gold, and it has a mask on, and as I watched, Bambo came out of another dressing room and put his arm round it. That's when I looked again at the body underneath the gold, and I

177

thought it was familiar, and then it spoke to Bambo . . . and I'm almost sure, that gold thing was Sammy!'

'With Bambo?'

'Yes, yes, that's what I said, and he must have made a joke because I saw Bambo laughing, and they didn't look like strangers to me. I wanted to be sure, I wanted to see what you think, because it looks like he's coming on stage next.'

'Did they see you?'

'No, I was hidden in a shadow. They went into another dressing room.'

Before I could question Alys any further the lights dimmed and conversation was drowned by a man's voice, issuing in amplified sepulchral tones from the loudspeakers.

'Oh Beings of the twentieth century,' it proclaimed, 'prepare to regress to an earlier life. Spin back through the aeons of darkness and see history reborn. Here in the Pyramid of the Pharaohs, prepare to fall under the mesmeric spell of the Boy King of the ancient Egyptians – here he is, resurrected from his desert tomb – the hypnotic *Tutankhamun* . . .'

An Egyptian sarcophagus emerged from the dark depths at the rear of the stage, slowly pushed forward by loin-clothed slaves. It reached the centre of the spotlight, and the slaves stepped reverently back as the gold lid of the sarcophagus began to rise. Even the chattering women were silenced by the spectacle appearing before them. The Boy King lay in his golden tomb, which was now tilting towards the audience by means of some hidden mechanism. His arms were crossed over his chest, which was naked. He wore only a gold wrap round his waist, which was knotted at the front to reveal a bright jewel winking in his navel. His skin was coated in gold and his nipples were encrusted with florets of gems. He wore a shimmering cloth head-dress, and over his face was a mask of gold.

Slowly, to the evocative Eastern piping of a flute, he opened his arms to the audience and stepped from his bier.

'You are Pharaoh's women,' he said, scanning the audience with his gold mask. 'Put your trust in me, your King.'

He stopped his scanning, and pointed a long, gold claw of a fingernail at a woman at the front – the same woman who had volunteered to stroke Bambo's pouch.

'You,' said the boy. 'Are you willing to be Tutankhamun's handmaiden, to do my bidding and obey my command? Are you ready to take this honour?'

The woman looked hesitant, but her friends urged her: 'Go on, Paula, go on, it'll be a laugh – you can do it.'

Paula nodded her short-cropped, streaky blonde head, and immediately the boy summoned his slaves, who descended to escort her on stage. An Egyptian throne was brought forward for her to sit on, and she clutched at the arms nervously. Then the Boy King approached her.

'Look at me, Paula,' he commanded, and as she did so he lifted the gold mask from his face, 'Look on the face of your master.'

Alys and I looked on the face also – and then looked at each other in recognition: despite the gold face-paint, despite the shimmering head-dress – it was indeed Sammy.

A minion had brought forward an amulet on a silken pillow. It was a glistening pendant which looked like jet, shaped like a scarab beetle and attached to a fine gold chain. The Boy King dangled it before his victim's eyes.

'Watch my sacred talisman, Paula, my handmaiden,' he intoned. 'Watch it swing back and forth in front of your eyes. Slowly, slowly, relax, you are in my keeping. Trust your master, trust me. You are growing heavy, you are growing sleepy. Listen to me, Paula, listen to my voice. You are beautiful, Paula, you are the most beautiful girl in the land. You feel beautiful, you feel languid, you feel the Egyptian sun on your body. And you are the chosen one, Paula. You are happy today, for I have chosen you, of all Pharaoh's women, to be my Queen. Queen of the Nile. How do you feel, Paula?'

The girl's body had gone limp in the chair, but she looked

at him with total trust as she said, 'I feel beautiful, I feel happy. I want to be Queen.'

Her friends in the front row glanced at each other, but there was edginess in their muted laughter. I heard them whisper to each other: 'She's gone under. He's hypnotised her. Do you believe it?'

'Good, Paula,' continued the boy. 'Now, in token of my love for my future Queen, I will invest you with my sacred talisman.' And raising the necklace over her head, he opened it and put it across her shoulders. The jet pendant stood out against her yellow strapless top.

With vacant eyes, she looked down on it and smiled, raising her fingers to touch it. As she did so, a general gasp went up from the audience – for the beetle had started to move. It was not a jewel at all, but real, a living black beetle, the size of a cockroach, and it was crawling up, over her bosom, dragging its chain.

Still she smiled, and looked lovingly up at the Boy King, who stood before her, his arms folded. Not once did she wince as the creature reached the lip of her clothing, and fell over on to her bare skin, continuing its crawl upwards towards her neck, under her jaw, across her mouth and round her ear into her bleached hair.

Her friends were cringing as they watched, grasping each other's arms in horror. One covered her eyes, refusing to look any more.

'Well done, Paula,' said the boy. 'You have taken my sacred creature to your heart. Do you love me, Paula? Would you like to lie on beds of rose petals and bathe in asses' milk? Would you like to be my Queen, Paula?'

'I love you. I want to be your Queen.'

With a sudden sweep he lifted the beetle on its chain from the crown of her head. 'That's a pity, Paula, for I have a fickle soul, and my eye has lighted on another, more beautiful than you.'

He pointed his golden claw into the audience at a slender,

lustrous-limbed black girl who choked on her drink and giggled. The slaves descended and led her to the boy's side.

'How do you feel now, Paula? How can you live with this shame?'

'I can't,' she said, tearfully, her naked shoulders beginning to shake. 'I can't, I can't.' She was not shamming. I began to feel extremely uncomfortable.

'Then do the honourable thing.' He snapped his fingers at an attendant, who came forward with a small gold casket. The Boy King lifted the lid and withdrew something that caused sharp intakes of breath across the room. For wrapped round his hand was a long black scaly creature with glittering eyes.

'Take the snake's kiss, Paula, let the asp assist you into eternity like the Queen of Queens, Cleopatra. Take it, take it.'

And she did. The girl Paula, who had shown so much spunk with Bambo, meekly put her hand out to take the snake from his grasp, and pressed its fanged mouth into her neck.

'The worm,' muttered Alys. 'That's what he must have done to me, only more so, worming his way into my head, making me want to be dead. All a bloody cheap trick.'

For a minute I thought she was going to stand up and loudly denounce him, and I saw the boy's body jerk, flashing a look in our direction as if he too felt the imminence of an uproar. Sharply he turned back to the girl, clapping his hands around her ears and eyes.

'Awake Paula, awake. Be reborn. Take on your new life. Be reincarnated in the twentieth century. Here and now, with your friends in the Pharaoh's Club. Arise and take your bows.'

She seemed to shake her head, look down at the black reptile in her hand, and come to her senses. Recoiling, she threw it across the room, where it fell on a table in front of four women, who screamed. But it lay there, inert. One of them plucked up the courage to touch it. 'Hey, look – it's rubber, it's only rubber!' she shouted. 'It's not real, it's a toy.'

And she lifted it up and shook it. The tension broke amid a burst of laughter and applause. Paula stood up, blinking confusedly, half smiling as if not knowing why people were clapping. The black girl took her arm kindly and drew her in the direction of the steps.

I looked sharply at Alys as the lights came up again and Sammy, having taken his bows, disappeared once more into the wings.

As soon as the applause died down enough for me to speak, I grabbed her arm. 'What were you muttering about, Alys? Worming his way into your head? What d'you mean?'

'It was him, Ans. As soon as I heard that low voice he used on the woman I knew then it was the voice from my nightmares when I disappeared. He must've hypnotised me and then made me suppress it in my subconscious. He plunged me into a black hole and all the time he was twisting my mind to make me have a suicidal breakdown.'

Her eyes were so intense, her neck taut. She was gripped with conviction and anger.

'But why?'

'To keep me out of the way? To make me decide to cancel our research programme? To make me kill myself? Any of those would suit their ends.'

'Why Sammy though? He's only a kid – why would he do it?'

She gritted her teeth. 'He was only being used – I shouldn't be venting my anger at him. You're right, he's just a kid, he's not who's behind all this. He's a corrupted kid, though, he's sold his body, and someone must've wanted him to sell his soul. Probably someone who saw his act recognised his skill could be used for their twisted ends. They must've paid him handsomely to do it and to keep quiet. The way Sammy's lived, I'll bet he'd do anything for money.'

'And Bambo too? He stole Harry's data from me.'

'They were probably both hired to do someone else's dirty work. Doesn't it make you disgusted that such an angelic-looking boy should be debased like that? Bambo I can take – he seems eminently expendable.'

And if the police were now doing their job as I hoped, his time was up.

'Let's get out of here,' I said. 'I've had enough.'

TWENTY

The next day Tom rang while Alys and I were having breakfast to say they had picked up Bambo – real name Gordon King – and they now had him sulking in a police cell awaiting charges of indecency and theft. I told Tom about Sammy and the hypnosis act, and Alys's reaction to it.

He gave a long, low whistle under his breath. 'Jay-sus, that's going to be a hard one to prove . . . she doesn't even know where he took her to do it?'

'No, all she can really remember is the voice, Sammy's voice.'

'Well I'll work on it, I'll try . . . I'll see what Mr Gordon King has got to say about young Sammy. But I can't promise anything. I'm sure pea-brain Patton thinks I've got a thing about the kid. He's already had words about it since he found out I didn't drop that line of enquiry in the Jansen fall case.'

'Well I'll see what I can find out too.'

'You and me together, eh? What a team.'

He laughed, and I laughed too, uncomfortably.

I was working that morning, going straight to a council meeting at the Town Hall. The council was receiving a delegation from NIREX, the government's nuclear waste disposal arm, which was still trying to find a suitable dump site for low-level waste. Northport already had a nuclear fuel enrichment plant within its boundaries, and it was set in a vast acreage of land which was geologically suitable for such an underground 'repository', as the officials called it.

The councillors and a vociferous band of townsfolk would accept no such terminology: to them it was a dump and would always be a dump and they were determined to have none of it. A demonstration had been organised to greet the NIREX delegation on the town hall steps, and I was to cover that as well as the council meeting.

Alys asked if I'd give her a lift to the town hall. Amphitrite had now submitted an outline planning application for its sewage treatment plant, and she reckoned she might be able to find some useful addresses and telephone numbers on the application, which like all such submissions, was open to public view on request.

Sure enough, as we walked up the street after parking the car, we could see a group of about thirty people massed round the town hall steps, holding placards saying 'Dump on your own Doorstep' and 'Northport says No to Nirex'.

'I think I'll hold my own demonstration against alliteration,' said Alys. 'They look like *Sun* headline writers.'

'After all the demos you've been on!' I exclaimed. 'You've done your share of slogan-shouting and placard-waving.'

'I know . . . maybe I'm getting old,' she said.

The protesters were handing out leaflets as the councillors went in. I took a leaflet and asked if the NIREX people had arrived yet. They said not.

I turned back to Alys. 'You may as well go on in,' I said, 'I'll have to stay out here to see what happens. I'm expecting a photographer.'

'No,' she said. 'I'll wait. It'll make a change to be just a spectator at a protest for once. I'm interested to see how they do.'

'I don't think they're quite in your league yet,' I said, looking at the cheaply produced, amateurish-looking leaflet. 'But, come on, you're not really just going to stand by, are you? Surely you want to join them.'

'On another occasion maybe, but I've got other things on my mind today.'

I saw a figure laden with a huge camera bag labouring up the street. I was pleased to see it was Greg and not one of the other photographers. I wanted to talk to him about seeing Sammy the night before.

I left Alys on her vantage point atop a low wall with ornamental flower-tubs that surrounded the town hall. Greg and I went to work on the demonstrators – him taking mug shots while I took their names and any inflammatory quotes I could press them to utter.

We paused when we felt we had enough, and I managed to quickly tell Greg about our visit to Pharaoh's Club, and Sammy being on the bill with Bambo.

His fist tightened hard about his camera and his jaw clenched as he fought to retain self-control.

'I shouldn't let this keep getting to me,' he said grimly. 'I should know what to expect by now with Sammy. He wins you over by acting what you want him to be, and then he goes behind your back and does the opposite. All he cares about is what's in it for Sammy Trickett. I ask you, how can he lower himself like that – prancing about with jewels in his navel?'

I saw through Greg's eyes the tawdry spectacle Sammy had made of himself, compared with the lithe image of perfection Greg had made of him in his pictures.

'Has he ever spoken to you about this Bambo?' I asked.

'Yes – he told me it was all over. Another of his lies. Gordon King's his real name, isn't it?'

'That's the one.'

'Yep, I've heard of him. Gordon was one of the low-life

characters Sammy got involved with when he first came here . . . If truth be told, I suspect Gordon first put the idea in his head of being a rent-boy. He was certainly a drug-dabbler, and he'd been on the game himself. He had a flat, and I know Sammy stayed there when he didn't have anywhere else. Gordon was branching out into the male stripper business, he had stage contacts. Sammy got in on the act, with his hypnosis. He'd prostituted his body, so he had no scruples about prostituting his talent, I suppose. Gordon must've tempted him back – Pharaoh's must pay well for acts like theirs on hen night.' Greg sighed. 'I was expecting too much of him too quickly. I won't give up on him, Anon. I can't. He needs saving from himself. He's worth it. It'll just take more time.'

I began to say I hoped Greg wouldn't need saving from him, but I stopped. Greg knew what he was dealing with in Sammy, he didn't need my warnings.

The revolving door of the town hall began to swing round and my attention was immediately focused on the emerging figure – the tall, slender-suited Giles Hurt. He looked round at the crowd in his slightly superior manner, before descending the steps into their midst. I left Greg kicking his heels against the wall while I went to see if Giles was going to say something to the protesters.

But all I heard him saying as he pressed his way through was 'Excuse me', 'Do you mind', 'I'm so sorry – may I come through?' Even when being jostled, his expression was cool and composed, not a hair of his dark, sleekly trimmed head out of place. Only a shaving nick near his temple gave away the fact that he, like the rest of us, might be subject to human failings. Today's plain, dark navy suit was double-breasted and set off with a small, neatly furled red rose in his lapel. As he reached the edge of the crowd he saw me and smiled, pulling his red handkerchief from his top pocket to dab at his nose, reminding me of gentry holding scented handkerchiefs to their faces to disguise the smell of peasants.

186

'Anna,' he greeted me. 'The populace seems to be revolting. Please rescue me with some civilised words, I'm getting rather tired of rant and cant.'

'They have a right to make their views known, Giles.'

'Oh, indeed, I don't doubt it, but sometimes I think we take democracy too far – I can hardly get my job done for protests and petitions.'

I saw he was being deliberately provocative, with his tongue figuratively but firmly in his cheek.

'I've come to see that our guests have a safe passage through,' he said. 'They're a little late. I wonder if they've seen what awaits them and decided to bide their time. Isn't that your Groundswell friend over there?'

'It's Alys, yes.'

'She's not joined up with this little local lot, has she?'

'No, no . . . she's just come to watch.'

'I see.'

He moved away, and I saw that he was walking towards Alys. I followed in his scented wake. She was still standing on the wall, and as I approached I saw him reach up to kiss her hand and hold her arm as she descended like a lady from a carriage.

'We wouldn't want to encourage the more oafish elements to emulate your wall-climbing and damage the flowers,' he was explaining. Only I caught the fleeting loathing in Alys's face at his obsequious treatment.

Giles turned back to look despairingly at the crowd. 'I'm afraid the NIREX delegation will have a wasted journey today,' he said. 'The closed minds you see before you are but a reflection of those in the council chamber.'

'Do you think there should be a dump here, Mr Hurt?' asked Alys, sharply.

'There has to be one somewhere, my dear. Some provision has to be made for the waste we have generated.'

'Yes, but not an underground dump,' said Alys emphatically. I knew she could not resist joining in such a campaign. 'What's needed is a secure ground-level storage facility where it can be monitored for dangerous emissions, and easily retrieved when science – *if* science, I should say – finds a proper way of rendering it harmless. To simply seal it away in an underground coffin is like leaving a time bomb for future generations. It's like burying your head in the sand along with it.'

'That's all very idealistic, my dear, but the fact is the waste is mounting up and it needs a disposal facility urgently.'

'The fact is it's sheer madness to go on producing the stuff when we haven't a clear idea of how to cope with the waste we've got.'

'But there are clear ideas,' he said, dropping his usual affectation, which made me think he felt very strongly about the subject. 'Other countries have developed a sophisticated technology in terms of disposal. Underground repositories provide the best protection – the longest pathways back to man. But NIREX faces such hostility in this country that one begins to doubt whether any repository will be allowed anywhere. Nobody has the political courage to say, yes, we'll have the best storage facility available, yes we'll spend as much money as it takes and yes, we'll put it there. It's not only the Not In My Back Yard syndrome, it's Not In My Term Of Office.'

'And that,' I commented, 'means from the PM right down to the good burghers of Northport who are going to throw in their four penn'orth today.'

'Exactly,' he said. 'My lords and masters.'

Alys was standing in front of him, and he looked up, over her head.

'I'm sorry, ladies, duty calls, I'm afraid. Here are our visitors from NIREX.'

He darted forward, but the protesters had already seen the large, official-looking car draw up and three men, carrying briefcases, get out of it. The NIREX name was seen clearly on a document case under the arm of one of the men, who all looked somewhat daunted by the approaching mob.

Riled by Giles, Alys could no longer stop herself joining the protesters. She pushed through the crowd, and began shouting her message about surface storage in front of the three NIREX men. Giles was angrily trying to make a passage for his charges through the shouting people. Alys obstructed their path and I saw him push her shoulder. Still she refused to give ground but the three men behind Giles were pressing forward. Alys moved backwards up the steps in front of Giles. When they got to the revolving door she stood still, and Giles, in frustration, pushed her into one of the door's compartments and got in with her to force it round. They both disappeared from view.

Greg had rejoined me, and as the crowd dispersed we made our way up the town hall steps unimpeded. We pushed through the revolving door, and the first thing I saw on the other side was Alys, sitting on the marble-tiled floor with her back against a column.

Someone had given her a glass of water which she was drinking thirstily.

'Alys, are you all right?' I said, rushing over to her in alarm.

'Yes, yes,' she replied, but her face was pale, her lips white.

'What happened?'

'I just fainted, I fainted, that's all,' she said, loudly so that people round her could hear. Then she lowered her voice to a near whisper, for my ears only. 'It was because I was cramped in that confined space with Giles Hurt.'

'In the door? What did he do?'

'Nothing dishonourable, don't worry. It was his smell, Anna, I knew it reminded me of something outside, but I couldn't place it. There, in the door, it was so strong, the memory overpowered me.'

'Memory? What memory?'

'From my nightmare, from my black hole, my lost days

with Sammy and his damned hypnosis. That smell was there. And it's not a common aftershave, is it? I've never smelt anything like it. I'm sure he must have been there, Anna. I'm positive.'

TWENTY-ONE

Giles was now my prime quarry. I needed to hunt down every detail I could find about him, any hint he was involved in something surreptitious, any inkling he was not all he seemed. I started on home ground – in the *Evening News* cuttings library.

In a free half hour later in the day, I went and asked for the file on Giles Hurt. While I waited for the girl to find it, I reflected on the way he had conducted himself at that morning's council meeting, with the NIREX representatives. Never at any point in the noisy, emotional debate did he betray a trace of opinion on the matter. Though I knew how much he must have wanted to bang certain of the more obtuse and vociferous councillors' heads together, he remained tightly impassive, giving advice only on points of order. Only at the end, when the vote showed an overwhelming majority against the dump plan, did his fine features lose their neutrality as he glanced at me for one second, as if to say 'I told you so'.

I looked back to the cuttings from when he had first joined the council, a couple of years before. Someone had interviewed him about his background for a profile, and it gave brief biographical details. He was the only child of an army colonel and his non-working wife, born while his father was serving with the British Army on the Rhine in Germany.

From the age of eleven he had been sent to boarding school in England, and emerged with a scholarship to Cambridge, where he studied law and economics. After that there followed a series of appointments with various councils; at each stage he climbed a rung up the promotion ladder until his present position as chief executive. So far, so unenlightening.

Only his German birth marked him out from the ordinary, and indeed I had heard him speaking German fluently to civic visitors from Northport's twin town, a resort near Hamburg. He had been instrumental in setting up the twinning arrangement, twelve months ago.

I looked more closely at his earlier periods of office with other councils. He had, it seemed, started to promote links between private enterprise and local authorities early in his career, developing an expertise which had greatly eased his path to promotion. Bearing in mind Harry's stress on Amphitrite, I looked for previous links with the company, indicating a perhaps suspicious tie. But the cuttings were no help. Other companies were mentioned, but not Amphitrite. Had he left local authority employment at some time, worked in the private sector, and there come into contact with Amphitrite?

I counted up the years spent with each council, and found that all were accounted for, except one. This, I calculated, must have been the year after he left university. He must have taken a year out. What did he do?

I put the cuttings back in their folder and wondered where else I could look to piece together the man's life. I had made a list of all the councils he had worked at, and their dates as far as I could deduce them. At least it was a start. Could I possibly ring all the local newspapers in each of those areas and ask what library cuttings they had on Giles Hurt – in the guise of preparing, perhaps, a special biographical feature? Of course I could. I would, but it was getting late. I'd start tomorrow.

When I got home I found Alys packing her bags.

'I'm off to London tomorrow, Ans,' she said. 'There's not much more I can do here. I've got Amphitrite's official address, and I'm going to check out the Companies House files to see if there's anything of significance there – I might find out what other business it's involved in.'

I felt a sudden pang at the thought of her leaving, and she stopped midway through folding a shirt, as though she felt it too.

'Don't worry Ans,' she said, 'I'm not going to let myself be kidnapped again – this lady will vanish no more. Hey, before I go though, I'd like to talk to Shelley. I've had an idea to try and help her.'

'Really? What exactly?'

'Well, I know you said she wouldn't take a holiday, but I still think she needs to get out in the world for a bit. She's already shown some interest in Groundswell – d'you think she'd go on a Groundswell campaign if I asked her? I mean, we're doing a lot of work to save the dolphins out in the Pacific and the Tasman Sea – they get stuck in the drift nets and die in their thousands. She could help on one of our boats, it'd be a totally new experience, and it'd get her out of the country while that court case goes on.'

I sat on the bed next to Alys and thought about it. It was a good idea for her to get away. It might open her eyes to fresh targets for humour – blinkered governments and rapacious commerce – and above all it would draw her out of the unhealthy self-obsession that had long troubled me. At the end of the season's contract she could afford to take the time off, and afford the break financially.

'But she's got no expertise,' I said. 'How could you use her?'

'We need support crew, deck-hands, like any ship,' said Alys. 'She'd soon get the hang of it. What d'you think?'

'Yes,' I said. 'Ask her tonight – I'll ring her. I only hope she takes it up – you may need all your powers of persuasion.'

'Don't worry,' she said. 'I know how to pitch it. Think of all the publicity angles, the jokes to be had out of trying to stay upright in a Force 9 gale. Lord, the papers'll be queuing up to hear her story.'

I hugged her. 'What's that for?' she said.

'Just for being you. Don't dare disappear again, you hear?'

Shelley didn't turn down the idea out of hand, as I'd feared. But neither did she leap at it. I sensed that so much was worrying her at the moment, she needed time to think it over – but I also knew the thought of an escape hatch when the court case came up was a real temptation. I didn't push it. I knew too well that forcing my own views on her simply had a negative reaction. The offer was there, I felt happier for it, but she had to make her own decision.

The next day, after Alys had gone, I used my spare moments at work to ring round the local newspapers in the towns where Giles had worked previously. There were five in all, ranging from Surrey to South Wales. I worked through them chronologically, going back from the one immediately before Northport. I quickly found that not all newspapers were as thorough as ours – from the first four I gleaned nothing I didn't know already – and the calls were arousing threatening glares from Ellis Clancy, wondering what I was up to. The name of Amphitrite had not come up at all, in any of the cuttings that were laboriously read out to me.

I had to break off as Ellis came over with a complicated eviction story for me to cover, involving a long interview with a tearful mother thrown out of her dingy flat with three children in tow. So it was a long time before I could get back to ring the last newspaper on my list, and by the time I did so it was obvious that the librarian at the other end had had a bad day, and wanted to get home, and a call like mine just on finishing time was the last straw.

Nevertheless she grudgingly did what I asked, and rattled through the information so fast that my shorthand could not keep up. It was on the third cutting that I inwardly shouted 'hallelujah!' It was evidently a chatty, diary piece on the exploits of the new young town hall legal assistant, who had joined them after spending a year working for a private company – in Germany. So that was the secret of the lost year. He had worked, it said, for the firm of Rumerstein, a waste-disposal company near Mainz, in their legal department – a contact made through a friend of his father.

The name meant nothing to me, but its line of business did. It was evidence, however tenuous, that Giles Hurt was no stranger to disposal companies.

Meanwhile Alys had been delving into Amphitrite's antecedents at Companies House. She rang me that night.

'I'm off to Germany, Anna,' she said, before I could begin to tell her any of my findings.

'You've found a German connection too? What is it? Tell me – not a company called Rumerstein?'

'No – what's that?'

'I'll tell you in a minute. What have you found out, first?'

'OK – Amphitrite isn't a British firm at all, although it operates to all intents and purposes as one. In fact it's a subsidiary of a giant multinational based near Hamburg, called the Tethys Corporation. As soon as I saw that, alarm bells began to ring in my mind. Tethys is a huge conglomerate, a holding company with its fingers in all sorts of businesses – chemicals, gas, oil and they run a nuclear power station. I know that German Groundswell has been suspicious that all's not above board with that company for some time. They've mounted an undercover surveillance operation. But quite what their suspicions are yet I just don't know, and I'm going over there to find out.'

'Well let me give you something else to find out about too, while you're there. Giles Hurt spent a year working in

Germany for this Rumerstein company, based in Mainz. It's into waste disposal, just like Amphitrite.'

'We need to find out if there's a link – right?'

'You've got it.'

The corporation she mentioned seemed familiar to me. 'Tethys . . .', I mused out loud. 'The Tethys Corporation – haven't they got a gas-drilling rig in the Irish Sea?'

'They have, yes. That's what made me even more convinced we're on the right track. Harry kept insisting we go back into the area of the gas field with the sonic survey. And there's something else, Anna. Remember the burnt piece of paper with Harry's writing on it that Mrs Jansen showed us?'

'Yes.'

'Well? The remains of a word at the top, with an arrow leading down to H, U, R, and below it to Jefferson?'

'Of course . . . it began with a T . . . It must be—'

'*Tethys!*' we said in unison.

'So what do you think he meant?' I asked.

'It looks to me as though Harry believed Tethys was putting some sort of pressure on Giles, or working through him.'

'But why?'

'That's for Harry to know and us to find out,' she said. 'Happy hunting, Anna.'

'You too.'

TWENTY-TWO

The mention of Harry's half-burnt piece of paper made me think back to the circumstances in which Mrs Jansen had said she saw him crouched over his whisky glass, writing.

He had been muttering something, she said, something she was sure referred to Dr Jefferson. It was, as far as I could recall, 'I shouldn't've asked him to do it, I shouldn't've put him in that position.'

The question was, what position did he mean? I wondered if Mrs Jefferson, that poor widow, half-demented with her grief, could shed any light on it. I wondered if she would remember me from the inquest. I took a chance on it, looked up the number in the directory, and rang. I was nervous as I waited for an answer – maybe she would not want to go back over her husband's death, raking up embers which could flare again. But I knew myself, having gone through the experience, that widows often want to talk about the departed – it was other people who shied away out of embarrassment or a misplaced sense of tact.

I took a deep breath as I heard the phone picked up at the other end. It was her, and she sounded much calmer than when I had last seen her. She listened carefully while I told her of the impression she had made on me after the inquest, how worried I had been about her husband's letter, and her conviction that it did not mean he was overworked. I said I would now like to talk to her, to see if I could find out what actually had happened.

I heard her give a long sigh.

'I would like to talk about it, yes,' she said, 'I really would. It will make a change to speak to someone who doesn't talk down to me as if I'd lost my brain as well as my husband. Perhaps I was too emphatic when it happened, perhaps if I'd wept quietly instead of shouting at the police they'd have taken me seriously.

'But to be honest I've just taken some sleeping pills, I'd be no use at all to you tonight. Come round tomorrow, about four o'clock, I usually take tea then.'

The house, as I drove up to it the next day, was set in a prosperous avenue where the cars in the driveways were Volvos, Jaguars and BMWs. It was a large, red-brick Edwardian-looking home, which hid its frontage behind a mass of trees in full foliage. I rang the doorbell and it was quickly answered by Margot Jefferson herself.

'Well,' she said, smiling. 'At least my hysterics at the inquest had one good outcome – they brought you here. I think Sonia was quite ashamed of me, the scene I made. Well, as you can see, I'm a bit calmer now. Come on through, it's such a nice day, I've put a table out in the garden.'

The house, from what I saw of it, was traditionally furnished with a great deal of care. The wood was highly polished, the Persian carpets spotless, and someone had a good eye for antiques.

The garden too was obviously cared for – professionally, I guessed – for its long, undulating lawn was neatly trimmed around luxuriant flowerbeds, and the tall trees gave a perfectly judged amount of shade.

We sat under a willow, where Margot Jefferson poured me tea and offered home-made shortbread. She seemed inordinately pleased when I complimented her on the garden.

'It was a labour of love for Iain,' she said. 'He planned it and pottered round in it, when he could, although of course later on he didn't have so much time and we hired a man to come in twice a week.'

He had been happy at home, I thought – this was no cold, spurning wife I was talking to. She spoke of him with warmth, with affection. She had a slight Scottish lilt to her voice which I found pleasant to listen to, and she had obviously taken care to dress neatly in a plaid skirt and crisp blouse, with her hair recently, tightly permed. She looked like a woman who had pulled herself together.

'I'm glad you've come,' she said, in a tone which implied that a 'but' was to follow. I knew what she wanted to ask me: Why now? Why not sooner?

'I've been to see your husband's friend, Harry Jansen,' I said, deciding I need not treat her with kid gloves. She would either know what I meant, or she would not, and that was an end of it.

'Ah,' she said, in such a guarded manner that I feared she might clam up. 'And what has Harry told you?'

'He's still very badly affected by a stroke. He can hardly talk. But his wife told me, before the fall happened at the hotel, she said he seemed terribly concerned about Iain's death. He seemed to blame himself in some way.'

'And well he might,' responded Margot bitterly, 'and well he might.'

'What d'you mean?'

She pursed her lips, reminding me strongly of a Scots Presbyterian teacher I'd once had, full of old-fashioned moral wrath.

'He had a hold on Iain,' she said. 'He's a damnable, despicable man. It started in Edinburgh, when they were students, and it's carried on all through our married life.' Her eyes glittered coldly. 'Iain was always a gentle man, and when he was young he was shy – especially with women. He'd gone to a male boarding school, he had no sisters, and when he came to university he was an innocent where women were concerned. They frightened him, he shied away from them and fell in with a pretty racy crowd of young men, a decadent bunch whose ringleader was Harry. I met Iain in his second year. I was friendly rather than flirty, and I didn't frighten him away. He was already beginning to recoil from the antics of that crowd, and I seemed to him a kind of rescuer, he found he could talk to me. He confessed to me he was homosexual, and to him that was a source of shame. He was relieved when I said that didn't upset me, and he was grateful too. You see I liked Iain despite all that, and I thought he would change. He cared what conventional people thought of him – his family would've been horrified if they'd known – and Iain wanted a normal, decent family life, with marriage and children.

'Well Iain did change, and we did have a normal, decent family life, all except for one interference – Harry Jansen. I never trusted him, never, but Iain would brush off my criticisms, he wouldn't hear a wrong word about him. He'd break off family arrangements if Harry wanted him, he'd dash off at a moment's notice . . . Harry still had a hold over him, you see, right from those early days before I knew him. Harry called the tune, and he had Iain dancing to it whenever he wanted. When Harry became a Euro-MP he was too busy to bother Iain so much. I was relieved. But then suddenly it started again, worse than before. In those last few months he was on the phone constantly; I couldn't get rid of the man. Even when I was downright rude, he'd still ring back, or he'd ring Iain at work and catch him there. Poor Iain was run ragged, no wonder Harry Jansen blamed himself. Hah! At least he does have some conscience then!'

'But why was he ringing him so much? Have you any ideas?'

'Ach, he was always asking Iain to do blood tests and such for that addiction clinic of his – on the cheap, you know, typical Harry. But then there was something else. Something more serious.'

She broke off, looking troubled. I waited while she shaded her eyes as if trying to remember something, or trying to decide whether to speak at all. Finally she looked up again, facing me squarely.

'I know I shouldn't have done it,' she said, 'but sometimes I used to eavesdrop on those conversations, I felt so uneasy about Harry. A couple of times I listened, and one night I heard Iain actually arguing with him – which hardly ever happened. 'You just don't know what you're asking me, Harry,' he said. 'A doctor can't do that, it's against all medical ethics.' And then there was a pause while Harry must've been arguing back, saying Iain must do whatever it was, for this reason or that reason. Iain still stood his ground, and they raged back and forth. Then suddenly it was as if Iain crumpled. Harry must have said something to him that was so decisive it broke all Iain's resistance. His voice became resigned, and he began to ask Harry what he wanted to know.'

'And what was it?'

'I couldn't really gather much, but it seemed to be to do with divers – the word "divers" kept cropping up again and again. I knew Iain was treating a couple of deep-sea divers at the time, they'd been brought to hospital after an accident in the gas field, and apparently they had some long-term blood problems. German I think Iain said they were. I gathered Harry wanted Iain to ask them questions about the accident, and about the gas field, and to pass their answers on to him. I couldn't imagine why he wanted to know such things, but it really rattled Iain. He cared profoundly about patient confidentiality.'

I remembered the accident – we had reported the airlift of the stricken divers from the gas field. Equipment failure had been blamed, and they were said to be suffering from the bends. But did Harry suspect there was more to it than the official explanation? That would fit in with Alys's theory that there'd been a catastrophe someone was trying to cover up. Was Harry trying to ferret out the truth by pressuring Iain Jefferson to pry secrets from his patients?

'It wasn't till after Iain was dead,' Mrs Jefferson was going on, 'that the significance of that argument with Harry really struck home. It suddenly hit me that it had been a turning point. His manner changed, he became angry whenever I mentioned Harry's name. The trouble with that suicide letter was . . . it was so ambiguous . . . you could read into it whatever you wanted. But to me it was clear as day. After our marriage we never discussed his early homosexual experiences, Iain wanted to put all that behind him. But Harry Jansen brought it all up again. I'm convinced that's what Harry must've used to get what he wanted out of Iain – the threat of exposure. He thought it would have blighted his career, not to mention his relationship with our sons. He couldn't face it, it was too much for him to bear.' Her hand shook as she drank some tea. 'But he wouldn't talk about it, not even in his suicide note. So all we got was that veiled explanation, and everyone else took it to mean he was overworked.'

'Did you tell the police your suspicions, Mrs Jefferson?'

'Yes, of course I told them. But Harry was still in perfect working order then – able to bamboozle them, pull the wool over their eyes. He made them believe I was making it all up – the delusion of a grief-deranged mind. He laid it on about how much extra work Iain had been doing for the addiction clinic. He denied everything I said about the divers, denied he'd ever asked Iain to interrogate them.' She smiled ironically. 'He's a real politician all right – they turn everything on its head to suit themselves. So he steered the police towards the overwork theory, and Iain's colleagues at the hospital backed it up because they want more staff. No one took me seriously.'

'I take you seriously.'

'Thank you, dear, I can see you do. And it's a relief to talk about it to someone who does understand. It's funny, when everyone else treats you indulgently, as if you're slightly demented, you begin to wonder about it yourself, sometimes.' She sighed. 'The pity of it is, it all happened so long ago – Iain's fancy for boys – and I came to terms with it even before we married. I'm sure our sons would've understood too, after the first shock – they're not narrow-minded – if only he'd told them.'

'Have you told them?'

201

'Yes – but I just get that indulgent treatment from them too. Harry blackmailing their father, it sounds so far-fetched, they don't know what to believe, and I can't prove anything.'

'Well, I hope I can help in some way, Mrs Jefferson.'

'I hope you can too – but beware Harry Jansen – I wouldn't trust him, even helpless with a stroke. Damnable man! He drove my husband to his death just as sure as if he held him underwater himself. Oh God, it was all such a waste. Not even Iain's colleagues would have held such a thing against him, so long ago, not in this day and age . . . he could've carried on working. It was all in Iain's head, his shameful past come back to haunt him . . . he just couldn't cope . . . and I couldn't help him.'

I took her hand to try and offer comfort. As it trembled in my clasp I couldn't bring myself to mention Sammy. To tell her Iain's fancy for boys had extended till his death would only hurt her more. And what good would it do? Iain was gone whatever ultimately drove him to it, and I was sure she was right about the bulk of the blame. All I could do was give her the comfort of believing her, and that I did, till her trembling calmed and we walked back to the house in the evening sun.

TWENTY-THREE

At my flat that night I tried to pore over Mrs Jefferson's revelations. But Shelley came round, telling me she'd decided to take up Alys's idea of working on the Ground-swell campaign. I was surprised how relieved I felt, especially when I saw her real enthusiasm. She wasn't just looking on it as an escape, but as a positive new direction, and I was grateful for that. I was perfectly aware that dying dolphins and threatened turtles could become the next vehicle for Shelley Chantelle's showtime, but they stood to gain from that. And so did she.

When she'd gone I felt hollow, plagued now by nagging thoughts of Tom and how to extricate myself as gracefully as possible from the affair. Finally I decided I couldn't possibly concentrate on Mrs Jefferson, and neither could I deal with Tom. To hell with graceful – I poured myself a stiff gin to drown the pesterings. I was tired. I didn't want to think any more.

But before I could sit down, the phone rang. It was Alys, her voice strained and urgent.

'Ans, I'm at Manchester Airport. I had to leave Germany in a hurry and I haven't much cash. How much is a cab back to your place?'

'A cab? Don't bother about that, it'd be a fortune. I'll come and pick you up. What happened?'

'It's too long to tell you on the phone – I've no more change.'

'OK, save it for the journey. I'll meet you at the information desk in the arrivals hall. I'll be down there just as soon as I can.'

I put the gin down, untouched, and raced down the motorway to Manchester.

Alys was waiting, looking travel-worn, with just a small canvas bag and an expensive-looking camera which she guarded against her like the crown jewels.

'Let's get out of here,' she said as soon as she saw me.

Once back on the motorway, headed for home, she started talking. The story came out in spurts, as though she was still trying to assimilate what had happened.

'When I got to Hamburg I made contact with one of our main organisers, he's called Gunther Metz. I asked him what they knew about the Tethys Corporation.'

I nodded, trying to keep half my mind on the traffic blazing past us through the night.

'Gunther said they suspected Tethys was illicitly dumping toxic waste. His group had recently had a breakthrough. They'd managed to infiltrate a Groundswell member on to the transport staff at Tethys. Hermann something . . . I can't remember his surname.'

'It doesn't matter. Carry on.'

'Hermann was working for them, co-driving a lorry down to somewhere in Southern Europe and back, taking a load to a Tethys chemical plant near Hamburg.' She rubbed her eyes before going on.

'Gunther's group had already mounted a secret watch on the traffic going in and out of that plant. A sympathiser let them use his house on the access road. They were taking photographs of the lorries and their number-plates, so that the Groundswell network could report sightings and track their movements. That way they could find out where the loads were picked up, whether it was likely toxic waste was involved, and where it was taken to.'

'You think they're dumping it on unlicensed sites – or perhaps sites only licensed for the less poisonous stuff?'

'It's possible – it would save them money. They could even be shipping it to sites in England.'

'Through the Irish Sea? Ah . . . your theory about the cargo overboard – the accident you thought Harry was trying to pin down?'

'Yes – I told Gunther, and he was alarmed. It could be true. Anyway, he took me to this house, where they were keeping watch. We parked the car down a side road and went into the house. It was only about a hundred yards from the main gate into the Tethys plant.

'We were there a couple of hours. The camera was rigged up behind a curtain, taking pictures of each lorry going in or out. Gunther had binoculars. As we saw one lorry approaching the plant, with yellow and black containers on it, he suddenly said: "This is Hermann, it's Hermann's load

– I can see him in the passenger seat." They photographed it as it went by, but when it got to the gates, instead of stopping only momentarily, like all the rest, we could see a car screech up from inside the plant, and two men got out, pulling Hermann from the cab. Gunther was looking through the field-glasses, and he said, "I know one of those men. He's head of security, from Tethys headquarters – they've got Hermann!" They bundled him into the car, and it sped down the road towards us, the girl on the camera was taking pictures all the time. We just had time to see Hermann's frightened face. He was alone in the back seat, and as they passed the house where he knew we were, he put his palm flat against the car window. We could see there was writing on it, but we couldn't see what – they were going too fast. Then I heard the squeal of brakes, and Gunther said, "Damn, they're coming back, they're looking at the house, they must've seen what he was doing." And he grabbed the camera and threw it at me. "Take it, Alys," he said, "take the car and drive as far away as you can. They don't know you here. I'll stay and keep them busy. Go out the back way. Drive!" He threw me the keys and I ran. The only route I knew was to the airport, so I got there and took the first flight I could to England.'

'And here you are.'

'Here I am – and more important, here's the camera, with the film still inside it. I only hope it got the writing on Hermann's hand. Does Greg do blow-ups in his dark-room?'

'I'm sure he does,' I said. 'We'll see, anyway, first thing in the morning.'

We roused Greg from his bed at seven in the morning to ask if he would develop the film. On the phone he was drowsy, too bemused to ask questions, but he said yes, and as soon as we got there we plied him with coffee to get him going. He was certainly wide awake some time later when we heard him shout from the dark-room: 'Eureka! I don't know what we've got, but we've got it!'

Alys and I shot up the stairs and saw him, standing in

the doorway of the dark-room, the picture still dripping in
his hand. Blurred and shaken though the image was we
could still see, written on three lines across Hermann's
palm:

KERN
KRAFT
MÜHL

'Nuclear waste,' said Alys, staring at me. 'They're dealing in nuclear waste. Oh God, the horror . . .'

Greg broke the silence with, 'Well, I reckon you two owe
me a breakfast. Where're you taking me?'

We went to one of the large hotels on the seafront. Greg
tackled a mound of scrambled eggs and toast while I
crumbled a croissant, waiting for Alys to come back from
the phone. She was ringing Gunther Metz in Germany.

Relief was in her face as she returned to the table.

'Gunther's OK – and so's the girl who was taking the
pictures,' she said. 'One of the Tethys men burst into the
house just as I was leaving. He didn't see me go, Gunther's
sure of that. This brute started asking questions: who they
were, whose house it was, what they were doing. When he
didn't get the right answers he started turning the place
over, but Gunther grabbed the phone to ring the police. He
got hit in the jaw when the man punched the phone out of
his hand, but it did the trick – the guy left before he could
find any evidence of what we were doing. They've still got
Hermann, though,' she said pensively.

'Did you tell him about the nuclear waste?'

'Yes . . . we've a Groundswell member on one of the
customs points that the lorry was driven through: Hermann's load was listed as scrap metal.'

Greg stopped mid-mouthful: 'So what the hell could they
be doing with undercover consignments of nuclear waste?'

'I shudder to think,' said Alys. 'But with a company like
Tethys one thing's for sure, they wouldn't do it unless

206

there was an awful lot of money to be made. It's easy to see how some countries would pay a fortune just to have their nuclear waste taken away. Nobody wants that stuff on their doorstep, nobody knows what to do with it properly. If Tethys came along offering discreetly to get rid of it for them, I can see they'd leap at it – and keep quiet. Whatever premium Tethys is charging, it has to be cheaper for them than storing the stuff for centuries on end.'

'But the question is, where does it end up?' I said.

'Could be anywhere – anywhere someone values money above lives, or anywhere people are too ignorant to know the risk. Chemical waste has been dumped in Third World countries – Tethys is quite capable of exploiting them to dump nuclear too.'

'It doesn't bear thinking about.'

Nevertheless we sat, thinking about it, in mounting depression until Alys said: 'Oh, Gunther had some news on the Rumerstein company, by the way, the one that Giles Hurt worked for.'

'Yes?'

'It was one of four companies which merged twelve years ago to form . . . guess what?'

'I can't – tell me.'

'The Tethys Corporation.'

I took a deep breath: 'So Giles could have links with Tethys – his old employers with a new name. I wonder . . . there were some mutterings among the councillors not long ago about Giles spending a lot of time away on twin-town business. It was him who really set up the twin-town link.'

'Where's the twin town?' asked Alys.

'About forty miles from Hamburg.'

'Bingo,' said Alys. 'The perfect cover for visits to Tethys.'

'You should spell your name like Alice in Wonderland,' said Greg, wiping his beard on a napkin, 'this whole thing gets curiouser and curiouser.'

I checked my watch and checked it again in disbelief: 'At the risk of sounding like the White Rabbit, Greg, we mustn't be late. We're supposed to be at work in two minutes flat.'

'Sod it,' said Greg, scraping his chair back. 'This is much more fun than work.'

'It's no Wonderland, Greg, believe me,' said Alys. 'Go on, you two, earn your crust – I'll make my own way back.'

TWENTY-FOUR

I had to find out more about Giles Hurt, and whether he was really working for the Tethys Corporation. I badgered the industrial correspondent for background on the conglomerate. He was an ageing journalist, perpetually harassed. He waved vaguely at his filing cabinet. 'Sorry – I've got a lot on. All bumf I keep in there. You're welcome to rifle my drawers.'

He had no filing system. I spent ten minutes sorting through sheafs of promo leaflets, press releases and company reports. Finally I found a glossy booklet wedged at the back of a drawer, its cover torn. Tethys Corporation Annual Report, I read. It was five years old. Quickly I leafed through it till I found a list of Tethys subsidiaries. No mention of Amphitrite there – too new perhaps – but two other company names looked familiar. I went back to the cuttings library to check Giles's file. I was right. He'd brought them in on co-operative ventures with his previous councils.

I had to find a way into his secret life. The more I

thought about it, the more I concluded that my only opening lay with Sammy.

Tom had failed to get any information out of the boy – but his rough tactics would always fail with a character like Sammy. I had a feeling I could engineer a way into his confidence that Tom never could. I would appeal to two facets of his make-up – vanity and greed.

Alys had said Sammy would do anything for money, and I suspected she was right. But I also sensed it would take a sizeable amount to tempt him to divulge all we wanted to know; after all, he knew what had befallen Jefferson and Jansen – his life could be at risk. If, however, in addition to the money, we could offer him a brief flare of fame – then maybe the bait would be hard for him to resist.

It was time for me to make a foray into chequebook journalism. This was way out of the Northport *Evening News'* league. But I knew the Northern news editor of a national Sunday tabloid – he'd worked on our paper a few years before. The story would appeal to the Sunday's appetite for sex and scandal. I rang him. How would he like the confessions of a rent-boy with certain 'friends' in high places? He would; he wanted more details. I gave them. He was interested, very interested. I asked how much they'd be prepared to pay. The answer was enough, I guessed, to tempt young Sammy. He would send one of his reporters as soon as I could set up a meeting. I thanked him and rang off.

My next task was to tackle Greg. Sammy had reappeared on his doorstep a couple of days after his Pharaoh's appearance. Greg was struck by how cast down the boy was, miserable and depressed, as if brooding on something. It seemed the change had come over him since Gordon King's arrest – as if the risks he had been taking finally hit home. Greg was doing his best to draw him out of it by working with him in the dark-room, making pictures. I reckoned Greg was my best bet for persuading Sammy to be interviewed by the tabloid reporter. I put it to him. We were sitting in the canteen at work and he almost choked on his coffee.

'Jeez, you don't ask for much, do you Anna? I'd be asking him to incriminate himself.'

'I know, but if he's been as miserable as you say since Gordon King's arrest, he probably realises it won't be long before the police are knocking at his door. This way he'd at least get a lot of money and his name all over the papers. And you could put it to him that if he was led into all this by Giles Hurt, and he's sorry he ever got involved, then confessing might do some good. The courts might be more lenient. Put it to him as a way out of his problems.'

'If there is going to be a court case, none of what he tells us can be printed anyway till it's all over.'

'I know, but that needn't make any difference to Sammy. If his story checks out the paper'll still pay him and keep the confessions till they can be printed.'

'I dunno, Anna. I just don't know. I'll try, but I can't guarantee he'll play for it.'

'It may be the only way we'll get enough info on Giles Hurt to be able to nail him.'

Greg sighed, 'Well, it is a way out for Sammy, I can see that. If he's going to be dragged in the mire with Giles Hurt anyway, the sooner he distances himself from him, the better chance he has of getting off more lightly. I'll put that to him. And the money of course; if that doesn't swing it, nothing will.'

He rang me that night. 'Anna, I've got Sammy to agree to it, but he's getting more nervous by the minute. If you can't get your man here first thing in the morning, I don't think you'll have a Sammy to interview – he'll have disappeared. He's jumpy as a cat, I'm sure he thinks the cops are on to him. But he does want the money, of that I'm certain.'

'All right, Greg,' I said. 'I'll have a reporter here, cheque in hand, by the morning – even if I have to drive to

210

Manchester and bring him myself. Just do your best to hang on to Sammy for us.'

Luckily it was my day off the following day, but I did not have to drive to Manchester. My news editor friend said a reporter called Neil Siskin would be on the train that arrived in Northport at 9.30 a.m. I said I'd pick him up.

Alys asked if she could come too – she wanted to hear what Sammy had to say. We picked up Neil Siskin at 9.30 prompt, and drove him to Greg's.

He was an over-friendly young man, plump and beaming, with thick curly dark hair, a jazzy waistcoat and bow-tie. Alys cringed away from his vigorous handshake and ebullient manner.

'So you've got a rent-boy who wants to kiss'n'tell?' he said in the car. 'And he's been seeing what – a Euro-MP, a chief executive, some big-wig doctor?'

'Those are the ones we think have been his clients, yes,' I replied.

'No pop stars then, that you know of? Or maybe a telly actor? No? Pity – they'd go down a treat with our readers. Still, you never know till you ask the questions – he may have one stashed away among his customers.'

Ignoring this, I tried to brief Siskin as much as I could on why we wanted him to interview Sammy.

Siskin whistled through his teeth in disbelief. 'You think the boy's willing to tell all?'

'Part of it, for money, yes. That's where you come in.'

'I usually do. I've got past the stage of thinking people want me for my wit and charm,' he smiled cheerfully, and pulled out a chequebook from an inner pocket. 'Hey-ho, hey-ho, it's off to work we go . . .!'

An anxious Greg answered the door and ushered us into the living room. I led the way, and saw Sammy, his slight figure dressed in white with a china-blue neckerchief, staring distractedly into the empty fireplace. He sat in the corner of an armchair, and seemed lost. But immediately I introduced Neil Siskin his face changed. He looked up at Siskin and I saw the light of anticipation in his eyes.

'You're going to publish my story in your paper?' he said.

'If it's true, and if it's exclusive, yes, Sammy, I think we will. But it must be genuine – I don't want any wind-ups – we've paid out enough in libel damages already, sunshine. If it doesn't check out – no go. OK?' His words were a serious warning, but he said them beaming all over his face, and Sammy seemed won over by his friendly manner.

'It's true,' he said. 'I've had some powerful men. This must be worth something – for the exclusive.'

He then sat impassively, and I knew he would go no further until he saw money. Neil Siskin must have known it too. He deftly produced his chequebook, and I watched Sammy's eyes widen as Siskin signed away thousands of his paper's pounds.

The cheque, however, remained on Siskin's side of the table as he produced his portable tape-recorder from his briefcase and placed it between them.

'Now,' said Siskin, smiling again at Sammy, 'I'll just switch on this little baby, and we'll start. Let us begin at the beginning – how did you get to know Giles Hurt?'

'After one of my stage nights. He watched the hypnosis show. He came to the stage door as I was leaving. It's not unusual. I've met several gentlemen that way. I thought little of it. I didn't know who he was – I didn't find out till later. I saw his photo in the paper.'

'Did he pay you for sex?' asked Siskin bluntly.

Sammy's face pinkened. 'It's not always sex you know,' he said defensively. 'Giles taught me a lot. He showed me paintings, read me poetry, he was kind to me, I liked that.'

'But did he pay you for sex?'

'Yes,' the boy said finally, as if preparing himself for what came next.

Siskin wanted to know all about it – where, how, when – teasing out the fine details with all the craft of his trade.

Alys and I stared at the walls. Greg disappeared to make coffee.

Finally Siskin exhausted this seam of enquiry. I saw my chance to slip in a question of my own.

'Did Giles ask you to use hypnosis for him, Sammy? On other people?' The boy flinched, but went on, as if he'd expected this.

'Yes . . .', he said slowly. 'But I trusted him, I looked up to him, that's why I did it. I didn't know what I was getting into, I didn't know it'd get so serious. I'm sorry I ever met him.'

'All right, all right, Sammy,' said Siskin, noting the fear in his eyes. 'Just tell us how you got involved.'

Greg returned with the coffee tray, and we waited while he distributed mugs.

'I thought he was just interested in hypnosis because of me at first,' said Sammy. 'I thought it was because he liked me, he wanted to find out what I did. But the more he went on about it, the more I thought he was only interested in me because of the hypnosis. He asked me if I could put someone under without them really knowing it, and make them forget all about it when they came round. I said I thought I could, but he made out he didn't believe me, said my show was a scam. So I darn well proved it to him – I wanted to please him, you see. One night I said I'd give him a massage – it's so slow and rhythmical, people relax, they don't realise what's happening, and if I just keep on talking gently, I can gradually slip into their subconscious. That night I had a tape-recorder hidden, to record what he'd said to me, and when I brought him round, he didn't remember a thing about it. But I had the proof, on the tape. He was very impressed. He said . . .', the boy looked down, 'he said I had a rare and valuable gift.'

'And when he asked you to do this on other people, what was your reaction?'

'I said yes . . . I told you, I wanted to please him. I wanted him to like me.'

'You did this for money, though?'

'Of course, he paid me, and he was generous. But he said he needed me to do it because these people were enemies who could threaten his career. I wanted to help him. I've stolen stuff before – stealing secrets seemed no different, not at first.'

'Like Harry Jansen's secrets, for instance?'

'Yes, and others . . . Dr Jefferson who – who drowned,' his voice tailed away.

'Never mind Jefferson for now,' said Siskin, who wanted to concentrate on the more headline-grabbing Euro-MP before netting the smaller fry. 'How did you get to know Harry Jansen?'

'Giles asked me to make friends with him.'

'How?'

The boy hesitated, and his voice was lower when he went on. 'Harry Jansen and his wife run a clinic for recovering junkies and alcoholics. I had a drug problem, pretty serious at one time. Giles gave me the money to go there, to the clinic, to come off the drugs and get therapy. It worked. I've a lot to thank Giles for. But at the same time he asked me to go all out to become friends with Harry Jansen, which I did.'

'Sexually?' pounced Siskin.

'No,' Sammy sounded disparaging at the thought. 'Harry's a raving hetero.'

Neil Siskin's mouth tightened, his vice angle on the Euro-MP evaporating.

'I tried to be a model patient,' Sammy explained, 'to be Harry's protégé in a way. He asked me to co-operate with him on an anti-drug campaign, so he could show me off as a success story. I didn't mind, I did everything I could to be nice to him, to keep in with him. It was what Giles wanted me to do.'

'So that you'd know him well enough to be able to hypnotise him?'

'Yes,' said Sammy.

214

'What did he want you to find out from him?'

'It wasn't anything sexy,' he said, eyeing the cheque as if it might disappear. 'It was boring stuff.'

'That doesn't matter,' I said impatiently. 'What did he want to know?'

'He wanted to know about the gas field,' said Sammy, sighing. 'I had to ask Harry what he knew about the gas field.'

'Well, go on,' I said. 'What did he know?'

'He knew they were drilling extra shafts,' said Sammy, turning defensive. 'Harry wasn't an easy subject, I found him difficult to get through to. Even under hypnosis there were layers of resistance. Giles wanted me to ask if he knew what the shafts were for, but Harry wouldn't respond to that question. He did say something else though . . . It was "Iain's grilling the divers. Alys'll prove what they're up to."'

I interrupted: 'No mention of a shipping accident? Or a cover-up?'

'No – no accident. Why, was there one?' He turned his face to the wall and said softly, 'Alys thought there'd been a shipping accident . . . Giles said she didn't know what she was talking about.'

'What d'you mean, Sammy?' Alys blurted out. 'You did take me away, you did hypnotise me – that's the only way I'd ever've told you about an accident.'

'Yes,' said Sammy, again in that still, quiet voice, 'I hypnotised you. You weren't easy to get to know, though. In the end we had to kidnap you and keep you drugged till it was over.'

'We? Who'd you mean?'

'I took you from London to a cottage Giles rented. Giles was there part of the time. Gordon King came later with some papers Giles wanted.' The papers he'd stolen from me, I guessed. 'When it was all over, Gordon was asked to dump you off, from his car. Giles paid him pretty well.'

Alys was white with fury: 'You little—'

Sammy put up his hand. 'I didn't like it either, but Giles

215

wanted me to do it, and I was in it too far by then. I felt sorry – you didn't react well – probably the drugs. I made sure Gordon took you back to your boat. I thought someone would find you.'

'Thank God they did,' she said, looking at me. 'Anyway, at least I'm not permanently damaged – unlike Harry Jansen. Did you throw him out of the window? Come on, Sammy – it's confession time, now. No use holding out any longer.'

'No!' he said angrily, his face red. 'Why is everyone trying to pin that on me? He was Giles Hurt's enemy, not mine.'

'But you did other things for Giles Hurt.'

'Not that. Ask him, ask him,' he said breathing heavily.

'Come on, come clean, Sammy,' I persisted. 'You must've had something to do with it. I saw you with Jansen that night.'

'All right I was there!' he retaliated. 'I met Harry to talk about the anti-drugs campaign. We went to his room. Harry wanted a shower. As he was coming out someone knocked at the door. He opened it, and Giles pushed his way in. Harry didn't even know I knew Giles. They stared daggers at each other, and Harry said, 'Beat it Sammy, this has nothing to do with you. If anything happens to me, you were never here tonight, understand? I won't let them frame you.' Giles never even looked at me. I ran and met Greg in the Townsman's Bar. That's what happened, damn it, is that enough for you now?'

Neil Siskin interrupted, anxious we were getting Sammy too over-wrought to carry on. 'Let's change the subject,' he said. 'Let's go back to the doctor – Dr Jefferson – did Giles introduce you to him?'

The boy calmed himself, nodding slowly: 'It was after Harry mentioned Iain's name under hypnosis. Giles already knew Iain, through some scanner appeal committee for the hospital. He sussed Iain was gay-inclined. He was, but he'd suppressed it for years. When Giles introduced me, I don't know, I seemed to have an effect on Iain . . . he melted, he wanted me. I knew he was trying to stop himself, but he couldn't.'

'You're a pretty boy, Sammy,' said Siskin. 'You can't've been surprised.'

'No,' said the boy, matter of factly. 'But if I'd known he'd die for it – I shouldn't've done it . . . and it was all for nothing.'

'What d'you mean?' I said.

'I hypnotised him, as Giles wanted. While he was under, I asked him about the divers from the ruddy gas field, as Giles wanted. But all I could get out of him was the same as we'd got from Harry Jansen: that the divers were helping build these extra shafts, it was a big job, very hush-hush. But as soon as I asked what the shafts were for, he started squirming, "I don't know, I don't know – you're just like Harry – I can't find out, they won't tell me. Why is this so important? Why won't you leave me alone?" And then he started talking as if I was Harry: "Why will you never let me go? I find this precious boy and then you use him against me. You know if this got out I'd lose my job, my boys, Margot. He's a prostitute! I may as well be dead – that's the only way I'll find some peace." And the more he went on, the more suicidal he became. Harry knew I was seeing Iain – I'd talked to him about my rent-boy experiences – there were no secrets at the clinic. He must've told Iain I was a prostitute – I never did, because Giles was paying me, there was no need. Iain was ashamed . . . frightened too . . . said he'd betrayed his patients' trust. He was spiralling down, getting deeper into this depressive state. I – I lost control of him. It was hellish difficult talking him out of the trance. When he woke he seemed dazed, as if the weight of it was still with him. I knew then he wanted to kill himself, I just didn't know when. I thought he'd shy away from me after that, but he didn't, he wanted to see me more and more. He seemed desperate. He didn't have to say anything . . . I knew he wanted me with him when he died . . .'

Silence followed. Alys broke it, her voice menacing. 'Don't try to pull that one, Sammy. Don't try to make out you didn't push him over towards suicide. I may not remember much about your hypnotising me. But I do remember your voice, dwelling on all my doubts and fears, dragging me down, making me wish I was dead. Did Giles tell you to do that? That's what it looks like to me, Sammy – so much easier for him if we did decide to knock ourselves off. Well – did he?'

Sammy glared: 'You can't make subjects do anything against their nature, not even under hypnosis.'

'No, but if the seed of depression was there, you could've played on it for all it was worth. Couldn't you?'

A pulse beat visibly in Sammy's cheek, but he made no reply.

Alys wouldn't give up: 'You did it to me, I reckon you did it to Jefferson, and you probably tried it with Harry – only you're right, you can't make subjects do anything against their own nature, and Harry was too full of life. You didn't have anything to work on. That's why Giles Hurt had to take more drastic measures. Isn't that what happened?'

His jaw gripped tight and his voice hissed: 'I don't have to answer that.'

Nobody spoke. Neil Siskin obviously felt it was time to quit while he was ahead. I guessed he planned to come back to Sammy later, when Alys and I weren't there making the boy feel uncomfortable.

Siskin cleared his throat and said, 'Well, it's quite a story, young man. But – ', and here he reached out and pocketed Sammy's cheque, 'I'm afraid I'm going to have to keep this back, just for the time being. It's not that I don't trust you Sammy,' he smiled at the boy's horrified eyes, 'but with a story like this my editor's going to demand legal back-up before any money changes hands. We have to have a cast-iron case these days, we can't afford the libel risks otherwise. It's for your own benefit too, Sammy, I assure you. There'll just be a little matter of swearing affidavits and getting corroboration. This Gordon King character, where – ?'

'In police custody,' I said.

'Ah, difficult,' sighed Siskin. 'Still I'm sure we can sort something out . . . ummm.'

He was staring at Sammy's face. The boy was sitting tense and white, emanating silent malice. Siskin looked away in embarrassment. His glance lighted on the drawing board at the far end of the room, where one of Sammy's works in progress was mounted.

'Ah, is this yours, Sammy?' he said enthusiastically. 'Anna told me you did these marvellous pictures on the way here. Let me look more closely.'

Alys, Greg and I followed him, anxious to break the tension that was radiating from Sammy. We stood round the picture – it showed a lonely loitering knight haunted by La Belle Dame Sans Merci. Only Greg and I knew the knight's face was Iain Jefferson's. I became aware the boy was beside me, watching Neil Siskin. Siskin, uncomfortable, picked up a fragment of silvery foil from the work table.

'I see – you're using this for the armour. Do you just stick it on the photograph? I must say, it's very good. How do you – ?'

'I use this,' said Sammy, picking up a spray can which smelt powerfully chemical. 'It's a special fixative.'

Before any of us realised what was happening, he had sprayed it straight into Neil Siskin's eyes, and as I tried to knock it out of his hand, Greg caught a blast in the eyes too. The two men fell back, groaning, rubbing at their faces in agony.

'I should never've trusted you – any of you!' shouted Sammy, 'it was all a con, you bastards, you were never going to give me money. Hurt always looked after me!'

219

Alys and I were desperately trying to help Greg and Siskin. I heard Sammy slam the front door as he fled, but I didn't see him go.

It was not for several minutes, after copious drenching with water to his face, that Neil Siskin blinked open his eyes and said: 'The tape – where's my tape-recorder? It was on the table.'

Alys and I looked at each other. It had gone. Sammy had reclaimed his confession.

TWENTY-FIVE

'We'd better call the police,' said Siskin. 'I want my bloody recorder back.'

I inwardly groaned at the thought of Tom finding out we'd been interrogating Sammy without telling him – still worse, interrogating him for a pretty sleazy Sunday newspaper. It'd been bad enough when I hadn't told him about Alys's research for Harry. I couldn't face his surly antagonism again.

'No,' I said, 'leave the police out of it for now – you want to get more out of the boy, don't you Neil? The police'd swipe the tape as soon as they heard it, and you'd've lost any chance of a story. Let me and Alys try and get him back – you and Greg are in no fit state to go anywhere right now. Give me the cheque, Neil, it's the only way he'll play.'

Siskin shrugged and retrieved the cheque from his pocket: 'OK, it's worth a go. We can always stop the bank paying out if it comes to that.'

'Greg, you know him best,' said Alys. 'Where d'you think Sammy'll go to?'

'Not his flat, that's for sure,' said Greg. 'That's the first place anyone'd look for him. I reckon he'll beat it out of town. He's no car though, and I did see him looking at a London train timetable card this morning. I'd try the station first.'

'OK, any other ideas?'

'Giles Hurt,' I said. 'He might've gone back to him. He said Hurt always looked after him just before he ran.'

'Anon, you're going to need help, you and Alys can't tackle Hurt. He's dangerous, and he'd be even more so if he was cornered,' Greg said.

'But look at you, Greg, your eyes are still streaming.'

'At least take this,' he said, pulling open a drawer and thrusting a mobile phone in my hands. 'Keep in touch and yell for help if you need it. Oh, and these may come in useful,' he opened another drawer and withdrew a pair of binoculars.

'Thanks Greg.'

'Just phone me every step of the way,' he said, still rubbing his bloodshot eyes. 'Damn this stuff. Damn Sammy. Don't leave me on tenterhooks not knowing what's happening.'

'I need a doctor,' moaned Siskin, 'I should get danger money.'

'Come on, Ans,' said Alys impatiently from the door. 'We gotta go.'

As I followed, Greg reached out and brushed his damp beard on my cheek with a wordless kiss. I smiled.

'Take care,' he said.

Northport railway station is a cavernous modern hall, and it echoed to the sound of hundreds of holidaymakers. Alys and I pushed through them to the ticket office.

'Have you seen a boy here in the past half-hour – about this high, thin, blond, looks about fourteen?'

The man gazed back at me blankly through the glass. He saw so many people in the course of a day, I doubt he even looked at their faces – just took the money and gave the tickets. His colleague, a woman, was no help either.

Alys asked the porters, I made for the ticket barriers. The first collector shook his head and carried on punching tickets, so did the second. I was beginning to think we had drawn a blank.

The third collector ignored my question, and I repeated it.

'I know, I know, I heard you the first time. Runaway kid, is he? I thought he looked a bit shifty like.'

'You mean you've seen him?'

'Can't be certain,' and he looked at me significantly.

I grabbed my purse and pulled out a pound coin, slipping it into his cupped hand.

'He's on the Birmingham train over there,' he said. 'Better be sharpish, it's due out any minute.'

I frantically looked round for Alys, saw her in the crowd and pulled her towards the ticket office. 'He's on the Birmingham train,' I explained breathlessly. 'The ticket collector saw him.'

A queue had built up. I had no option but to shove myself to the head. 'Sorry, sorry – our train's due out in one minute – please, d'you mind?'

'You should leave yourself more time,' said an officious-looking man whose turn it was. 'It's not fair on other people.'

Still, he let me in and I asked for two singles to Birmingham. Then I found I hadn't enough cash, and neither had Alys. It took another precious half-minute while I wrote a cheque and the man scrutinised my cheque card, laboriously copying the number on the back. Finally we had our tickets and we raced towards the barrier just as the whistle blew to send our train on its way.

'Come on,' shouted Alys, 'we can make it.'

We practically pushed the ticket collector back into his

hut, determined not to let him stop us boarding the train now beginning to edge away from the platform.

Running flat out, Alys reached the door, wrenched it open, and we flung ourselves in. An angry guard slammed the door shut behind us, and we looked up at the startled faces of our fellow passengers.

We found a couple of vacant seats and sat a few minutes to compose ourselves and catch our breath back. Then we started a steady progress down the aisle, me checking one side, Alys the other.

We received some indignant glares for our seeming rudeness in staring so openly.

'Sorry,' I apologised at first, 'we're looking for someone – a blond boy, on his own, looks about fourteen?'

But no one responded, and I got tired of repeating the refrain as we moved from carriage to carriage. Alys tried it too, with no more success than I. No one admitted seeing him – not the passengers, not the guard, not the inspector, not the buffet-car assistants – no one. By the time we reached the end of the train we were totally dispirited.

'I reckon that ticket collector was having me on,' I said. 'He never saw Sammy at all, he just saw the chance of a handy tip.'

'Seems like a wild-goose chase,' agreed Alys. 'What should we do now?'

'Stay on till we get to Preston?' I suggested. 'We can get a non-stop express back to Northport from there.'

Alys nodded. We made our way back to the buffet car for a cup of tea. While I was waiting at the counter, Alys grabbed a table. We pulled into a station serving a small commuter village about fifteen miles from Northport, not far from the coast. The train waited and then jerked, ready to depart. I was about to lift the teas from the counter when Alys snatched at my arm.

'I've seen him!' she said urgently. 'He's got off the train. I just saw him going through the ticket barrier.'

Our carriage had already left the platform as we opened

the door. Alys leapt out on to the grassy embankment and I tumbled on top of her. I heard the door slam as the train gathered speed, and a curious stationmaster gazed down at us from the platform.

'Cut it a bit fine there, didn't you ladies? Not hurt, are you?'

'No, no,' I replied, as we brushed ourselves down. 'We're looking for someone. We saw him on the platform as the train started to move off. A boy, blond, looks about fourteen,' I reeled off the litany. 'Did you see where he went?'

'If he's the one you mean, he asked where the taxis were. I told him, over there,' he indicated through the wire-mesh fence to a small line of cars across the road. 'Is that him in the front one there, just pulling out?'

Alys and I looked. We just had time to see the unmistakable blond head in the passenger seat as the car turned away from us.

'Thanks,' I said, already running, Alys beside me.

'Tickets please,' he reminded us. A precious minute was lost as I searched for them, eventually unearthing the wretched things from a side pocket of my bag.

We ran across the road to the remaining car on the rank. The driver, a young man in his twenties with Latin good looks and an earring, lounged languidly in his seat. He perked up immediately we told him we wanted to follow the bronze-coloured car that had just left.

'A chase?' he queried. 'Great stuff – just what I need.'

At our puzzled looks, he explained: 'I'm an actor, I just drive cabs while I'm between parts. A chase is good experience – get in.'

True to his word, he flung the car round the corners as if rehearsing a cop movie. Alys and I braced ourselves as best we could in the back seat. Hanging on to the door handle grimly, Alys said: 'Are you sure they came this way?'

'Reckon so, we're just coming into the village. I know

John, the driver – he usually gives the thumbs-up to the other drivers if he's going anywhere else, 'cos it normally means a good fare. But he didn't this time.'

'Can't you contact him on the radio?'

'Nope,' the driver shook his head. 'Not with the same firm, see. It's the boy you want, is it?'

'Yes.'

'Nice-looking kid – whoahhh! There we are – I told you they came this way. See, straight ahead, just going through the traffic lights.'

We saw the bronze car turning right at the junction about two hundred yards ahead.

'We'll get him,' said our driver. 'You're in good hands with Jason Milo, don't you worry.'

But I was worried as he put his foot down hard, overtaking with inches to spare from an oncoming lorry. As we approached the traffic lights they turned amber, and I thought for a minute that Jason Milo was going to dash through on red. But he slammed the brakes on hard, lurching his back-seat passengers almost to the floor.

'Sorry about that, girls,' he said into his rear-view mirror. 'Not bruised are you? All part of the thrill of the chase.'

We gritted our teeth, not so much at being shaken up, as at being called 'girls'.

'Have we lost him?' I asked anxiously.

'Nope,' Jason flashed a winning smile at me in the mirror. 'There's only one place they can be going to down there. Interested in boats, your kid, is he? That road leads to the creek, and nowhere else.'

Alys rummaged in her large bag and pulled out the mobile phone. 'Here,' she said. 'Tell Greg where we are.'

The car roared off as I got through to him and told him where we were going.

'Wyre Creek?' he said. 'I've never heard Sammy even mention it before. I can't think what he's doing.'

We dropped down a hill and I saw a flotilla of little

225

pleasure boats – a motley bunch of yachts and cruisers – moored alongside wooden duckboards which extended into the creek.

The bronze car was just turning round as if to leave, and I saw Sammy's blond head bobbing as he ran along the duckboards. Alys had the binoculars out as we sped down to the quay, and I saw Sammy stop at one of the larger cruisers. A man came out of the wheelhouse and flung out an arm to help him on board. Then the man undid the rope tethering them to the mooring.

'Blast!' said Alys, glued to the binoculars. 'It's Giles Hurt. They're leaving. The boat's pulling away. We're going to lose them.'

Still on the phone to Greg, I told him what had happened as Jason brought the car to a stop on the quayside.

'You realise what's going on, don't you?' said Greg. 'That estuary leads out into the Irish Sea. They're making a run for it, both of them. I'm going to call the police, Anon, it's got to be done.' He rang off, and I got out of the car deflatedly. Jason got out too.

'You're not giving up, are you?' he said.

'My friend's calling the police,' I said.

'But it'll take them time to get here. Your boy'll be well away by then. You'll lose him. Look, one of my mates has a boat down here – he lets me use it sometimes. If you could just wait here while I go up and get the keys – his house is only in the village.'

I looked at him dubiously, then at Alys, who was kicking gravel in irritation.

'No extra charge,' urged Jason. 'Honest, I want to help.' His eyes glittered, I could see he relished the drama we had brought to his dull afternoon.

'Let's do it, Anna,' said Alys.

'OK,' I said, and Jason leapt into the driving seat with that flashing smile.

We waited, listening to the roar of his engine and the squeal of tyres as he progressed back up the hill, through the village, stopped half a minute, roared again and finally reappeared, skidding to a halt beside us. He waved a set of keys at us in triumph, locked the car and trotted over.

'Cap'n Milo at your service,' he said. 'Let me pipe you aboard, me hearties.'

He led us to a small but nippy-looking glass-fibre craft, her white hull painted with the name, *Marlin*. We jumped aboard and he started up the engine as Alys untied us. The motor powered into life, the water churned, and he carefully steered us away from the moorings out into the creek.

'They went north,' said Alys. 'I saw their boat heading for the north side of the estuary.'

But as we drew out of the creek there was no sign of Giles's cruiser. Alys scanned the horizon with the binoculars. Fishing craft plied homewards and we bounced over their wakes as we aimed for the opposite side of the estuary. Alys grimaced, her face turning paler, and I knew she was anticipating seasickness. She clung on to the binoculars as we rounded the headland into open sea, but as the waves became more choppy she moaned and handed them over to me before going to sit down at the stern of the boat.

'You all right?' asked Jason as she passed the wheelhouse. 'There's some seasick pills in the first-aid box if you're not feeling too good.'

He gave them to her with a bottle of water and I took over the lookout station in the boat's prow. Jason hugged the coastline as I scoured both sea and land, the *Marlin*'s spray salting my lenses so I had to wipe them repeatedly. Giles's boat had looked large, modern and fast – it could probably far outstrip the little *Marlin* – but still I kept looking.

A tongue of land jutted out into the sea, and Jason steered a wide arc round its jagged rocks. As we turned back towards the deserted landscape I saw a white blur through my salty lenses, on the other side of the inlet – it must have been half a mile off. As we grew closer I wiped the smear away and looked again. It was a boat – a large, powerful-looking cruiser, and it seemed to have stopped. I watched as it drifted in the current – there seemed to be no one at the helm. The boat swung round, and revealed a man leaning over the side, a large bundle in his arms.

'Step on it, for Christ's sake, Jason,' I muttered to myself, for there was no way he could hear me above the engine's noise.

We grew closer, and at last I could define the man's features. I gasped. It was Giles Hurt, and the bundle in his arms was Sammy, lying absolutely limp. With a gentle gesture, almost of regret, Giles Hurt slid his body into the water.

'What the bl—?' I whispered under my breath. 'He's knocked him out, or worse – dear God!'

I dashed back to the wheelhouse and told Jason what I'd seen. He rammed hard on the accelerator and through the binoculars I saw Hurt look up, startled by the noise. He disappeared inside, and his boat immediately swung round, swirling water as he slewed out of the inlet and set off at high speed on his northward course.

The *Marlin* hurtled to where he'd been. I prayed he hadn't weighted Sammy's body. White foam crested from every wave, and I realised Sammy's white clothing would effectively camouflage him.

All three of us, even the wan Alys, were scanning every inch of the water. Suddenly Jason pointed: 'What's that?'

'A seagull,' I said. 'Two of them.'

'I know,' he replied. 'They've seen something. Look, more of them are coming.'

The seagulls sheered down from the sky ready for food. Jason made towards them. And it was then we saw it – a white hand thrust upwards, dashed by the waves.

I'm a good swimmer. I didn't hesitate, as soon as I saw the hand I mounted the side of the boat and plunged in, feeling the breath knocked out of me, tasting the salt, caring for nothing save rescuing that white hand, and the body with it. I only hoped it was alive.

I powered my way towards the shape under the water, touched it, only to feel it slide from my hands, pulled by the current's undertow. I grasped again, snatched at the slippery clothing, and hauled it back towards me. I had him then. I looked him in the face, the mouth open, eyes closed, lips blue.

I heard Jason shout as he flung out a lifebelt on a rope and I swam towards it, breathing hard as he hauled us in. They both took Sammy's arms and heaved him over into the well of the boat. Then Jason came back to help me while Alys tended to the boy.

'Well done, Anna! You were amazing,' he enthused, as I clambered back aboard. 'You're shivering. Look, sit down, let me bring you a blanket.'

Alys was crouched over Sammy, pumping water out of his lungs, trying to breathe life back in.

'You need help?' I asked.

'No – no – not yet,' she said between gasps, 'I've got a rhythm going – it's OK.'

I sat and watched her working on him in fierce concentration. Then gradually she slowed, watching his face. Pink began to fill his lips, and his chest rose slowly. He was breathing, he was alive. It was only then I saw the blood in his hair, matted with seaweed.

'Damn it, Anna!' exclaimed Alys, trying to staunch it with a handkerchief. 'Why's Hurt done all this – what's so important?'

'Giles Hurt, that's what's so important – to him anyway,' I replied, screwing my lips in disgust. 'Sammy got too wound up with him for his own good. It strikes me that all Giles cares about is ambition, and that makes him ruthless. Tethys gave Giles leg-ups in his career – the Amphitrite sewage scheme would've been another achievement on his CV. He'd've gone on to bigger and better councils. He's always fixed deals between councils and companies, many of them tentacles of Tethys. He's a fixer – he looks after their interests and they're good to him. So he's been looking after this gas field business, making sure no one gets close enough to scupper whatever it is Tethys wants kept secret. Sammy was simply his tool – and his knowledge of Giles was dangerous. He was always going to be expendable.'

'Well it all stinks,' she said as she began rubbing the boy's limbs to warm him. Still he lay unconscious.

Jason reappeared with blankets, covering Sammy, easing an old folded sweater under his head, and turning back to me. A drone of engines sounded across the waves and a pair of boats appeared, behind but coming towards us, cutting fast across the sea's surface.

Jason wrapped a blanket round me, and began massaging my shoulders. 'Stick close to me,' he said, 'you'll soon get warm. You deserve a medal for all this, both of you.'

With an actor's demonstrative ease he had his arm round me, hugging the chill from my bones. He lifted a lock of damp hair from my cheek and smoothed it back, gazing admiration into my eyes.

The noise of the approaching boats was upon us now. I looked up, and saw Tom Irving in the leading one, leaning out to get a better view of our craft. His gaze fell on Jason, still hugging me close, and his face turned thunderous. I knew he'd misread the situation, and I was glad. It would make cutting him off rather easier. I was aware I'd be playing him false, but neither of us were strangers to lies, and I preferred a short, jealous rupture to rumbling hostilities. There could be no soft let-down with Tom, he was a man who bore grudges.

A flurry of activity followed. The police were in two hefty power-launches. Tom barked questions and orders, avoiding my eyes, and finally Sammy's inert body was passed into the second boat, where they had proper medical equipment. The boat swung round to race him back to shore and hospital. Alys told Tom which way Giles had gone, and his helmsman needed no prompting – the boat took off in pursuit, drenching our deck in its wash.

'Now what?' asked Jason. 'Home James, and don't spare the horses?'

Alys and I exchanged glances. We both knew we wanted to see this through. She didn't feel seasick any more, and Jason found me some spare clothes in the cabin. I took off my wet trousers and shirt, and donned the old jeans and fishy-smelling sweater. At least they were dry. We turned the *Marlin* northwards and out to sea. Alys kept a keen eye on the white wake of the police launch.

'They're moving away from the land,' she said. 'They're steering north-west.'

The *Marlin* ploughed gamely on. I took the binoculars. The steel structures of gas rigs appeared ghostly out of the sea mist, far away, and I realised that had been Giles's aim all the time: the Tethys field – his protector, his home. I only hoped Tom's boat was powerful enough.

The waves came stronger and harder, but somehow the *Marlin*'s lightness came into its own. She skimmed over them, slicing from wave to wave. I faced into the wind and almost felt exhilarated. We were closing the gap between us and the police boat – I could even see what must be Giles's craft far ahead, homing in on the gas rigs.

A huge boat was drawn up beside one of the structures – an enormous yellow bulk that dominated the water. I guessed it was a supply boat for the rig workers.

A low beating fanned in from up above. I looked skywards, and saw a helicopter fast approaching from the south. 'Crikey, he's coming low,' gasped Jason, and he was. The helicopter was bearing down on us – we could already feel its down-draught. The *Marlin* began to toss wildly, the waves spreading outwards in the whirlwind. All we could do was grip tight and watch helplessly as the helicopter dipped in front of us as if in warning, before wheeling upwards and onwards again.

'They're trying to scare us off,' shouted Alys.

'But we're not scared that easily, are we?' responded Jason, regaining control of the *Marlin*'s course and revving the engine to full throttle. We skimmed the waves once more.

'He's doing it again,' said Alys, peering through the binoculars. 'The helicopter's having a go at Tom's boat now. Only he's going much lower, he's really close.'

Even Jason and I could see with the naked eye what was happening. The police boat, more powerful than ours, swerved away from the whirlwind, but the chopper only followed, twisting this way and that, forcing the launch round in an arc. The boat nosed into a crashing wave – and suddenly all the power went out of it.

'It's stalled,' said Jason as we watched figures frantically trying to revive the crippled engine while one man at the prow – it could only have been Tom – raged at the droning machine in the sky.

The helicopter rose away and dipped down again, and I could see Giles's boat beneath it. As the *Marlin* grew steadily nearer we saw a ladder uncoil out of the chopper towards his boat. Still the police launch drifted helplessly only a hundred yards away.

I grabbed the binoculars, and saw Giles reaching for the ladder, which dangled tantalisingly out of his grasp. A burst of sound roared from the police launch as its engine swelled into life again – just as Giles succeeded in getting a hand-hold on the ladder. He started to climb it, seizing each rung as if it were life itself. He was getting away, climbing higher and higher. Suddenly his foot slipped and he lost his grip. He slid erratically from rung to rung, trying to regain a hold, but his own weight pulled him implacably down. Finally he reached the bottom rung, and swung by one arm above the waves. Tom's boat sheered round Giles's abandoned cruiser. Without anchor or helmsman, it rocked in the swell just as Giles's foot hung above. Its high wheelhouse rose up, hit him and he fell, disappearing into the waves between his own boat and the police launch.

Immediately two of Tom's men were over the side, lifting his head and arms above the waves. Tom himself performed the final act of pulling the bedraggled Giles on board, and I suspected that nothing would give him greater pleasure than seeing this refined man brought low.

An audience of workers had gathered on the gas rigs and on the yellow supply boat. They turned away and disappeared as they saw what happened to Giles, and the helicopter thundered down on to a landing pad without its precious cargo.

Alys was peering hard at the supply boat. She grabbed the binoculars from me and stared again. 'Ans,' she said. 'I think I understand. Look there, at the containers – that one just being swung off the boat.'

'Yes, I see it.'

'I've seen those containers before, the same colourings, the same markings – on Hermann's lorry, in Germany.'

'You mean the nuclear waste?'

'Exactly – it makes sense, doesn't it? That's what the extra shafts were for – undersea storage. They thought they could get away with it – they were drilling for the gas field anyway. Who would know if an extra shaft or two was not for gas but for nuclear waste? When they were full they'd seal it up with concrete and no one would be any the wiser – except Tethys would pocket the profits for getting rid of it. God, they could store tons of the stuff out here . . . just waiting for an earth tremor to crack the concrete . . . who cares if it's a hundred years away? We won't be here . . .', she ended dryly.

'So that was what Harry was hoping you'd find: seismic patterns to prove the existence of the dump.'

Alys nodded and sighed. 'You know, I don't think you were quite right about Giles. Ambition was only the half of it – arrogance drives him just as much. Remember the speech he gave me about safe nuclear repositories? He and his kind think they know better than the rest of us. We're just too ignorant or pig-headed to know what's good for us – that's their view. And so they went behind our backs and did it anyway. Him and Tethys, they think they're above the rules.'

'Giles Hurt's above nothing now, my love,' said Jason, who'd been listening to this in some puzzlement. 'Just look at him.'

We saw Giles's bitter face in the back of the police launch. Drenched and dripping, he still shrugged off a police blanket with a violent swipe. All of Tom's assistants crowded round him to suppress further struggles, and I saw Tom himself at the helm. The launch swung round and he revved the engine. It gathered speed.

'What the bl—?' exclaimed Jason, jumping for the wheel of the *Marlin*.

'Alys – he's aiming for us!' I shouted. 'Get ready to jump!'

But though I said it, I couldn't quite believe it. I looked again – yes – I saw his face through the window of the wheelhouse, mouth open as if shouting while the launch powered towards us and the *Marlin* lurched helplessly on the waves.

Alys and I clambered the rail, sure he was going to hit us. But just before I jumped I looked up again. With seconds to spare the police launch swerved to avoid us, and I saw Tom's face now laughing behind the wheel. Still half over the rail, Alys and I clung together until the *Marlin* ceased its wild rocking and we could come down. So Tom had had his little spit of vengeance at me, he had to have the final gesture.

Alys, face wet from the spray, looked at me knowingly: 'Big joke, huh? You won't be seeing him again.'

'Too right I won't.' I put my arm round her shoulder. 'Let's go home.'

More Deadly, Delectable Detection from Virago

CHILDREN'S GAMES
Janet LaPierre

Romance, blackmail and murder on the Californian coast

In Janet LaPierre's supremely atmospheric mystery, schoolteacher Meg Halloran and her young daughter Katy move to a small town to start a new life. Soon Meg receives anonymous letters and suspects they originate from her former student, religious fanatic Dave Tucker. Dave accuses Meg of making sexual advances, and when he's found murdered, his father, a prominent banker, and many of the townspeople are convinced Meg is responsible. Her reputation and livelihood at stake, Meg, with the sympathetic support of Police Chief Gutierrez, strives to clear her name. Her enquiries uncover shocking and unsavoury secrets. But for Katy's survival and her own, she persists in finding the killer.

NORTH OF THE BORDER
Judith Van Gieson

'Carl Roberts. The name left a lump in my stomach like a cold burrito'

Meet Neil Hamel, tough, witty, fast-talking, a small-time lawyer in Albuquerque, New Mexico. Here she's cajoled by Carl Roberts, former lover, former boss, and probable candidate for Congress, to sort out a dangling thread in his life. Who's sending him anonymous letters hinting at the illegality of his Mexican son's adoption? Neil crosses the border to question the Mexican attorney who handled the paperwork. And finds him with his throat slit . . . Combining a powerfully atmospheric plot with magical descriptions of Mexico and Albuquerque, Judith Van Gieson puts Neil through her paces in this superb debut.